The Legend Of Aranrhod

Acknowledgements

Thanks to my wife, Lynn, for her patience; to Pete and Naomi for their encouragement in the early days; to Mike Hale, Brian Lux, Roy and Margaret, for their words of wisdom when the first drafts appeared; to Jenny Sanders, an editor with an eye for the Big Moment; to Dave at ideas4writers for being as meticulous as I hoped he'd be; to Imogen Hallam for the cover, and Lili Bagby for the illustrations, and to Catherine McIntyre. There are people with whom I may have only exchanged a few words, but who helped – like the couple who ran the B & B in North Pembrokeshire.

The Legend Of Aranrhod

Geoff Anderson

i4w²

ideas4writers

ISBN 978-0-9550116-1-0

First published in Great Britain in 2007 by

ideas4writers
PO Box 49
Cullompton
Devon
EX15 1WX

Cover illustration by Imogen Hallam
Text illustrated by Lili Bagby

Printed and bound by CPI Antony Rowe, Chippenham

For Zak and Eve
and their future siblings and cousins
who may read this book one day

On August 17th 1920, the Welsh historian, Professor Sion Llewellyn, was digging in one of the many hills in Pembrokeshire that claim to hold the body of Merlin the magician, when he unearthed a silver cylinder, sealed at both ends. It was no larger than a cigarette. Inside he found a tiny parchment scroll. When translated, the writing on the scroll read:

The Legend of Aranrhod:

When Aranrhod joins with Cadwaladr,
She'll be the Finder, and He the Wielder.

Nobody knew what this meant. Until now.

Part One

Aranrhod

He paid, he was wearing a suit of mustard and orange checks. When Carys caught his eye to apologise, she felt as if she were falling... Carys raced along the platform through a thick cloud of steam, and crashed into a man who was stepping down from his carriage. Tall and

Chapter 1 · Merlin's Farm

'Dad! *Dad!*'

Carys raced along the platform through a thick cloud of steam … and crashed into a man who was stepping down from his carriage. Tall and bald, he was wearing a suit of mustard and orange checks. When Carys caught his eye to apologise, she felt as if she were falling into a hole, as black and as deep as the well on Merlin's Farm, back home in Brynmyrddin. The well was dry, so when she hit the bottom, she –

'Carys! Wake up, girl!' shouted Branwen, shaking her daughter by the shoulder.

Carys awoke with a start. She was sweating. She tried to sit up but had no strength.

Branwen sat down on the bed.

'Was it that same man again? In the coloured suit?'

Carys nodded, and wiped her damp face with the sleeve of her nightdress.

'Where were you this time?' asked her mother.

'I – I didn't notice,' Carys lied. 'Nowhere special.' She wasn't going to tell her mother that this time she had bumped into the man on the platform of Foregate Street Station in Worcester. *Imagine what Mum would read into that!*

'I don't like it, not one little bit,' said Branwen. She went over to a chest of drawers and started removing colourful tops and throwing them into a battered suitcase. 'I wish you'd let me do a proper reading.'

The thought of her mother getting out her crystal ball was enough to bring fresh energy rushing back into Carys's body. She threw the duvet back and leapt out of bed.

'You know what I think of *that* idea, Mother.'

Carys didn't believe in premonitions and stuff. She was sure she would not be bumping into any tall, bald men in loudly coloured suits. Anxiety about leaving home was giving her nightmares, it was as simple as that. Even so, she couldn't help noting the fact that in her dream the train was of the old-fashioned steam variety – nothing like the one she would be taking to Worcester later that morning. *So much for premonitions,* she thought with a smile. She moved towards the door. 'And you're wasting your time packing those tops, they're ancient. I don't want the suitcase either.'

'Why not?'

'You know why not. It was Dad's – and don't pretend it wasn't. My rucksack will be enough. The big one.'

'So what will you take to wear, then?' asked Branwen, shuffling after her daughter along the dark, narrow corridor of the old farmhouse. Carys dodged into the bathroom and poked her head out.

'Nothing,' she said, hardening her soft, North Pembrokeshire accent so it bristled with sarcasm. 'I'll be their poor relation from the country with absolutely nothing to wear.'

With that she closed the door, leaving her mother shaking her head and clicking her tongue as if she had something stuck in her teeth. Branwen looked older than her years, her silvered hair done up in a bun. She had a handsome face, with pale blue eyes that might be reflecting a late summer sky. Branwen wore an apron as if it were a uniform, a symbol of her work-centred life. Moving closer to the bathroom door, she shouted to make herself heard over the rattling of the boiler.

'Carys? In your dream, you weren't falling, were you?'

'Into a black hole!' Carys replied, sounding faint and far away.

Branwen shook her head and went to find the rucksack. When she got back to the bedroom, Carys was already dressed. She was wearing a short skirt, leggings and desert boots – all in black. Her black denim jacket had faded to grey in parts. Carys's concession to colour was her vest top, which was brown.

'You were quick,' said Branwen. 'Let me look at you.'

She ran a hand down her daughter's coal-black hair, fine and straight, hanging past her shoulders and accentuating the pallor of her face.

'You might have washed your hair.'

'There's no time, Mum. And anyway,' Carys added, scrunching up her nose in mock distaste, 'they won't expect me to be clean, coming from a farm in deepest Wales.'

She removed some of the clothes that her mother was stuffing into the rucksack. 'I told you I didn't want these.' She threw them onto the bed in frustration. 'Why do they have to be English relatives? I mean, they don't even have the same name as us.'

'Of course they do. It was anglicised along the way, that's all. But the Cadwalladers are Cadwaladrs, believe me.'

Branwen put a couple of the rejected items back into the rucksack and this time Carys was too upset to protest. She sat on the bed, looking glum. Branwen sat down next to her and put her arm round her daughter. 'It isn't everybody who can take in a thirteen-year-old girl at short notice like this, but Stephen and Helen didn't hesitate.'

Carys sighed. 'I'm sure they're very nice.'

'And haven't you always wanted a sister?'

'But Bethany's a child!' exclaimed Carys.

'Get away with you. You'll get on fine, I'm sure.'

She patted her daughter's knee and got up to carry on packing. But when Carys didn't move to help, Branwen turned and spoke more firmly. 'Look you, it was either the Cadwalladers of Worcester or Great Uncle Elwin.'

5

Still no reaction from Carys.

Branwen continued, 'I didn't think you'd appreciate living with an eighty-five year old widower in Caerdydd ... and it's not proper Wales down there anyway – you might as well be in Worcester.'

Carys couldn't help laughing at this. Not at the idea of living with Uncle Elwin but at her mother's dismissal of everything south of the Landsker Line as 'not proper Wales'. To hear her talk, you'd think that everyone born in North Pembrokeshire had a certificate saying: 'My ancestors fought against the Saxons alongside King Arthur himself!'

A young man appeared in the doorway, dressed in a bathrobe a couple of sizes too big. He was shaking his head.

'Is Ma slagging off them southerners again? They've got a nerve, all those people born in Cardiff, calling themselves Welsh!'

'You can mock your mother, Dylan,' said Branwen, 'but I know my history.' She pulled the linen off the bed and forced her way past her son to make a pile of it in the corridor.

'The people in this part of Wales carry a huge responsibility,' she added, in a tone that mixed pride with resentment.

'A huge responsibility, is it?' Dylan shouted, striding off down the corridor.

'That's right, son – and none more so than our family.'

Outside the bathroom, Dylan turned. His face was flushed as he stripped off the bathrobe and flung it in a heap. 'Then it's a shame Dad let the side down, eh Mother?'

He disappeared into the bathroom, slamming the door behind him. Like all the doors in the farmhouse, the bathroom door shut with a latch which had to be lifted, so it rebounded on its wrought iron hinges and creaked to a stop.

Branwen and Carys followed. Dylan was sitting on the bathroom floor, fighting to hold back tears. While his sister kept a tactful distance in the corridor, his mother dropped down beside him and gave a deep sigh, as if hoping to breathe out Dylan's pain.

'Dylan, my boy, when are you going to forgive your father?'

Carys stepped inside the doorway.

'Mum, we're never going to catch that train.'

Then Dylan spoke. His voice barely rose above a whisper. 'Don't worry sis, I'll drop you in Worcester on my way to London.'

Carys looked surprised. 'I thought you were staying 'til Saturday?'

'If you're sure,' said Branwen to Dylan, 'it would be a great help. To be honest, I never liked the idea of Carys travelling all that way on her own.'

'Mum, you never said!' exclaimed Carys, with a flash of annoyance. 'I'd have been all right.'

Branwen got up and gave a helping hand to Dylan – as if he were an old man, not an eighteen year old. He was well built, though he'd lost his rugby player's physique. Taking her arm, he almost brought his mother down on top of him, but she stood her ground.

Dylan grinned as he dried his eyes.

'I don't know another woman who could take my weight like that, Ma. You're amazing.'

'There's no "amazing" about it. If they mauled sheep about, chopped up logs and raised bucketfuls of water from the well, those fancy women you cavort with in London would be as strong as me.'

'Mum, come on, when was the last time you raised water from our well? It's been dry for years.'

Dylan was a happy lad with sunny features and light brown, curly hair. Some people laugh with their mouths alone, but Dylan laughed with his whole body, which shook like the rabbit-shaped jellies that he and Carys used to have for their birthday teas when they were little.

Branwen slapped his backside so he felt it through his boxers.

'Look at you, all that surplus baggage! You couldn't raise an *empty* bucket now, I'll warrant. You should start playing again.'

'I shall, I shall, Ma, just don't hit me again, please!' he screamed, as he went running out of the bathroom. Dylan's body shook as he laughed his way to his room. He went in, switched on his radio and called out, 'Carys, we should set off before lunch, okay?' Then he shut his door without waiting for an answer.

Branwen perched on the rim of the huge Victorian bath.

'What am I to do with him, Carys? Tears one second, laughter the next – and it's me they're calling crazy.'

'Mum, nobody's calling you crazy. Dr Williams is concerned about you, that's all.'

'Concerned about me, is he? More like he's concerned over the patients I keep taking from him. Well, if he cured more of them, they wouldn't need to come to me, would they? And *you* can shut up!' she added, banging the boiler with her fist. The boiler gave a disgruntled gurgle and lapsed into silence.

Carys led the way back to her room.

'Don't worry about Dylan,' she said, 'we all need time. And I bet he's not like this in London. Coming home disturbs him, but he needs to see we're all right.'

Branwen took her daughter's hands in hers. Standing this close, she had to look up into Carys's eyes. 'Look at you, counselling your own mother like you were Pastor Lewis himself. When did you grow up, girl? I think I missed it.'

Carys put her arms round her mother and gave her a hug. 'You've had other things to think about, Mum. We all have.' As Carys moved away to finish packing, she added, 'Do I have to go?'

Her mother clicked her tongue. The time for emotions had ended; it was down to business again. 'Of course you have to go. And I'm glad Dylan is far away in London too. I have to face this alone.'

'Why won't you at least tell me what's going on?'

'Because,' said Branwen with a cheeky smile, 'even though you're older than Bethany, you're still a child, and the less you know the better. Anyway, in these matters it isn't always a question of knowing, but of being ready. That's why I need to be alone, to concentrate my forces.'

She was holding her head back as she spoke, staring through the skylight in Carys's sloping ceiling, as if reviewing invisible armies ranked in the sky, waiting for her orders. Then her tongue clicked, the spell was broken, and she said as she strode out, 'I'll get breakfast ready while you finish packing. Then I want to take you for a short drive. I've a surprise for you.'

She stopped at the doorway. 'I'm glad Dyl offered, you know. It was going to be an awful rush.' As she reached the top of the stairs, she called out, 'Delicious farmhouse breakfast in fifteen minutes. Better make that half an hour – I haven't collected the eggs yet!'

Carys smiled a grim smile. She was happy to live with English relatives she'd never met, if it meant that Mum's life would be less stressful. Deep down, Carys would have preferred to stay and face the challenge with Mum, whatever it was. *But then,* she thought, *how do you fight imaginary foes?*

Carys lingered over her childhood treasures: holiday souvenirs, birthday presents from friends, the poster from her first pop concert. They all brought back happy memories, but Carys was surprised how little she wanted to take with her. Then she saw the music box, a present from her father on her fifth birthday. Seeing again her father's laughing eyes, her own eyes brimmed with tears.

Her reverie was interrupted by the bell ringing for breakfast. It was a huge fire bell, fixed to the outside of the house, which could be heard in the farthest reaches of their land and beyond – a proper fire alarm, able to run on batteries if there was a power failure. It had been made partly redundant by mobile phones, although these didn't always work in the hills and valleys of North Pembrokeshire, but it wasn't needed at all now that the sheep had been sold and no one worked on the hills any more. For some reason, Branwen persisted in using it at meal-times, even though Carys was always within hailing distance. She sometimes wondered if her mother was letting the neighbours know that there's still life on Merlin's Farm. But to the young girl's ears, it had a hollow sound, an echo of happier, busier times.

Carys was quiet when she sat down to breakfast, thinking about the music box.

Branwen caught her eye. 'Anything you leave and then decide you want, anything at all, I can always post it, you know? And it's not as if you're never coming back.'

Dylan arrived, looking smart in a grey suit, with a pink shirt and tie.

'Ma, what's wrong with people who have M.E.?' he asked.

9

'Why, love?'

'It was on the news. There's been an outbreak of something like it.'

'People with M.E. are always tired. Sometimes they can hardly move their limbs, it's so bad. Did they have an explanation?'

'As if! But they sounded worried.'

'Maybe it's the beginning,' said Branwen under her breath.

Carys heard her. 'The beginning of what, Mum?'

As Carys watched, the light faded from her mother's eyes. Although these eyes had been clouded with grief, their old sparkle had been returning. But at this moment they spoke only of fear – presumably, thought Carys, of the great evil that she'd prophesied was coming.

'Any more eggs, Ma? You never see eggs like this in London.'

It was Dylan, breaking the silence. As quickly as Carys had seen the look appear in her mother's eyes, it vanished.

'Three eggs in one day is more than enough, Dyl, you know that.'

Branwen turned from her son to her daughter, eyes warm and optimistic once more.

'Come on, my dear, eat up. You've a long journey ahead of you.'

'I'm only going to Worcester, Mum. It's not the end of the universe.'

'Well, we hope not,' said Branwen, with a nervous smile.

Chapter 2 · Dredge's Riddle

On the morning the Cadwaladr family were having their breakfast on Merlin's Farm, a tall, bald man wearing a mustard and orange check suit strode into an antique shop in Worcester. A tiny brass bell jingled as he opened the door, but no one came to attend to him.

'Dredge!' shouted the man.

The shop was situated in one of the city's more secluded side streets. Unlike normal shops, it didn't have a frontage of plate glass displaying the items for sale, nor did it have a large sign above the premises. It was more like a cottage, with small, dirty windows. There was a rectangle of cardboard pinned to the top of the door with rusty drawing pins. *Dredge's Emporium* was written in ink that had run in the rain. Not everyone who saw the sign ventured in, for it would have felt like entering someone's home without knocking.

Those who did summon the nerve to go into the premises had to wait for their eyes to grow accustomed to the dim interior. Then they had to endure the heat generated by a central wood-burning stove, which was lit all year round. As if this weren't enough, there was a faint but pervasive smell, reminiscent of a school chemistry lab.

'Dredge!' repeated the loudly-dressed man, 'where the devil are you?'

The antique dealer appeared at last from a back room, went straight to the door and locked it. He had the appearance of an antique himself, a medieval piece in need of restoration. Bent over a cane, dressed in baggy trousers and threadbare tweed jacket, with a shawl around his shoulders, it was hard to believe the amount of money that passed through his gnarled, grubby hands during an average week.

Dredge's Emporium was well known to dealers who specialised in artefacts of the Middle East. Dredge had contacts there with access to rare treasures. In the trade there had been rumours of grave robbing, smuggling, even murder, but nothing had ever been proven.

'Balimm,' he said, 'I wasn't expecting you.'

Dredge was annoyed, but beneath the surface of his irritation fear was lurking. In an effort to conceal it, the old man straightened his bent figure, but he reached no higher than the top button of his visitor's cherry red waistcoat.

'Didn't we say the end of August?' asked Dredge, his tone half-assertive, half-pleading.

'We did,' replied Balimm, 'but I can wait no longer. I need it now.' If his voice had been a blade, it would have sliced through steel.

'B-But I don't have it yet.'

'Do not worry, my friend. I will understand if you do not have it with you. There are always loose ends to be tied up – bodies to be disposed of, a trail of evidence to be destroyed. I appreciate all of that.'

It didn't sound like he appreciated any of it. Furthermore, Dredge didn't like the way Balimm had looked him up and down as he talked about disposing of bodies.

'We're not talking about any old artefact, you know,' Dredge said. 'Aaron's Rod is unique.'

'That is why I gave you so much time,' Balimm insisted.

He was idly thumbing through a large book, bound in dragon skin and lying open on a sideboard. He didn't look up as he added, 'But Dredge, you have *found* it, have you not?'

The dealer knew the danger he was in. He might be the best in his field, but he wasn't indispensable. 'We've – we've made progress. We know it can be wielded only by a particular man.'

Balimm banged the book shut, raising a cloud of tiny, silvery scales.

'You told me that six months ago and I acted upon your advice. But information about wielding the rod is not much use if we do not have the rod to wield.'

Dredge's fear was no longer lurking; it had come to the surface and was dancing a jig all over his face.

Balimm continued, 'You have never let me down, Dredge. You can dig up facts forgotten by the gods. This is why I find it hard to believe that you have given my assignment the attention it deserves. I was expecting to find the rod waiting for me.'

Dredge had to sit down before his knees gave way beneath him.

'With Aaron's Rod,' he whispered, his breath coming in short gasps, 'it's hard to separate fact … from legend.'

'You are too modest, Dredge. You have an instinct for this kind of thing.'

Dredge wasn't fooled by the compliment. He had to regain his client's confidence. 'We know that the rod became the symbol of Aaron's priestly power and was kept in the Ark of the Covenant.'

A flicker of life registered in Balimm's eyes. 'Aaron's Rod was more than a symbol of his power, it was its *source*. Think of it, Dredge, spiritual power that springs from the infinite godhead. My plans for this world are perhaps too modest. Should I be thinking on a grander scale? The galaxy? The universe!'

He bounded across the room to stand before the mirror of an Edwardian wardrobe, and struck a pose befitting the future ruler of the universe. 'I can do a certain amount with my present forces, but to achieve my goal I need the power contained in Aaron's Rod. You have to find it, Dredge.'

He was almost begging. Almost.

Seeing how desperate Balimm was, Dredge became more assertive. After all, he was the expert – Balimm no more than a client. He should dazzle Balimm with his knowledge. So the dealer stood up and, as far as his twisted frame would allow, adopted an upright, professorial stance.

'According to Kebra Nagast –'

'Who?' interrupted Balimm. He tore himself away from the wardrobe and came striding back to Dredge. The dealer found it harder to be assertive when Balimm was towering over him, but he knew he had to persevere. 'Kebra Nagast is not a person, but an ancient, Ethiopian bible – a reliable source.'

This felt good. This was keeping Balimm in his place.

'According to Kebra Nagast,' Dredge repeated, relishing his own expertise, 'Aaron's Rod was broken into three pieces.'

'Broken?'

'The rod had to be broken to fit it into the Ark.'

Dredge waited a moment while Balimm absorbed the implications, then he continued, feeling that he was in control of the deal once more.

'I don't need to tell you,' he said, 'being in three pieces, the rod will be harder to find. This may not matter. In my experience of similar artefacts, the separated parts still deliver some power. But with Aaron's Rod, I don't know, different rules may apply. You may need the whole thing.'

Dredge shouldn't have said that. He'd become overconfident.

Balimm wrapped long, slender fingers around Dredge's scrawny neck and lifted him clear off the floor, until the dealer's face was level with his own. 'I *may* need the whole thing? Listen, Dredge, we are not playing with possibilities here. I want the whole of Aaron's Rod ... and the whole of Aaron's Rod, I ... will ... *have!*'

Balimm roared this last word until the Queen Anne chandeliers tinkled. Then he threw Dredge across the room like a bag of bones. The old man landed on a 17th century dining table, knocking aside two Georgian candlesticks as he slid towards an oak Welsh dresser, which brought him to a stop. He caught three of the Wedgwood plates that crashed down upon him.

'You are giving me nothing but bad news,' said Balimm.

Dredge crawled back along the table and climbed down.

'I-I can only give you … what I have.'

He limped to his chair and pointed to the large volume which Balimm had banged shut.

'That book … didn't turn up 'til … yesterday,' said Dredge, nursing his sore neck.

Balimm went over to the book.

'What, this? Nothing but a cheap book of spells.'

'You're right. Nothing special, apart from a couple of Merlin hexes. But turn to page forty-two, if you will.'

Balimm rifled through the pages. 'I cannot *find* page forty-two. It is missing.'

Dredge joined Balimm at the sideboard. 'Let me tell you, when a page number is missing in a book of spells, it doesn't mean a *page* is missing, just the number. It means the book has a message for its owner. I'll show you.'

'You had better not be trying to trick me,' said Balimm.

'You'll see, you'll see. I have to multiply the missing number by my astrological number to find the relevant page …'

Dredge leafed through the vellum pages. Some of the pages emitted sparks as he turned them, while others gave off distinctive odours, such as sulphur, chlorine or peppermint. Once or twice, snatches of self-incanting spells could be heard – Dredge turned these pages quickly, before the spell could finish. At last, he found the page he was looking for.

'Ah, yes, here we are – here in this margin, in silver ink. As I suspected, it's a message written in Merlin's own hand. Merlin had the rod last, remember, with Arthur.'

'Arthur?'

'Indeed. The legend of Excalibur –'

'But Excalibur was a sword!'

'No, no, in legend it became a sword. But in reality it was the rod. I explained all this when I told you who can wield the rod at the present time, and how it can be drawn from stone by the Wielder and nobody else.'

'I hate wizards,' Balimm complained. 'They always play silly games.'

'That's because, to a wizard, life *is* a game,' Dredge pointed out.

Balimm leaned over to read Merlin's message.

'Show me the message. I see nothing.'

'Ah … this particular game is for two players, Merlin and myself.'

Balimm frowned. 'Hmm. I am going to have to trust you, Dredge, and I do not like trusting people.'

The antique dealer swallowed hard but bided his time. It wouldn't do to make his task appear too easy. He pretended to be struggling to make out the message, even though to his eyes it was easy to read.

'Well?' said Balimm in an urgent tone which pleased Dredge. 'What does the almighty wizard say?'

'*By a silver … circle … in a … silver circle,*' murmured Dredge in a halting voice. 'Merlin valued silver highly, which was unusual in his day.'

Balimm began pacing up and down the shop.

'What silver circle does Merlin refer to here? Does he mean that the rod is *by* the circle or *in* the circle? Which?'

'I-I need time to work on it. It's a riddle.'

'A riddle?' echoed Balimm with a look of exasperation. 'I might have known – more silly games.'

'I need to brush up on Merlin's riddling style. I'm a bit rusty. But don't you see? It proves I'm on the right track. I know Joseph of Arimathea brought the rod over here with the Grail. I know Merlin found it and Arthur withdrew it from the stone to bring peace to his land. I worked out, because of that, who can withdraw the final piece from the stone now. And this riddle, in Merlin's hand, is the last piece of the jigsaw. It reveals how the wizard arranged for the rods to be *found.*'

Feeling pleased with himself, Dredge rose from his chair and turned to face Balimm.

'I feel I've achieved a lot in half a year,' he declared.

Balimm said nothing. He went over to the stove. Smouldering logs were visible through the glass window in the door. He walked in a circle around the stove.

'This presents a fire hazard, surely? Some of this furniture must be drier than your skin.'

Dredge didn't like where this was leading.

'I-I keep an eye on it.'

Balimm held a hand over the stove, as if to warm himself.

'I shall return after you close tomorrow – that gives you two full days to crack the riddle.'

The logs began to burn brighter.

'I shall expect you, Dredge, to know the location of at least one portion of the rod.'

The flames grew bigger and stronger. Now the fire was shining white like a furnace. Dredge could feel the intense heat now. The varnish on the furniture nearest to the stove was beginning to pucker. Fearing that the skin on his face would soon peel away like a cheap veneer, the old man retreated behind a tallboy. He heard the mirror on the Edwardian wardrobe crack from top to bottom, followed by the jingling of the door bell.

With Balimm gone, the heat died down. Dredge came out of his hiding place and surveyed the damage. *This will all have to wait,* he thought. *I'd better get to work on that riddle.* By a silver circle in a silver circle. *Classic Merlin.*

Chapter 3 — Branwen's Surprise

After breakfast, Branwen took Carys for a drive, as she had promised. It had started to rain, but not heavily – the Preseli Hills were taking their morning shower. For a while, mother and daughter rode along in silence, except for the swish and squeak of the windscreen wipers and the brush of the tyres on the wet road. The Land Rover reeked like all farm vehicles, a sweet and sour mix of muck and manure, mingling with the scent of sweat that comes from honest labour.

High up in the hills, Branwen turned and parked in a lay-by. Before them was a panorama stretching all the way to the coast. The sea was a silver ribbon, almost indistinguishable from the sky – the huge sky that loomed so close to the land in these parts, as though the gods were reluctant to leave. The shower had cleared. Big clouds were rolling in from the sea, casting moving patterns of dark and light on the patchwork of fields, most of which were dotted with sheep. A kestrel hovered above the verge of the road lower down the hill, hoping for prey disturbed by passing traffic.

Carys let out a deep sigh. It was such a peaceful scene. She glanced at her mother. Branwen had an open, honest face; it was impossible for her to hide her emotions. At the moment, her jaw was set and features drawn.

'Can't you relax, Mum? It's so peaceful here.'

'Everything looks peaceful from a distance,' said Branwen. 'From far away, people can't see the pain and heartache that generations of farmers have suffered to create this peaceful scene, including Bryn and me.'

Carys sighed again, this time from frustration. She loved her mother, but sometimes she found her hard to understand.

'Why did you bring me up here, Mum? Not to gaze upon Dai Jones's sheep, I'm sure.'

Carys was glad that her comment raised a smile at least.

'No, you're right. Those are Dai's sheep and that's his land, but I wanted to remind you, love, that all of this, including what belongs to Dai,' – and her mother made a sweeping gesture with her arm – 'is your land. You belong here, Carys. If you never come back to live here, it won't matter, because nothing can change that fact. City people don't appreciate it, how the soil gets under your fingernails and into your soul.'

When her mother spoke like this, Carys *did* understand her. Looking at the gentle slope of the hills and the different coloured grasses in the fields, she knew what her mother meant. Carys was as rooted in this landscape as the hawthorn hedge which marked the boundary between Jones's land and Merlin's Farm.

From surveying the land of her fathers, Carys's thoughts turned to the city of Worcester, where she was heading.

'What does Bethany think of my coming to live with them?'

Her mother hadn't heard. She was transfixed, as if listening for something, or someone. At last she spoke. 'Look in the glove compartment, love. That's where you'll find my surprise.' Branwen smiled her crooked smile, as she added, 'And no, it's not the gloves.'

Carys loved it when her mother cracked a joke. It made her seem normal. Carys played along.

'Oh Mum, why not? I'm sure all the girls in Worcester will be wearing bottle green woollen gloves, caked in sheep muck, with the finger ends missing!'

Now they were both laughing; a mother and daughter whose lives had not contained enough laughter in recent months. As she laughed, Carys trailed some strands of hair across her mouth, as if she were embarrassed to be having fun.

'Are you … are you sure it's in here, Mum?'

Then she saw it. Behind the spanners, the half-eaten chocolate bar and the inevitable oily rag lay a small, white box.

'What is it?'

'Open it and see, you tuppen!'

Carys was half afraid it would be a dried newt's leg or a bottle of moon dust – dust gathered during a new moon – so she couldn't believe it when she took the lid off the box to find a silver ring, lying on a bed of cotton wool.

'You mean …?'

'Well, it's too small to go on your finger, that's for sure. You should've seen Mrs Evans's face when I asked her if she stocked nose rings. 'Nose rings? Are you getting a bull then, Mrs Cadwaladr?' No, I said, it's not for a bull, it's for my Carys. She nearly spilled her morning pick-me-up over the first class stamps. I had to go into Caerfyrddin to find one.'

'But why? Why now?'

Carys had been pestering her mum all year to let her have her nose pierced.

'I didn't want you buying something nasty and having it done in a back street in Worcester, on the cheap. I've written a note – in my best English, look you – giving my permission. It means you can go into a proper shop.'

Carys was delighted, but couldn't help wondering.

'Have you … *done* anything to the ring, Mum?'

Silence.

'Mum?'

Branwen clicked her tongue against her teeth. 'Well … I might have said a few words, I can't remember.'

Carys smiled through tear-filled eyes. She wondered what spell had been cast over this innocent piece of jewellery. Was it now a ring of protection against demons? A charm so she could make ethereal contact with her mother?

'Does it make any difference, Carys? Don't you want it?'

The car's bonnet was beginning to steam as the late July sun rose higher in the sky.

'Of course I want it. But it's so typical of you.'

Branwen looked hurt. 'What do you mean, typical?'

Carys felt mean. Her mother wasn't well, she'd done something that she must have found difficult, and yet all Carys could think to do was criticise her. The ring was gorgeous.

'Typical of you … to be so kind, I mean. I shall wear it and think of you.'

Carys had to try not to think of her mother as her school friends did: 'two bat wings short of a witch' is what they called her. She leaned across and kissed her mother's cheek.

'Thank you, Ma.'

'I'm glad you like it. Mind you …'

Despite herself, Carys thought she heard the flapping of bat wings getting louder.

'… if you're ever in trouble, I mean serious trouble, it wouldn't do any *harm* to hold the ring and repeat the name we share, would it? Who knows, I may be able to send help?' Branwen took Carys's hand. Her tone became urgent. 'Remember, love, we have a strong bond, we who bear the name Aranrhod, stronger than between a normal mother and daughter.'

Oh no, not the Aranrhod legend again. Carys had never been able to tell Branwen how she envied daughters who had a *normal* bond with their mothers. Lots of people have embarrassing middle names – but not many, Carys was sure, were lumbered with the name of a moon goddess, passed down the female line for a zillion generations. There would be no stopping Mum once she was in full flow about 'the secret responsibility that is borne by all who are given the name, Aranrhod'. So Carys decided to take the initiative and risk offending her mother.

'It was thoughtful of you, Mum –'

'Yes, but Carys, I want –'

'And it's so clever because Aranrhod means 'silver wheel' and a wheel is a ring –'

'Yes, but –'

'And that's why I shall treasure it, always. It's an 'aranrhod' – for me, Carys Aranrhod!'

With that, Carys slipped the box into her denim jacket, and fastened her seat belt. 'I think we should be heading home now, Mum – you never know, Dylan may be preparing our packed lunches to surprise us.'

Branwen started the engine and laughed. 'That wouldn't be a surprise, love – it'd be a miracle!'

They set off down the hill, remembering the time Dylan had nearly burned the house down trying to cook his own breakfast. After coasting for a hundred metres or so, Branwen stopped the car. 'Did you see that?'

They left the car and walked a few paces to where the kestrel had been hovering.

'I never would have believed it,' said Carys, as she examined the bird. 'It dropped like a stone.'

Branwen bent down. 'I didn't hear no shot.'

'It's not been shot, Mum, but I think her neck's broken.'

'I'm not surprised. It's a long way to fall.'

'But Mum, birds don't fall. They can fly – that's why they're birds!'

'Listen!' said Branwen, 'd'you hear that? A humming …'

'It's the wind coming over the hill, Mother,' said Carys, climbing back in the car.

Branwen was about to get in as well, when she changed her mind. She went and picked up the kestrel and gently handed it to Carys to hold, before climbing in behind the steering wheel and setting off again down the hill.

'What are you doing, Mum? The bird is dead.'

'I know, I know, poor thing. But if she had the good grace to act as a sign for me, the least I can do is give her a decent burial.'

Branwen was leaning forward, scanning the horizon. There was a film of sweat on her brow and her eyes were bright. She was high on omens – in another world, where every event has significance. She began mumbling to herself.

'First, Carys falls into a black hole, then a kestrel falls from the sky. This morning I saw three buzzards flying into the rising sun. All my life, I've seen this coming. Branwen Aranrhod, are you ready?'

She turned to Carys, who by now could hear those bat wings hammering on the car roof to be let in. 'Carys Aranrhod, you're my only daughter. The sooner you leave this place, the happier I shall be.'

Chapter 4: Dylan's Dilemma

Dylan's car was packed and ready to go. All that remained was for Branwen to prepare food for the journey. She insisted on doing this by herself, sending Carys and Dylan out to play, as if they were still her little children.

They wandered over to the old apple tree that stood near the farmyard's boundary wall. It was all that remained of an orchard that used to occupy a large area next to the farmhouse. Carys loved to watch from her bedroom window as the tree's appearance changed from season to season. Sadly, it hadn't produced a good crop in a while. When Carys was little, one of its bright green cookers, with the core replaced by raisins and cinnamon, used to provide a delicious pudding for the whole family. The smell of baked apples was an enduring memory of her childhood.

The tree was gnarled but strong. Bryn had fixed a small swing to one of the overhanging branches, but the children had long since grown too big for it. Bryn had always meant to make the swing larger as the children grew, but it was one of those jobs he'd never got round to. So Carys now idly pushed the tiny swing back and forth and remembered the fun times she and her brother had enjoyed up and around that old tree.

Dylan leant on the wall and looked past the farm's dried up well, into the valley beyond. He began tossing small stones, trying to hit the well.

'Did you ever forgive me for throwing your doll down the well?' he asked.

'I can't remember,' Carys answered. 'I was very young.'

'I suppose I was old enough to know better, but it was a hot day and I thought she'd enjoy a cool dip,' said Dylan, laughing. 'I never thought about how I'd get her back – typical!' he added with a grin.

Carys joined him in throwing stones but she couldn't reach the well.

Dylan continued, 'When the well ran dry, I wanted to climb down and look for the doll, but Dad wouldn't let me.'

'Really? I never knew that.'

'He said it was too dangerous. He said there'd be rats down there as big as cats.'

Dylan found his range and began peppering the well with stones. 'You don't have to go, you know.'

'Yes I do. Mum thinks I'm in danger here from the great evil that's coming.'

'You don't believe that do you, sis?'

'No, of course I don't. But if I stayed here and Dr Williams had Mum taken away, even for a short time … well, you know how things work.'

Dylan didn't know how things worked. In fact, he didn't know much about anything. For a few years now, Dylan had been known as 'the brother of the clever one'. He hoisted Carys up so she was sitting on the wall.

'Is Ma really that bad?' he asked.

'You should have seen her this morning.'

'The kestrel, you mean?'

'She sees everything as a sign now,' said Carys.

'I'm not with her enough to judge, I suppose, but she seems okay to me.'

'That's because you're good for her, Dyl. You make her laugh. In fact, you make everybody laugh.'

'What you mean is, I'm a simple clod!' he said, with exaggerated indignation.

Carys laughed and chewed on some strands of hair. 'If Mum gave her clients their potions and crystals and left it at that, she'd be fine. But she gets carried away talking about angels and demons –'

'And the coming of a great eeevil!' interrupted Dylan, in ghoulish tones. He lifted Carys from the wall, threw her over his shoulder and ran round the tree making monster noises. Carys screamed and laughed and beat his back with her fists.

They both stopped when they heard a car door slam. Branwen was standing by Dylan's car, which was parked near the farm gate. It was starting to rain.

'Get off with you now!' she shouted. 'And mind how you go!'

Then Branwen ran into the house. Carys understood that her mother wasn't simply getting out of the rain.

The car rolled down the long drive. Carys looked back. Merlin's Farm was her home; she had known no other, and the Cadwaladrs had known no other for countless centuries. The house was made from the same stone as the Preseli hills that rose behind it. As she watched, the hills reclaimed the house, dissolving it in the fine mist of a summer shower.

'Maybe it won't rain so much in Worcester,' said Dylan.

Carys said nothing.

Changing gear, Dylan put his foot down and the BMW convertible accelerated out of the valley. 'Get the map book, will you love, and find Worcester. I haven't the faintest idea how we get there.'

Carys had memorised the route. 'M4 past Swansea and Cardiff, A449, A40, M50, M5, off at Junction 7 and we're there. Or we could cut across through the Brecons, but the motorway is easier.'

'I'll go with that.'

They drove for a while in silence.

'I hope Mum will be all right,' said Carys, at last.

'Now don't get me wrong, Cass. I'm concerned about Mum, you know I am, and she's having a rough time of it –'

The radio came on. Dylan shouted over it, 'But it'll pass, you know?' Tom Jones was singing. 'Look you,' said Dylan, bopping his head to the beat, 'I control it with these buttons on the wheel. Magic, see?' He turned the volume up high, a wild grin lighting up his face, then turned it down again. 'Sir Tom – now there's a Welshman who's made it big.'

'You're not doing so bad yourself,' said Carys.

'No, but I mean big. It would be great to have his kind of money. Ma could take on some workers and build up a new flock. With enough cash, I bet we'd solve the water problem as well.'

Carys was intrigued. 'If you were rich, you'd help Mum build up the business again? You never struck me as that interested.'

'No, you're right; I wasn't much help, was I? I suppose, if I'm honest, it was too much like hard work. But I wouldn't mind paying others to do it.'

Carys laughed. 'Sir Dylan Cadwaladr, gentleman farmer!'

Dylan joined in, his whole body shaking and shifting in his seat.

Carys looked around, admiring the car's interior. She loved the luxurious smell of the leather upholstery.

'Here's a thought,' she said. 'This car would pay for a few sheep.'

'You're not wrong there, sis. In fact, it'd buy half of blinkin' Wales!'

They both laughed again.

'But it's not mine, is it sis? It's the company's.'

With that Dylan shrugged and turned up the volume. Carys wondered what her brother's company did, that it could afford to hand out such generous perks.

After a while they swung onto the motorway, and made good progress. As they passed the first sign for Cardiff, Dylan dug out some wine gums and handed them to Carys, who chose her favourite, black. Then he opened his window and screamed out, 'Ma says none of you lot are proper Welsh!' which made Carys laugh so much that her hair became tangled up with her wine gum.

28

On the day Carys left home, Helen Cadwallader strode down the Great Hall of the Old Palace in Worcester, towards the room near the end, which was serving as her husband's study. She was of medium height, with a trim figure, of which she was ever so slightly proud. It prompted her to wear colourful, waisted dresses.

Helen had the peculiar habit of starting a conversation before she entered a room and, more annoyingly, drawing it to a close after she'd left. Drawing level with the Great Hall's enormous fireplace, she called out, 'Darling, did you get the message?' Several metres from the study door, she added, 'Carys is not coming by train after all.'

Entering the study, Helen couldn't see her husband anywhere.

'Stephen, where are you?'

'Over here, by the window.'

Like the Great Hall, the room Stephen was using looked out over the river Severn. He was sitting in a capacious wing chair, enjoying the view, which is why Helen hadn't spotted him.

'Did you know,' he said, 'when it floods, the river at this point turns into a lake? On the other bank, fortunately.'

'That's fascinating, darling, but did you get the message?'

'Yes, I did. Her brother is driving her,' said Stephen. 'I must admit, I thought it was strange, Carys travelling all that way on the train by herself. We'd never let Bethany, would we?'

'Of course we wouldn't,' replied Helen. 'But Bethany is younger, remember.'

Stephen reached over to the table next to his chair for his cup of tea.

'I could get used to this, Helen. Waitress service, real china, log fires in the baronial hall. Would you like a cup? I could ring for one.'

'*Ring* for one?'

Helen looked round the room for a tapestry bell-pull hanging on the wall somewhere.

Instead, Stephen took his mobile phone from his pocket and pointed to it.

'Since we're here for the summer, the lady in charge of the Palace Restaurant has assigned Hilda to respond to my calls.'

Helen dropped into an armchair and laughed.

'Only you, Stephen, could pull a trick like that and get away with it.'

'As the new Dean of Worcester Cathedral, I'm discovering that I can get away with all kinds of things – a lot more than ever I could as an ordinary vicar.'

'Darling, you were never an ordinary vicar. That's why they were desperate to get hold of you. They want you to work your magic here, as you did in all your parishes.'

Stephen got up and filled his cup from a tray on his desk. 'I mean, look at this: a silver tea set! Did you know, darling, this was actually the Deanery for a hundred years, until the Second World War? The Dean and his family lived here. I tell you, I could get used to it.'

Helen nestled deeper into her chair.

'Enjoy it while you can, dear. In a few weeks it'll be back to chipped mugs and frozen meals.'

'So, shall I ...?' asked Stephen, getting out his phone and pointing to it.

'Oh, go on then – and while you're at it, ask Hilda if there's any cake!'

*

Carys and Dylan stopped at the next service area. Carys reached for the lunch that their mother had prepared for them. As she unpacked the bag, the dashboard began to resemble the counter of a delicatessen.

'Good old Ma – never lets me down,' said Dylan, eyeing the feast to come. He poured them both some coffee from an enormous flask, while Carys unwrapped the first sandwiches. Home-made bread, each slice an inch thick.

'Beef or ham?'

'Any horseradish on the beef?' asked Dylan.

'Loads. They must be for you. What about the crumbs?'

'I told you, it's a company car.'

'So what's your company do, then,' asked Carys, 'besides handing out posh cars with magic radios?' In truth, what Carys wanted to know was how her brother had bagged himself a dream job, despite having few qualifications. But she didn't want to hurt his feelings.

'Professor Nash – he founded the company, see – has contacts working for him all over the UK. He wants to go global at some point.'

'That's great Dyl, but what does the company *do?*'

Dylan squirmed in his seat. 'It's something to do with the environment.'

'And ...?' added Carys.

Her brother took a huge bite out of the triple-decker sandwich that he'd constructed for himself. Through the mountain of bread, meat and horseradish, he explained:

'Sapih-ushush.'

Carys was unfazed. She was used to her brother's total commitment to the process of consuming large quantities of food.

Dylan spoke again, or at least made a valiant attempt.

'Sapihu-shush!'

This time Carys received a few damp crumbs on her lap, but no understanding of what Dylan had said. Finally, when he had devoured the whole sandwich, he explained that his work 'is a bit hush-hush'. The idea that her brother was engaged in some kind of top secret project increased the mystery for Carys.

Dylan continued, 'You know how sensitive the ... ah, Government is about ... this kind of thing.'

'What kind of thing? Nuclear waste? New airports? *What*, Dylan?'

'You know, the environment in general, I suppose.'

Carys sighed. She was getting nowhere. 'It is legal, isn't it? I mean, I don't get where all the money comes from.'

Dylan placed his coffee on the dashboard. The windscreen steamed over. 'Look, Carys Aranrhod, you moon goddess you, I can see you're worried about me and I love you for it. But I promise, we're not harvesting poppies from Afghanistan or anything like that. I told you, it's just ... hush-hush ...'

31

'Can't you tell me *any*thing?'

Dylan thought hard for a moment. 'The Professor has talked about "restoring the earth's energy", or something? That's about all I know at the moment. Honest!' He shrugged in his innocent way, then drank all his coffee in a few quick mouthfuls.

'The fact is,' he said, 'it's embarrassing for me right now – my job and all.'

'I must admit, Dyl, it does sound weird.'

'No, it's not that. What's embarrassing is I'm not needed yet. But Professor Nash told me, when he took me on, that I'm the ideal person for the job.'

Carys looked sceptical. 'So ideal that he's willing to pay you to do nothing?'

'He doesn't want to risk losing me, see. Money's no problem for him. He's one of those billionaires who want to do some good with their money. It's not a business, look you, it's an Institute. Anyway, I don't do *nothing*. I help out where I can.'

Dylan started on his second pork pie and held his cup out for a refill.

'Let me put it this way: I'm not complaining.'

Carys poured him another coffee, which her brother sipped at, chewing on his bottom lip and from time to time turning away from Carys to look out of his window.

Carys was worried that she'd pushed him too hard. 'Well … I think it's wonderful, Dyl. I'm happy for you.'

Dylan smiled. 'What about you, though, sis? Tell me about these English relatives. All right, are they? I mean, they can't help being English. Shows, though, how desperate Ma must have been.'

'It was either them or Uncle Elwin. At least Helen and Stephen have a daughter.'

'What's her name?'

'Bethany.'

Dylan started on Branwen's fruit cake, more fruit than cake. 'What's he do, then, this Stephen?'

'He's the new Dean of Worcester Cathedral.'

'Blimey, sort of bishop, is it? What did Pastor Lewis say when you told him you'd be living with a bishop? An English bishop, mind.'

Carys smiled. 'Not a bishop, Dyl. A dean's job is a lot like Pastor Lewis's, except he runs a cathedral instead of a fellowship, see.' She started packing stuff away.

Dylan scoffed a last slice of fruit cake, downed the rest of his coffee and swept all the crumbs onto the floor. 'I'd have been terrified at your age, going to live with strangers. You always were the brave one.'

The car eased back onto the motorway. On the radio, Abba were singing about money; Dylan sang along with gusto. After a while, the news summary came on and Dylan changed channels.

'Hold on,' said Carys, 'can we hear that?'

Dylan changed it back, in time to hear that there'd been a drop in people reporting the symptoms of extreme fatigue.

'I wonder what that was all about?' asked Dylan.

As they approached the Worcester exit, Carys began to feel nervous. What if they didn't like her? What if she didn't like them? Bethany was an only child, so if they didn't get on, there would be nowhere to hide.

Dylan went to speak, then stopped. After a lengthy silence, he tried again.

'Sis, um … can I give you some brotherly advice? Ditch the black, why don't you? Colourful clothes suit you far more than all this black kit. And Ma told me about the nose ring. Is that such a good idea? People are going to think you're a goth. Not that there's anything wrong with that,' he added, 'if that's what you want.'

Carys folded her arms and looked out of her window. 'People can think what they like.'

Dylan took a deep breath, which turned into a sigh.

'It's been six months, Carys. We have to move on, you know.'

'You're a fine one to talk,' Carys snapped. 'Who was crying in the bathroom this morning?'

Dylan didn't respond.

'I'm sorry, Dyl. That was mean of me. It's not been easy for any of us.'

'No, it hasn't. You're dead right there.'

He gave another deep sigh.

'Look, sis, at least promise me you won't cut your hair short, or shave your head, or anything silly like that? Long hair suits you. If I was tall like you, I'd grow my hair long. As it is, it would hang around my knees!'

Carys laughed despite herself. 'I promise. If you promise the same.'

'What, not to shave my head? That's easy. Professor Nash is bald, so I wouldn't want him to think I was making fun of him or anything. Between you and me, I don't think there's a single hair on his body – anywhere. Must be a condition.'

At this mention of a bald man, Carys felt a tingling sensation behind her ears, spreading across her neck. As her brother was chattering away about his boss being an eccentric, his voice sounded distant, while her own voice inside her head was shouting, 'I don't want to know! I don't want to know!'

But there was no escape. She had to know.

'– and you have to see his suits to believe them … Stripes and checks, in all colours of the rainbow.'

Chapter 5 : Stephen's Canon

Carys watched the car head up the street until it was lost in a line of traffic. She had asked Dylan to drop her off near Foregate Street station, so that she could walk the route she'd originally planned from there. She was pleased that her brother liked his boss, who sounded like a generous eccentric. Carys wasn't stupid. Despite her tingly neck, she knew that Professor Nash's resemblance to the figure in her nightmare was mere coincidence. She hadn't told Dylan about her dreams; the last thing she wanted was to sound like her mother.

Carys was walking past the station entrance when she had an idea. It was a silly idea, yet in her present mood it made a twisted kind of sense. She would call her nightmare's bluff. She would prove it wasn't a premonition by re-enacting her latest nightmare on the station platform.

She went into the station and walked down the platform, as fast as her rucksack would allow. No collision occurred. *Mum would be furious,* thought Carys with a grim smile. She trotted down the stairs, her rucksack feeling like a feather. There was a spring in her step as she walked out of the sta –

BANG!

Carys had collided with a large man, but he was neither tall nor bald. And far from wearing a multicoloured suit, this man was dressed in a black cassock. He had been clutching an ice cream until the collision. The ice cream now lay on the pavement, a squishy mess, being lapped up by a short-haired terrier.

Carys expected the man to be angry, but he was smiling.

'I'm so sorry, young lady. I should learn to give corners a wide berth in view of my wide girth.'

Then he laughed at his own play-on-words.

Carys insisted it was her fault. 'I'm sorry about your ice cream.'

'Don't be silly, don't be silly,' he said. 'Do you honestly think I needed those calories? You have saved me from exploding over the good people of Worcester.'

Carys giggled. He couldn't be Stephen, could he?

'In any case it serves me right,' he continued. 'Suzy begged me to buy her a triple cone and I refused. I said it would make her fat. Call me a hypocrite and I couldn't deny it, could I?'

He pulled on the dog's leash. 'Sit, Suzy, sit and prepare yourself to be introduced.' The clergyman stuck out his hand like a paw and the little dog sat and lifted its right paw.

Carys's heart melted. All the fun she used to have with her father's dog, Vala, came rushing into her mind.

The man bowed in the direction of the dog. 'This is Suzy. She has no pedigree. Mind you, she's from a dog's home, so she might be the lost heiress to a Crufts fortune, but I doubt it. Suzy, I assume this young lady from Wales, with the sweet North Pembrokeshire accent, is Carys Cadwaladr. If I'm wrong, I shall be extremely embarrassed and run down the street screaming.'

Carys giggled again. She didn't think of herself as a giggler, but this man was funny. Also, deep-down, she was relieved. For a split second, when she'd collided …

'Yes I'm Carys,' she said, shaking Suzy's paw, 'but how did you know?'

'Forgive me, forgive me. I don't know what came over me, introducing a dog before myself. She's not mine – belongs to my son, Zach. That's as may be. I am the Reverend Canon Roland Thomas. Call me Tom. I am a canon at this great city's cathedral, where Stephen Cadwallader is the new Dean.'

The canon started walking down the pedestrian precinct and so Carys went with him.

'That rucksack looks heavy,' Tom said. 'I would offer to carry it but I fear it wouldn't fit round my shoulders. I propose –'

He stopped and put his hand up in the air as if he were at a meeting.

'I propose that we ring the Dean, to inform him of our encounter, so he can make certain the red carpet is in place. The whole of Worcester is a-quiver with excitement at your arrival. Would you take Suzy while I call?'

He handed the dog's leash to Carys.

*

The first line of 'Jerusalem' rang out in thin, electronic tones. It was Stephen's mobile phone.

'*Right. Good. Excellent. How serendipitous indeed. Bye.*'

He went and stood by Helen.

'That was Tom. Carys is here. In Worcester, that is. Would you believe it, he bumped into her in Foregate Street.'

'Foregate Street? Did she come on the train after all?'

'That's a point. Do you know, that never occurred to me.'

Stephen placed his cup on the tray and flopped down in his favourite armchair. His hair was white, peppered with ginger – a relic of his Celtic roots, perhaps. He wore half-moon, rimless spectacles, which gave him the air of an academic. In fact, three years' lecturing had been enough to convince Stephen that he wasn't the scholarly type. His shoulders were narrow and sloping and he occasionally hoisted an invisible academic gown that he imagined was slipping off to one side.

'We've done the right thing, haven't we, Helen?'

'What, coming to Worcester?'

37

Helen was distracted.

'No,' said Stephen, 'I mean taking Carys. Did we give Bethany enough say in the matter?'

'Stephen, which way is south?'

'To your left. Why?'

'Doesn't the Severn run south to Bristol? Come and look, it's flowing the wrong way.'

She was gesturing to Stephen to hurry. He struggled out of the chair and took long strides to her side. He looked down at the river.

'What do you mean?' he asked. 'I said to your left, darling. That's the way it's flowing.'

'I could have sworn it was flowing from left to right.'

'An optical illusion, dear. It happens when the current isn't strong.'

'Of course. Silly me.'

Helen glanced at her watch and frowned. 'Bethany is supposed to be home by now. I want her here when Carys arrives.'

'Where is she? At Zach's?'

'Where else? In a way I wish she hadn't made a friend so soon.'

Helen picked up Stephen's phone and punched in a number.

'It might make it more tricky for – *Hello? Zach, is that you? Helen here, Bethany's mum. Can I have a word with her?* – more tricky for Carys to fit in – *Bethany? You were supposed to be home half an hour ago ... What? Well, bring Zach with you and you can carry on the conversation after tea – and then Carys could join in ... Why on earth not? ... Suit yourself, but I'll see you in five minutes.*'

Helen switched off and handed the phone to Stephen.

'What was all that about?' he asked.

'It's complicated.'

'Try me,' said Stephen mischievously, 'and I'll stop you if I don't understand.'

'Well, Bethany's having a marvellous time with Zach and she's not keen on bringing him to meet Carys. Not today, anyway.'

'I must confess to feeling a little nervous myself,' said Stephen, sitting down behind his desk, and shuffling through a few papers.

Helen followed him, embraced him from behind his chair and whispered in his ear.

'You've nothing to worry about, darling. Carys will fall under your spell – people always do. I fall every day.'

Stephen leant his head back.

'I'm not Merlin the magician. I think you should know that this is the Dean of Worcester Cathedral you're canoodling with.'

Helen asked, 'Aren't deans allowed to canoodle with their wives?'

Stephen's phone rang. He hesitated and then answered it.

Helen straightened up and walked towards the door.

Stephen's conversation came to a close. *'Right, I'll see to it. Thanks, Bill.'*

'What's up?' she enquired.

'Bill says the alarm has gone completely now. I'll have to deal with it. But first!' he shouted, to stop her continuing out of the door.

She popped her head back inside and asked in a resigned tone, 'But first what, darling?'

'First I'm going to ring the bishop and ask him to spell out what a dean's canoodling rights are.'

Helen laughed and blew Stephen a kiss. 'Are you sure you aren't Merlin?'

After his wife had closed the door, Stephen heard her say, in a voice amplified by the acoustics of the Great Hall, 'You mustn't be in your study when she arrives. I suggest you loiter in the lobby!'

Stephen smiled, and left his study.

*

As soon as Carys took Suzy's leash, the dog sensed there was scope for a bit of fun. She kept tugging at her collar. Carys loped along for twenty metres or so. It wasn't the same as a downhill race with Vala on the Preseli Hills, but Carys decided that if Suzy was going to be her friend, then the city of Worcester wouldn't be such a bad place after all.

They waited for Tom to catch up. As he approached, Suzy went rigid, yelped and then growled. It was as if her worst enemy had trodden on her tail. Tom stopped and looked puzzled.

'Are you all right, Suze?'

He picked the dog up and hugged her, as if she were a frightened child. After a few moments of being reassured by Tom, Suzy relaxed, licked his face and jumped back to the ground. She was her old self once more.

'I've never known her to growl before. Extraordinary.'

Carys was used to being with animals in wilder surroundings, so she didn't direct her attention to Suzy when the dog went rigid. Instead, she scanned in all directions to catch sight of whatever it was that Suzy had sensed. For a moment, Carys thought she glimpsed a brightly patterned trouser leg, disappearing round a corner. But though Carys had become jumpy about the man in her nightmare, Suzy would have no cause to be on the alert for him. Would she?

'Suzy was onto something,' Carys said to Tom. 'Vala – he was Dad's dog – could sense a fox on the move at the other end of the field. He wouldn't even be looking that way. Amazing, he was.'

'Was?'

'He was killed six months ago.'

Before Tom could question her about this, Carys handed Suzy's leash back to him and asked, 'Are you Welsh?'

'Thomas, you mean? No, I'm afraid I'm a boring Englishman. But I adore Wales, especially North Pembrokeshire. My son Zach shares my love for the area, so he's dying to meet you – oops, don't tell him I said that, will you?'

'What do you love about it?'

'The people, the sense of mystery, the light, the unspoiled landscape, the legends, especially about Arthur and Merlin – did I mention the people?' and he laughed.

He leaned closer to Carys, as if sharing a secret, and put on a dreadful Welsh accent.

'Where the spirits of the Welshry still roam, that's where I'd like to call home.'

'Is that Dylan Thomas?'

'Heavens no! *Roland* Thomas. I spout all kinds of drivel. Make it up as I go along. You should hear my sermons – utter nonsense, but nobody notices.'

They came to a large roundabout. On the other side, stood the cathedral.

'What do you think?' asked Tom.

Carys stood and gazed in wonderment. When she had said goodbye to her mother that morning, looking down over the Preseli foothills, she had felt a sense of peace. And now, to her surprise, she experienced a similar feeling. There were no sheep quietly grazing; instead there were cars streaming around the traffic island. There was no expanse of water shimmering on the horizon, only a sea of people rushing about their business. And yet, in the midst of twenty-first century mayhem, this medieval cathedral had put down a marker: here is peace to be found. In the thickness of its walls, in the massive tower which raised the eye heavenward, in its gracious permanence within the fluctuations of history, the cathedral proclaimed Peace.

'It's lovely.'

'Glad you like it,' said Tom. 'Be it ever so humble, it's what I call ... work!' and he chuckled mischievously.

Carys couldn't take her eyes off the cathedral as they walked round to a pelican crossing.

'It's huge!'

Tom laughed. 'It's bigger on the inside. We need to cross here to get to the Old Palace. The Old Palace is huge as well, but the cathedral makes it seem small. That's what cathedrals are for – to make everything and everybody seem small. That must be why I enjoy working in one.'

He slapped his bulging cassock with great glee.

Chapter 6 : Balimm's Plan

Although Dylan didn't need to return to work until Monday, he headed straight for the Nash Institute as soon as he arrived back in London. The conversation with his sister on their journey from Wales had troubled him. Not about their mother, for he was sure she'd be all right with the passing of time and the removal of stress. It was the questions that Carys had asked him about his work that had unsettled Dylan.

Yet there was no reason why her questions should have disturbed him. Carys had been shocked that he was being paid to do nothing, yet who in his right mind would complain about that? No one. Carys had also expressed surprise at Dylan's ignorance about the company's current project and his future role in it. But did he need to know these details? He did not.

So why was he in a lift, climbing towards the top floor of the building, the floor which contained Professor Nash's private offices? Dylan couldn't have explained it, other than to say that he valued Carys's opinion of him. It had been embarrassing to admit to his sister that he didn't know what the Nash Institute was about, after working there for six months.

The lift came to a stop, the doors slid open and Dylan stepped out. He hadn't been to this floor before. He found himself in a circular reception area, with six doors leading off. His shoes sank into deep-piled, burgundy carpeting that was emblazoned with the Institute's logo, an intertwined 'N' and 'I'. Dylan noticed that all the doors had digital keypads for feeding in access codes, so he couldn't go striding unannounced into Nash's office even if he had the nerve, which he didn't. He was about to return to the lift, when one of the six doors opened.

A man was backing out of the room, bowing and repeating, 'Yes, Balimm, of course, Balimm.'

This struck Dylan as odd until the man turned round to reveal oriental features, which explained the bowing – and 'baleem' must be an expression of respect. When the man saw Dylan, he was startled, as if it were unusual to see a visitor in the reception area. He was wearing white overalls and carrying a flask of green liquid that was bubbling. It gave off a faint, yellow vapour whose smell reminded Dylan of something, but he couldn't remember what.

This lab assistant walked over to one of the other doors and was about to punch in the access code when he realised that Dylan was standing behind him. He turned round. A cloud of vapour from the man's flask went up Dylan's nose, and this time Dylan recognised the smell. It was Professor Nash.

'What do you want?' the man asked, in perfect English.

The man's tone riled Dylan. 'I want to see Professor Nash. It's important.'

'That is not possible.' The man smirked, walked over to the lift and pressed the button. 'The Professor is in a high level meeting. I must ask you to leave.'

The lift doors swished open.

In that instant, Dylan knew how wrong he'd been not to insist on knowing more about the Nash Project. He had the uncomfortable feeling that this lab assistant knew more than he did.

'I am Dylan Cadwaladr,' said Dylan, brushing the man aside and pressing the button so the lift doors closed. 'There is no one more high level than me in this Institute. I am sure Professor Nash will see me. Please tell him I'm here.' In a flash of inspiration, Dylan bowed low and said, 'You know, baleem?' as a sharp reminder of the lab assistant's lowly position.

A look of terror came over the assistant's face. 'B-Balimm?' he stuttered. He bowed so low he almost fell onto his face.

Dylan smiled and bowed back.

'I'm so sorry, I didn't realise ...' the assistant said. 'Balimm, I will tell him ... please, forgive me, I did not recognise that you were ... I assumed you were ... I will tell him, please, wait a moment.'

This victory boosted Dylan's confidence. In truth, he wasn't looking forward to confronting his boss. A roar vibrated through the building, followed by a shrieking sound. They should have the air-conditioning serviced, for that air lock happened far too often in such an expensive office block. A couple of minutes later, a different lab assistant, carrying what looked like the same flask of green liquid, came out of the room and indicated with a low bow that Dylan should enter.

There were two people in the room – Professor Nash and a short, stout man. They both stood when Dylan entered. It was like walking into a sauna. The Professor must definitely have a skin condition, as Dylan had suspected, if he needed to have the heating on in his office at the height of summer. Dylan loosened his pink tie and undid the top button of his pink shirt, and tried to hide his disgust at the chemical smell in the air.

He approached Nash's desk, which was round, and bigger than the kitchen table back home. It was bare; no papers, pens, telephones or computers. As Dylan drew near, he realised why. It wasn't a desk, but a lab bench. A metal surface sloped down from the edge to the centre, where there was a large drainage hole, but no plug. Traces of wet slime clung to the surface near the hole, as if something had recently been poured down it.

Professor Nash pointed to a chair. 'Dylan, welcome. Get yourself a chair. I am glad you have come – and I apologise for the misunderstanding in the lobby. I assure you that assistant will not make that mistake again.'

This effusive welcome felt good to Dylan after the way he'd been treated.

'We were reviewing progress, Dylan. This is Professor Tomkinson, a colleague of mine – he has made a lifetime study of stone circles.'

Dylan looked into eyes that were blue circles behind a pair of round, rimless spectacles. Tomkinson's mouth formed the letter 'O' while at rest, and on top of what was clearly a bald pate sat a circular ginger wig. With his round face set in a permanent smile, he was like a stone circle himself. His voice, however, gave the lie to his cherubic appearance, for it sounded like sandpaper being rubbed over a gravestone.

'Stone circles,' he rasped, 'were built thousands of years ago by the human species, when they were at a more primitive stage in their –'

Nash interrupted him. 'Before you continue, Tomkinson, I should introduce Dylan properly to you. This is Dylan Cadwaladr, vital to our project. Dylan is one of the finest human beings I have ever met.'

Tomkinson got the message. He gave a nod of appreciation towards Dylan and then re-phrased his opening words. 'As I was saying, when *we* were but a primitive species, we built thousands of stone circles around the world. Are you familiar with the theoretical science behind stone circles, Mr Cadwaladr?'

Dylan returned the question with a blank stare. Nash, who was aware of Dylan's intellectual limitations, posed the question in a simpler form: 'My colleague is wondering if you know how stone circles worked, what they were for?'

'You mean like Stonehenge and that? They were used as calendars.' Dylan knew what he was talking about, for the bluestone used in the inner circles of Stonehenge was quarried from the hill behind Merlin's Farm. 'By lining up certain stones with the sun, moon and stars, they knew when it was time to sow or reap.'

Nash leaned forward and placed his hands palm-downwards on the lab bench. 'That may be true, but stone circles had another purpose, far, far more important.' He removed his hands and left a faint outline of his fingers burned into the metal surface.

The ointment to treat the Professor's skin must be powerful stuff, thought Dylan.

'You see, Dylan,' Nash continued, 'people in Neolithic times believed that the divine was within all creation –'

'You mean like tree worshippers?' interrupted Dylan. 'We've got a few of them back home. They reckon there are spirits in the rocks as well. A bit loopy, but harmless enough.'

'Ah, but sir, what if they are not "loopy", as you put it?' This was volunteered by Nash's circular colleague. 'Stone circles were built over sensitive points on the planet's surface, places where positive energy – divine energy if you will – bubbled not far below the surface. It was like sinking an oil well, only instead of physical energy, these primitive people tapped into spiritual energy.'

Nash took up the story.

'Tomkinson is right. This energy that they tapped is still available today. But humankind has become so obsessed with withdrawing *physical* energy from beneath the earth, in the form of oil and coal and so forth, that they have neglected to draw on the planet's *spiritual* resources.'

Tomkinson backed his colleague up: 'I'm certain we can restore the circles to working order –'

'But they will require a massive input of power,' interrupted Nash.

'Yes,' said Tomkinson, 'it will be like starting a car that's lain unused in the garage for years.'

Dylan could identify with that idea. Farm vehicles lie unused from one season to the next and need to be stored carefully if they are not going to seize up.

'What kind of power?' he asked.

Tomkinson and Nash leaned forward and, with one voice, said, 'Aaron's Rod!'

'Aranrhod?' echoed Dylan, looking puzzled. 'The Welsh moon goddess? Isn't she a legend?'

It was the professors' turn to look puzzled.

'Aaron's Rod,' repeated Nash. 'God's own staff, which he gave to Moses and Aaron. Do not tell me that we know your bible better than you!'

'Ah, Aaron's Rod, yes, yes!' exclaimed Dylan, relieved that the professors weren't relying on a mythical Welsh goddess to power their scheme. His brow furrowed as he strove to recall distant Sunday School lessons. 'Aaron stuck the rod in the ground, I think, and overnight, look you, it sprouted blossom and fruit, marking Aaron out as Israel's first high priest.' Then it dawned on him. 'You mean you've *found* Aaron's Rod?'

'Shush,' whispered Nash. 'This must remain within these walls.'

This was more like it. Dylan sat up straighter in his chair. 'And my job?'

'It requires a special man to wield Aaron's Rod,' said Nash, throwing a quick smile at his colleague. Tomkinson smiled back.

Dylan's head was reeling. He would hold in his hand the rod that Moses and Aaron had used to free the Israelites from Egypt. He didn't doubt that these clever men had found it.

'When –?'

'Soon, we hope,' the circular professor replied. A look of impatience flitted across his face.

Nash took the hint. He stood up. 'I am so glad you popped in, Dylan. Now we can move forward as a team. We must speak again, you and I – soon.'

Dylan walked towards the door. He opened it and turned round as Professor Tomkinson called out his name.

'Dylan! I can see why my colleague chose you.'

'And remember,' added Nash, 'not a word of this to anybody, including your family. We are trusting you.'

'I won't let you down,' said Dylan. He left the room and closed the door.

Dylan would have liked to stay and learn more details, but he felt more than satisfied with what he'd achieved. He now knew what the Institute's project was and how they would achieve it. Most important, Dylan knew what his own role was. He was dying to tell Carys. She'd be so proud of him. He couldn't tell her now, but one day she'd know.

Back in the office, the professors were congratulating one another on their masquerade.

'A masterly deception, Bagrimm – you make almost as good a professor as me!'

'Thank you, Balimm. These humans make it almost too easy.'

Balimm faced the wall of windows that looked out over Fulham. He could see the M4 snaking its way west towards Wales. 'Do not be deceived, my friend. Not all humans give in so easily.'

Then he opened his mouth wider than humanly possible and let out a mighty roar. The windows shimmered and bent out of shape. They weren't breaking or melting, simply disappearing. Soon, there was nothing in the whole end wall of the office but a gaping cavity.

Balimm's roaring continued until there appeared before him row upon row of unearthly creatures. It was as if they were suspended in the air on the same level as Balimm's office. However, if that had been the case, people in the streets below would have seen them. They were demonic beings, assembled in their own dimension. There were thousands of them, stretching to the horizon.

It was a good job that people couldn't see them, otherwise there would have been mass hysteria. They were all shapes and sizes, with no order or beauty. Some had bodies with limbs, but not in the right places, and out of proportion with each other. Others were amalgams of various earthly creatures. Others again had no discernable shape at all, being blobs of goop.

'I am sorry to take you away from your work,' Balimm declared. 'I wanted to congratulate you on what you have achieved using your own pathetic powers. Following the method worked out by Bagrimm here, you have restored several stone circles to working order and reversed their energy flow. The effects were localised and short-lived, but they did happen as Bagrimm predicted. Birds fell from the sky, rivers reversed their flow and – yes, my demons, human beings have been mysteriously short of energy.'

He began to laugh. A demon laugh is not a funny sound. A demon only laughs when others suffer. They laugh in contempt, from pride, or out of cruel satisfaction. Never in fun. Evil doesn't have fun or know humour. The legions joined in, though not many of them could laugh properly since they had no mouths or throats. But in their own ways they expressed their satisfaction at the thought of killing and causing pain.

'I can tell you now that I am close to obtaining the power we will need. I have discovered a vital clue, which is being solved as I speak. Once I have Aaron's Rod, its limitless power will be passed to you through me. By reactivating all the standing stones on this planet, and reversing their energy flow, we shall succeed in drawing out of the world all that is good, all that is positive and hopeful, including the spirit of love, and burying it in the earth for ever. We will convert this planet into a beacon of negativity and despair!'

Such a roar went up from his legions that it caused all the church bells in London to tremble and the clergy to drop to their knees in prayer, without knowing why.

Chapter 7 Bethany's Idea

Tom said goodbye at the entrance gate to the Old Palace. 'I feel privileged to have been the one to welcome you to Worcester, Carys. Suzy, of course, will expect you to toss her an ice cream every time she sees you!' He pointed to the building. 'You don't need to knock. Your family's quarters are up the stairs. Ciao.'

The Old Palace was a long building made of stone, with many windows and a decorative arch over centrally placed doors. As Carys was crossing the car park, one of the large doors opened and out stepped Stephen.

'Ah, Carys? I'm Stephen. Come in, come in.'

Stephen ushered her into a large entrance hall. The uneven black and red tiles underfoot and the smell of polish reminded Carys of home, but the staircase, which was wide and imposing, did not. Nor did the gallery of large portraits, in faded gilt frames, that covered the walls.

'Are they old deans?' asked Carys.

'They might be – or old bishops,' replied Stephen. 'You see, Carys, this was the *Bishop's* Palace until the 1850s. Then it became the Deanery until the Second World War, since when it's been the Worcester Diocesan Offices. A sad decline, I'm afraid.'

When they reached the landing, Stephen pointed to the left. 'Your room's down there, but come in and meet Helen and Bethany.'

Stephen turned right and led Carys into the Great Hall. Carys stopped and looked around her in wonder. The whole of the Cadwaladrs' farmhouse would fit in this room twice over – four times if the Great Hall's height was taken into account. Stephen responded to Carys's reaction.

'I know,' he said, 'ridiculous, isn't it? Imagine the dining table you'd need …'

Helen and Bethany were at the far end of the Hall, sitting on the window seat that ran the full width of the room and overlooked the river. Bethany had thick, light brown hair that fell to her shoulders in irregular waves and kinks. She had her mother's hazel eyes and button nose, set in an attractive face. Her cheeks had that wonderful English complexion that almost glows, rosy and ripe like a September apple.

'Stephen,' said Helen, 'take that thing off her back, for heaven's sake.'

While Stephen struggled to remove the rucksack without sending both himself and Carys crashing to the floor, Helen steered her daughter the length of the room. Then she put her arms round Carys and gave her a tight, maternal squeeze, which took Carys by surprise, and which threatened to go on and on. Carys's eyes met Bethany's, and for a moment she thought Bethany was going to smile a kind of 'Well, that's my mother for you' smile, but before it could move from her eyes to her face, the smile faded away.

'Welcome, Carys. I'm Helen, of course, and this … is Bethany.'

Bethany stepped forward and shook hands with Carys, with no hint of an embrace.

'Hi, I like your boots.'

She paid this compliment with so little feeling that it was obvious her mother had prepped her to make a nice remark about *some*thing. The fact is, Bethany would look dreadful in desert boots, or indeed in anything else that Carys had on. Carys weighed up what Bethany was wearing and decided that one thing they would not be sharing was their wardrobes. A loose, floral shirt hanging out over baggy blue jeans and trainers was not Carys's style.

Helen led everybody back down the room to the windows. 'Come and look at our view of the river, Carys. It's absolutely stunning.'

Carys knelt on the window seat and looked out.

Before she could respond, Stephen was pointing out the large number of swans. 'For some reason, they gather along this stretch of the river. I love watching them – such graceful creatures.'

'Swans are incredibly strong,' Carys said. 'A man in our village had his arm broken by a swan. Its leg was tangled up in a fishing line and Dai was trying to get it free.'

'That one doesn't look very strong,' said Bethany.

'Which one?' asked Stephen.

'That one on the bank, farther downstream.'

'Goodness me, yes. Birds don't sleep lying down do they?'

Carys was reminded of the kestrel. Was that today? It felt like a week ago.

Helen took Carys's arm. 'You look exhausted. Come with me, my darling, and I'll show you your room.' Then Helen tried to pick up Carys's rucksack. 'How on earth do you carry this? Hold on.'

Running up some steps at the top end of the Hall, Helen disappeared through a door marked 'Palace Restaurant'. She reappeared a moment later with a woman who was wearing a white coat.

'Hilda, this is Carys. Remember I told you she was coming to live with us for a while? Carys, this is Hilda. She's the Palace cook.'

Hilda laughed. 'You make it sound like I cook for the Queen. Did you hear that, Dean? I'm the Palace cook.'

Stephen chuckled. 'I'm sure Her Majesty eats no better than we do here.'

Hilda and Helen carried the rucksack between them, and Carys followed behind, still wondering at being called 'my darling'.

Their footsteps echoed on the bare oak boards of the landing, and along the warren of corridors. Helen's voice could be heard from the Great Hall. She was telling Carys how the entire diocesan education department had removed itself, so she and Bethany could have adjoining rooms.

After a few moments, Hilda returned. 'She's a nice girl. What's her name again?'

'Carys.' Stephen spelled it out. 'It's from the Welsh for 'love'. She's from North Pembrokeshire.'

'She grew up on a farm,' added Bethany.

The way she said it, it might as well have been a zoo.

Hilda headed for the study. 'I'll get the tray. Then I'll make you and your wife a fresh pot.'

When she emerged, Stephen said, 'Marvellous. I don't imagine Helen will be long.'

Stephen and Bethany watched Hilda walk the length of the Great Hall and disappear into the restaurant.

'I don't think I'm going to like Carys,' said Bethany in a mournful voice.

Stephen could counsel the bereaved and those about to be married, but sit him down with his own daughter when she was in emotional turmoil and he invariably said the wrong thing.

'Darling,' he ventured, 'we did say if it doesn't work out ...'

That must have been the wrong thing to say, for the dam burst, the tears flowed and Bethany threw her arms round her father.

'Oh Daddy, it's going to be awful!'

Helen's footsteps sounded in the corridor. When she entered the Great Hall, she was already halfway through telling Stephen and Bethany how amused Carys had been by the idea of keeping her clothes in a filing cabinet.

'So she's okay, then?' asked Stephen.

'A bit teary when I asked after her mother,' Helen replied. 'I can't blame either of the girls for being emotional. It's been a strain for all of us.'

'Has Carys rung home yet?'

'She can't – her mother refuses to have a telephone. Part of her paranoia, I suppose.'

Bethany unfurled herself from her father's lap and said to her mother, 'Doesn't she have any other relatives? We can't be the only ones.'

Helen began to clean her daughter's tear-stained face with a corner of her handkerchief.

'No, we're not, that's true. But the others are either ill, or too old, or don't have the room, or couldn't cope with having a thirteen-year-old girl living with them. Let's at least give Carys a chance.'

'But Mum, she's gorgeous!'

Stephen laughed out loud at this. 'Gorgeous? Darling, she's only thirteen.' This was another wrong thing to say.

Helen frowned. 'Weren't you doing something about the cathedral alarm system?'

'They won't come now, it's too late,' said Stephen, looking at his watch.

'So the sooner you get an appointment booked, the better. How will it look if the silver is stolen during your first week in charge?' By now Helen was gesturing with her head. Stephen retreated to his study.

'*You* know what I mean, don't you Mum?' asked Bethany when he'd gone.

'Carys is striking,' replied Helen, 'but she's no prettier than you.'

Bethany screwed her mother's hankie up into a ball. 'I must weigh twice as much as her.'

'Don't be silly! Carys is taller than you, and black is slimming, that's all.'

Bethany looked down and twisted the hankie round her fingers. 'Zach and I were going to have such fun this summer.'

'I'm sure Carys will be more interested in older boys.'

'I know that, Mother, I'm not stupid. I'm worried that she'll ruin things for me and Zach, just by being here.'

Hilda arrived with the fresh drinks. She placed the tray on a table by the window seats and returned to the restaurant.

'Thank you, Hilda,' Helen shouted after her. 'You are spoiling us rotten!'

Helen poured the tea and handed a cup to Bethany. 'Now, be a love, and take your father his tea.'

When Bethany came back, a smile was lighting up her face. 'Daddy says you were right. If he hadn't phoned the alarm people today, they couldn't have come 'til next week.'

Helen laughed. 'I'm not always right. I just give that impression.'

Bethany sat next to her mother, took her arm and squeezed hard. 'I'm being selfish, aren't I?'

'Well, perhaps a little.'

'It must be awful for her, losing her father. How did it happen?'

'Branwen didn't say. Carys will tell us about it, when she's ready.'

'I wish there was something I could do with her tonight. I'd like to get to know her before Zach meets her.'

'That sounds an excellent idea,' said Helen.

Stephen came in from his study, carrying his teacup. 'They'll be here tomorrow. We have to hope that thieves don't strike tonight.'

'That would be terrible!' said Bethany, diving onto the window seat. As she looked out over the river, her parents didn't see the gleam that had come into her eyes.

'I wonder what happened to that swan?' she asked, innocently.

Carys walked into the Great Hall at that moment. Bethany jumped off the seat and ran towards her. She grabbed Carys by the arm, took her to one side, and whispered something in her ear. Carys didn't respond until Bethany whispered a second time. Then they both ran off to their rooms, laughing.

'Did you see that, Helen? Talk about a quick turn around.'

Helen looked wistful. 'I was the same at her age. It's those hormones kicking in.'

Stephen frowned. 'I confess I don't remember being their age.'

Hilda opened the door of the restaurant to see if they had finished with the tea things.

Stephen called out, 'Hilda, stay there. I shall bring the tray to *you!*'

So saying, he balanced the tray on one hand like a waiter, and waltzed with it the length of the Great Hall, watched by Helen at one end and Hilda at the other. When Stephen reached the steps to the restaurant, Helen applauded and Hilda could hardly take the tray, she was laughing so much.

'It's going to be magic,' she said, 'you all living here this summer.'

Chapter 8 · Carys's Destiny

'Carys – it's locked!' Bethany whispered.

The moon, almost full, was being pestered by low, scudding clouds.

'Carys, where *are* you?'

Bethany had a busy voice that crackled with energy, like her mother's. Her words echoed in the night air, even though they were muffled by the scarf she'd wrapped around her face. Now, with her back to the gate, she scanned the garden through the narrow slit that she'd left for her eyes.

A tree moved. This was either a magic garden or it must be Carys, invisible in black jeans and sweater, her hair done up inside a navy blue baseball cap. She'd been more adventurous than Bethany, smearing her face with ash off the big log that lay in the Great Hall's hearth.

'What's it doing locked?' asked Carys. 'It wasn't locked when we tried it earlier.'

She was so indignant that she forgot to whisper, but luckily Carys had a low voice, almost husky as it nestled in the lilting embrace of her accent.

'Dad must lock it at night to keep people out of the garden.'

'Maybe he locks it to keep people *in*,' said Carys with a sinister laugh.

Carys was enjoying herself for the first time in ages. When Bethany had suggested a midnight feast, she hadn't been too sure. But when Bethany had added the idea of holding it in the cathedral, Carys's imagination had been fired. She loved old buildings, and to explore such a magnificent building, at night, would be fun.

For Bethany, it was a tried and tested formula. She and her friends in Sheffield had held several such feasts. They were fun because most of her friends had found being in a church at night a frightening experience, whereas churches held no fear for Bethany. Well, not much.

'We'll have to feast here, in the garden,' said Bethany, 'but it won't be the same.'

Carys tried the handle herself, but it was definitely locked. 'Can't we go round?'

'It would be too risky with you looking like a cat burglar – the police might pick us up.'

The noise of pubs disgorging their customers drifted across the garden.

'And I wouldn't like to bump into *them,* either.'

'A party, is it?' Carys asked.

'No, the pubs are emptying.'

'We don't have that in Brynmyrddin. Mind you, we don't have any pubs!' Carys would have laughed out loud if Bethany hadn't launched a series of shushes.

'So,' said Carys, 'we can't go round, and it's too high to go over.' She put on an American accent: 'We have no choice, Sarge – we have to go through.'

'How can we? I only brought the cathedral key.'

Carys stepped up to Bethany, toe to toe. 'Then it's a good job I brought these, isn't it?'

Bethany heard the muffled jingling of keys. She looked up into Carys's face. All she could see were the white orbs of Carys's eyes, shining like two tiny moons against the clouded sky.

'You've brought them *all?*'

'It pays to be prepared,' replied Carys.

The fourth key she tried was the one. The gate was actually a door, set within a pair of enormous gates. It was not a full-sized door, so Carys had to duck as she eased her long limbs through the frame. This added to a strange feeling that was growing inside her, a mixture of excitement and apprehension.

Carys locked the gate and put the keys in her bag. Then the two girls turned and almost jumped, because there it was. The cathedral. Towering over them as if it had caught them in the act. The girls stood there, looking up, mesmerised by the weight of it.

'It's weird,' said Carys. 'It looks bigger in the dark.'

The porch was twenty metres away, but in crossing that short distance they would be visible from the road. The two girls waited until the coast was clear and made it without mishap. Bethany unlocked the huge door and strode in, but Carys lingered on the threshold.

Bethany was signalling frantically. 'Come on, before someone sees you!'

Carys didn't move. She was holding her head as if listening for something or someone. She'd seen her mum do this many times and always wondered what she was listening to. Now Carys knew. It was as if she were on a boat, listening to the wind that was about to change direction, but knowing about the change long before the sails began to rattle and complain.

Carys walked in and Bethany locked the door. As Carys heard the clicking of the lock, she shivered – was she being locked into something greater than a midnight escapade?

Bethany noticed that Carys was shivering. 'Do you want to do this?'

Carys turned. 'Yes of course I do. I didn't realise it would be this cold in here, that's all.'

'I should have warned you. It's the thick walls. Are you sure you're all right?'

'Yes, I'm all right,' Carys insisted. 'It's a bit spooky, but I don't mind that.'

Bethany had known it would be spooky. Indeed she'd *wanted* it to be spooky, but nothing is the same in the middle of the night when the sun gives its warmth and light to the other side of the planet.

'I've always been at home in my dad's churches,' she murmured, 'but I'm not sure about this place.'

The moon was shining through the north windows, throwing down patches of cold light onto rows of pews, and casting deep shadows. The two girls walked into the centre of the nave and stood looking up at the ceiling. It was far, far away.

'I thought Tom was joking,' said Carys.

'What about?'

'He said the cathedral is bigger on the inside. But he's right. It's like the Tardis. We let ourselves in with a small key and there's all this space going on forever.'

'You mean it's a time machine?' said Bethany, playing along.

'Well, in a way it is. How old is it?'

'What, the cathedral?' Bethany paused. 'I think it's twelfth century.'

'That's funny; I thought it might be older.'

'There've been churches on this site since goodness knows when,' said Bethany. 'Nothing this grand, of course.'

'I wonder when the earliest was?'

'I think Daddy said sixth century, but it might have been six hundred and something.'

They had walked the length of the nave by now. Ahead of them were steps leading through an ornate rood screen to the chancel, where the choir sang during services. Bethany and Carys were speaking normally now, their voices echoing round the vastness of the vaulted ceiling.

'Shall we have our feast up by the altar?' asked Bethany.

Carys had never liked the word 'altar'. In the Welsh girl's mind, an altar belonged in a stone circle and was used by pagans for sacrifices. 'I don't think we should,' she said.

Bethany took a step closer to Carys and linked arms. 'I'm glad. I wouldn't have wanted to walk between those choir pews. I'd feel like someone was watching us.' Carys felt the tension in Bethany's grip.

'Look,' said Carys, putting on a slight shiver, 'this was a great idea, but I'm beginning to get cold. Let's find a place to have our feast and go home.' Bethany's arm relaxed.

Carys pointed to a door in the south aisle. 'Where's that go?'

Bethany sat down on the chancel steps. 'To the cloisters, but I'd rather not go there, thanks.'

Carys was already on her way. 'Why ever not? Cloisters are romantic.'

'They're also haunted!' Bethany's shrill voice bounced around the huge pillars. The echo lasted long enough for Carys to have retraced her steps before it died.

She sat down next to Bethany. 'You mean *these* cloisters are haunted?'

Bethany lowered her voice. 'I read somewhere that more ghosts are seen in cloisters than anywhere else.'

Carys spoke normally, refusing to be drawn into Bethany's fear. 'That doesn't make sense, Beth. Think about it. Why would monks want to hang around in draughty old cloisters when they could be getting their reward in heaven?'

'So how do you explain what people have seen?'

Carys jumped to her feet and started walking back towards the door. 'Simple. People imagine things.' She turned to see Bethany hadn't budged. 'Come on, Beth, this was supposed to be an adventure.'

'All right, but promise me, if we see a ghost, we'll make a run for it.'

'I promise. No stopping for a chat.'

They found the door ajar.

Carys couldn't resist it. 'Somebody's expecting us,' she said.

'Don't *say* that – I'm scared enough as it is.' Bethany hooked her arm through Carys's and drew her close, so they went through into the cloisters together. They decided to leave the door exactly as they'd found it.

'Seriously, Beth, that door shouldn't have been open like that, should it?'

'Probably not, but it's only an internal door. The main entrance from the cathedral close is down there, and that'll be locked.' Bethany pointed to the southeast corner of the cloisters, to the massive oak door straight ahead of them; a door which, even as they watched, began to creak open.

Carys thrust a hand over Bethany's mouth before she could scream, and bundled her through a nearby open door; wondering, as she did so, whether anybody bothered to lock *any*thing in this cathedral.

Making it clear to Bethany that she had to stay quiet, Carys closed the door until there was a narrow crack to look through. With the moon still masked by cloud, there wasn't much light coming into the cloisters from the courtyard, but Carys was able to make out a large, hooded figure, coming closer and closer.

His footsteps, assuming it was a man – assuming, indeed, the figure was of this world – were slow, and made an eerie, scraping sound. Where was this apparition heading? Into the cathedral? Or the room where they were hiding? She could see that he was hugging something to his chest like a tiny baby. A baby! Carys drew a sharp intake of breath. Was some evil, bloody sacrifice about to take place on the altar? What other explanation could there be for bringing a baby into the cathedral at this witching hour?

The figure drew level with the door. Carys sniffed a distinctive aroma … and nearly laughed out loud. There would be no sacrificial ritual. She knew of only one large creature that would presume to eat fish and chips in the cathedral – Canon Roland Thomas. As Tom walked past and on into the cathedral, she noticed he was wearing mules, whose soles scraped on the stone floor with every step.

Carys came back to Bethany. 'It's all right, Beth, it wasn't a ghost. It was Tom. He's eating fish and chips right now in the cathedral. He doesn't know we're here.'

Bethany kept catching her breath as she spoke. 'That was s-so scary. I've never been s-so frightened in my life! When that door opened just as I pointed to it, like it was me that made it happen. And then you put your hand over my mouth. That hurt!'

'I thought you were going to scream.'

'I was! That's why it hurt!' Bethany blew her nose noisily. 'Why weren't *you* scared?'

'The important thing was to hide. I suppose I didn't have time to be scared.' Carys had to get Bethany thinking of other things. 'Any idea where we are?'

Bethany stood up. 'I wish the moon hadn't deserted us. It's almost pitch in here.'

'Do you want to leave?' asked Carys. 'I don't mind, it's up to you.'

'What, and go back into the cloisters? No thank you.'

'You stay there, then, Beth. I'll grope around for a couple of chairs.'

'Carys, wait a minute, there's something weird about this room. Where are you? Slide your hands along the wall. It's not right.'

Carys was growing tired of Bethany's tendency to find everything weird or scary. 'It's only because you can't see it, Beth. Everything's different in the dark.'

'No, no, please, Cass, feel along the wall ... it's ... what *is* it?'

Carys decided it was easier to humour Bethany than to argue, so she slid her hands along the wall. To her astonishment, she had to agree – the wall didn't feel right. She found herself echoing Bethany's words ... 'What *is* it?'

Then it clicked.

'Bethany! The wall – it's curved!'

'Of course!' exclaimed Bethany. 'I know where we are, Cass – the Chapter House. It's a circular room.'

'What's a chapter house?' asked Carys.

'It's where Daddy will meet with the cathedral staff when the restoration's finished.'

'What restoration?'

'Oh dear,' muttered Bethany under her breath.

'What? What's the matter?'

'I've just remembered – this room is falling to pieces. Nobody's allowed in until the stonemason has finished. Nobody.'

Carys got the point of the repetition. *Nobody, not even the Dean's daughter.*

'Are your midnight feasts always this entertaining?' asked Carys, in as playful a tone as she could muster.

She'd hit the right note, for Bethany spluttered a giggle and asked, 'What shall we do?'

'Well, it's your choice. Either we share our feast with the cloistered ghosts, running the risk of bumping into Zach's dad when he goes for a curry, or we have our feast in a forbidden room that's falling down around our ears.'

Another splutter from Bethany. 'I choose this room. I feel safe here, somehow. I mean, it can't actually be falling down, can it – not falling *down*, otherwise it wouldn't be here, would it?'

Carys wasn't listening. As soon as Bethany had said she felt safe here, Carys knew that this was where she, Carys Aranrhod Cadwaladr, was intended to be.

'Good. I agree. It's a circular room, you say? So Beth, if you carry on going around the wall that way, and I go this way, we should end up meeting. Watch out for stuff on the floor.'

Almost immediately Bethany bumped into something. 'It's fixed to the wall. It feels like a stone bench. This must be where the chapter sit.'

Carys soon bumped into the other end. They continued round until they met somewhere in the middle. Sitting down next to Carys, Bethany reached into her shoulder bag and produced crisps, chocolate, and cans of cola. She gave Carys her share.

'Thanks,' said Carys, 'You can be the Dean for this *very* important meeting.'

'No, you're older than me – you be the Dean.'

'But you're a real dean's daughter. It's better if you're the Dean.'

'Oh, all right, you asked for it,' said Bethany, giggling. 'Knock! Knock!'

'Who's there?'

'Dean.'

'Dean who?'

'Dean-a, dean-a, dean-a, dean-a, Batman!' sang Bethany, although she could hardly get it out for laughing.

'Beth, don't you know that it spoils it if you laugh at your own jokes?'

'I can't help it,' replied Bethany, stifling more giggles.

'You were right,' said Carys, laughing. 'I should be the Dean – someone has to take control of this meeting.'

'You need one of those hammer thingies.'

'I'll use my fist,' said Carys. 'Order!'

She thumped the wall behind her. There was a loud cracking sound.

'Ow, that hurt!'

'Are you okay?' asked Bethany.

Carys felt her hand and wrist.

'I think so ...'

'I was afraid you'd broken something.'

Carys found a sliver of cement on the seat. 'Perhaps I have.' She found the hole where the cement had fallen out. The more she explored with her fingers to see how bad it was, the worse it got, as more bits broke away.

'This cement is crumbling at the slightest touch. You were right, Beth, this place is falling –'

Carys was interrupted by a beam of light which burst from the hole, shot across the room and splashed against a column.

Carys jumped up as if she'd received an electric shock. 'Where did *that* come from?'

Bethany giggled. 'You don't know your own strength – you must have broken through to next door.'

Carys was sceptical. 'Beth, even if I had, the light coming through wouldn't throw a beam across the room like that.'

Although Carys knew that the source of the light had to be something extraordinary, she felt no fear. On the contrary, she was experiencing an inner calm that she hadn't known for a long, long time. Carys was reminded of Bethany's comment when she opted to stay in this room – that she felt safe in here.

It was clear that Bethany was still feeling safe, for she was *playing* with the light. She was holding an empty crisp packet in its sharp-edged beam. After being frightened silly by her own imagination, Bethany was now showing no fear in the face of something that might hold real danger. She changed the angle of the packet and made the light bounce around the room. 'This is fun!' she cried.

'Sit down, Beth, please,' urged Carys. 'Doesn't it occur to you that this light might be dangerous?'

'How can it be dangerous?' Bethany replied. 'It's just a bright light. It doesn't even glare my eyes when I stare at it.'

'It might be radiation of some kind,' suggested Carys.

'What – there's a chunk of uranium in the cathedral wall?'

'It might be a laser, then.'

'It would have burned a hole in my crisp packet. Look, it's just ordinary light –' and before Carys could stop her, Bethany had put her hand in the light's path. 'See? It's harmless. And anyway, if you think it's so dangerous, what are we still doing in here?'

Bethany had penetrated to the heart of the matter – Carys wasn't afraid of the light either.

'You're right, Beth, I'm only saying what I feel I *ought* to say, whereas in fact I feel drawn to this light, as if …' Carys paused, surprised by the audacity of her own thought. *It's expecting me!*

There were now several beams shooting out from a growing number of holes in the cement that surrounded a smooth stone slab – the backrest for whoever sat in that spot on the bench seat. The slab was looking increasingly unstable. Soon, there wouldn't be enough cement to hold it in place.

'Move well away, Beth,' Carys warned. 'I think the slab of stone is going to fall off the wall.'

Beth moved along the bench seat. 'I wonder what's –?'

CRASH!

The stone slab fell forwards onto the bench seat, snapping neatly in two. The larger top section continued to the floor, where it broke into more pieces. The bottom piece stayed on the bench. Free at last, a tunnel of light shot across the room.

Presented with an opportunity to see the source of the light, Bethany hung back. But Carys didn't hesitate. She bent down and peered into the cavity.

'I can see it, Beth. It's a kind of …'

Carys reached inside.

'I … *think* … I can … just about … *get* it.'

She stood up. 'There!'

The light then exploded to fill the whole room. Carys was holding in her right hand, like a sword, a glowing rod. It was about sixty centimetres long by four centimetres in diameter. There were a few strange markings on it, which stood out against the light.

Bethany couldn't take her eyes off it. 'It's beautiful!'

She was so fascinated by the rod that she'd failed to notice that Carys hadn't spoken since taking it out of the wall. And that she was swaying from side to side. And that her eyes were shut. Then, as soon as Carys's strange condition caught Bethany's attention, the light went out.

'Dad!'

Carys knew this hillside inside out and backwards. She had played with Vala so often on these slopes – racing, wrestling, and games of hide-and-seek. She would hide behind the sparkling, bluestone rocks that littered the ground, like the jewels of a broken necklace that had been carelessly abandoned by one of the gods. But she never stood a chance against the tracking skills of Vala. Even when she hid downwind, the dog picked up her scent.

And there was Vala, up ahead, chasing after Dad and herding imaginary sheep. Dad whistled the dog to heel and spoke a few words to him, after which Vala followed quietly behind. Carys smiled. Dad always said that she played too much with Vala; he was a working dog, not a pet.

It was early morning. The sun hadn't yet risen, but it had sent heralds ahead, in the form of pink, fluffy clouds set against a pastel blue sky. It was very cold – Carys saw the trail of Dad's footsteps in the frost-covered path leading up the hill. He had his shotgun under his arm. When he reached the top, he turned, silhouetted against the pale dawn light. Did he see his daughter? Was he waving to her, asking her to follow?

Dad!

Then she fainted. The rod clattered among the scaffolding poles. Carys crumpled so silently to the floor that Bethany didn't realise what had happened.

'Carys! Why did you drop the light rod?'

There was no answer.

'Did it get hot? Are you all right?'

Still no response.

'This is not funny – I can't see a thing. Answer me – *please!*'

Carys groaned.

'Where are you?' asked Bethany.

'On the floor. I must have fainted.'

Bethany's eyes were adjusting to the shock of losing such a bright light. She bent down and helped Carys to her feet. 'You dropped the light rod. Did it get too hot to hold?'

Carys was dusting herself down. 'No. I told you, I fainted.'

'I'll soon find it,' said Bethany. 'I can see better now.'

'Don't bother – we'll find it later.' Carys's voice sounded strained.

'I don't mind –'

Carys interrupted, her tone severe: 'I said we'd find it later. Right now, I'm hungry. All right?'

Bethany didn't argue further. They found the remains of their feast and tucked in.

'What do you think happened?' asked Bethany.

'It was like a dream. I saw my dad, in the distance. He was on the hillside back home. With Vala, his dog. It was like a dream, but more real, somehow.'

'Your *dad?* Oh, Carys, how exciting!'

'No it's not, it's awful. I used to dream about him every night, and wake up crying next morning because it was nothing but a dream. It's not exciting at all.'

Bethany took Carys's hand. 'But maybe this was different. Maybe that light rod put you in touch with his spirit.'

Carys snatched her hand away. 'Don't talk like that, Beth – I have enough of that nonsense with my mum. You don't understand. I was beginning to have fewer dreams about Dad and now that … that rod thing might have set me back months.'

70

'But you said it was more *real* than a dream.'

'Yes, but it was messing with my head in the same way as dreams do.'

'What was your dad doing? Did he say anything?'

'I don't know. I can't remember. I don't *want* to remember! Now leave it, okay?'

Bethany recoiled from Carys's anger. She'd been drained by this whole escapade. Firstly, there was the disappointment of the garden gate being locked; then she'd had that awful scare when the south door had opened. That had been followed by the excitement of finding an ancient object hidden in the wall; then Carys had seen her father and fainted. And now Carys was angry with her. Very angry.

Bethany couldn't help herself. She started to cry. She dropped her head onto Carys's lap, and said through her tears how sorry she was. About everything. About the midnight feast, which had been a disaster; about Carys's father, who shouldn't have died; about Carys's dream, or vision, or whatever it was, which had been so weird.

Seeing Bethany cry like that, Carys felt ashamed.

Bethany had meant well. She'd been scared, and yet she'd carried on with the feast. Bethany had made such an effort to make her feel welcome and all Carys could do was get angry with her. If only Dad were here, he'd make everything right. Tears began to fall …

Suddenly the room filled with light.

Bethany and Carys instantly stopped crying and fell into uncontrollable laughter at the sight of Bethany's father, who was standing by the light switch. The new Dean of Worcester was in his pyjamas, holding a cricket bat, and asking them to explain *exactly* what they thought they were doing.

Part Two

Aaron's Rod

Border text (clockwise from top): the town centre. She'd ask Zach to join them, along with his dog, Suzy. Zach was twelve, small for his age in both height "It must be incredible to live on Merlin's Farm!" exclaimed Zach. It was after lunch the next day, and Bethany was showing Carys

Chapter 9: Zany Zach

'It must be incredible to live on Merlin's Farm!' exclaimed Zach.

It was after lunch the next day, and Bethany was showing Carys the town centre. She'd asked Zach to join them, along with his dog, Suzy. Zach was twelve, small for his age in both height and build. His face had a delicate appearance, with pale skin and high cheekbones. But his hair was his crowning glory: tawny brown, thick and wavy, it cascaded onto his shoulders.

The four of them were strolling up the Shambles, Carys and Zach lagging some distance behind. From time to time, Zach had to perform a little skip and a jump in order to match Carys's longer stride.

Carys laughed. 'Merlin's Farm is only a name – the wizard's not our landlord or anything.'

'Well, it wouldn't surprise me, not in Pembrokeshire. It's a magical place.'

'North Pembrokeshire,' Carys corrected him.

'*North* Pembrokeshire, yes, I'm sorry.' Zach did an extra skip and a jump. 'Is it true the Romans never penetrated the Landsker Line, or is that a legend?'

'No, it's true. Not even the Roman army could get through a line of Welsh castles. But I'm impressed – you knowing about the Landsker Line, I mean.'

Zach knew all kinds of odd things. He was an individualist, immune to normal peer pressures. Fated to be different because of his slight stature and powerful intellect, he had chosen to celebrate his uniqueness rather than deny it. Today he wore a green velvet jacket, and fawn trousers that had a large check pattern. His shoes were green suede, tied with brown laces. A coffee-coloured, polo neck sweatshirt completed his outfit.

'I only know about the Landsker Line because we've been on holiday there. My dad loves Celtic myths, stone circles and stuff. I'm the same.'

'What about your mum?'

'She's a landscape painter, so she can't get enough of the place. I can see them retiring there.'

Carys's face lit up as she pictured the wonderful views around her home. 'Tom mentioned he'd like to live there, but I didn't think he was serious.'

'That *can* be a problem with Dad,' said Zach. He hopped and skipped in front of Carys and began trotting backwards, so he could challenge her face to face.

'I've thought of a Roman who made it past all your defences – King Arthur.'

'Ah, yes,' Carys fired back, 'but Arthur came as a friend, not an enemy. We Welsh have always been quick to spot the difference!'

Zach came back to her side.

'You know, I've always wondered, why hasn't the Welsh Tourist Board identified Excalibur's lake?'

'You must be joking,' said Carys. 'All that Arthurian stuff is medieval legend.'

'So? Is the Loch Ness Monster real? People love legends – especially tourists. I can see them now, arriving at Merlin's Farm by the coachload. First they make a wish as they throw a replica sword into Excalibur Lake, and then they partake of a Wizard Tea on the farm.'

'Sorry to disappoint you, but Excalibur Lake can't be on Merlin's Farm. Our land's bone dry.'

'Pity,' said Zach, 'it would have been a nice little earner for you.'

Carys looked closely at Zach, but he was being serious.

'Dad was telling me about your escapade last night,' he continued. 'He was – '

Carys interrupted him, excused herself and raced on ahead.

'Well, what do you think?' asked Bethany, when Carys drew level.

'He's fun – but does he ever stop talking?'

'I know. And when he's not talking, he's reading books about history and geography. He wants to be an archaeologist.'

Zach caught up with the girls and took Suzy's leash.

'Dad's sorry about last night. If he'd known it was you, he'd have joined you in your feast. He rang Stephen because he saw the light and assumed you were intruders.'

Carys laughed. 'If we *had* been intruders, I'm not sure Stephen in his pyjamas and wielding a cricket bat would have been much use.'

Bethany joined in. 'Poor Dad, he looked so funny!'

Zach continued, 'You do realise, don't you, that you chose the only ten minutes all night when no one was keeping watch?'

Bethany stopped in her tracks. 'I've just thought – I hope we didn't get your dad into trouble.'

'Not a chance. I heard him and Stephen laughing about it this morning. I suppose it might have been different if the silver had been stolen. What about you two?'

'We were ticked off, but that's all. Dad was most annoyed that we went into the Chapter House, where we could have been seriously hurt. So Carys said –'

Carys shook her head angrily. 'I said if it's so dangerous, it should be kept locked, not left wide open for passers-by to stumble into.'

Zach yelped with delight. 'You *didn't!* And was the door really open?'

'Of course it was,' said Bethany, 'but they didn't believe us. I can't imagine how they'd react if we told them what happened to us while we were *in* the Chapter House. Not that we ever would – tell them, I mean.' Before Zach could respond, Bethany seized Carys's hand. 'Come on, I'll show you the market.'

The girls ran off together, leaving Zach to play catch-up once more. He found them at an accessories stall, inside the market entrance. He tried on a pair of dangly earrings and asked Suzy's opinion. The dog shook her head.

'So what happened in the Chapter House, then?' Zach asked Bethany. 'Did you break something?'

Bethany was sorting through lip glosses. She casually asked Carys if they should tell him about the rod.

'What rod?' asked Zach.

'Oh, nothing,' said Carys. 'We found an old candlestick, that's all.'

Bethany held out a purple stick of gloss towards Zach.

'What do you think?'

Zach took it off her and smeared a trace on the back of his hand. 'Not for me; doesn't suit my colouring.'

'Not for you, silly, for Carys.'

Carys took it off Zach and returned it to the stall. 'Sorry Beth, I don't wear lip gloss; mouth's too big.'

'You couldn't have found a *candle*stick,' persisted Zach. 'Dad cleared everything out of that room for the restoration work.'

'You're right, it wasn't a candlestick,' said Bethany, 'it was a magic wand. So what about eye shadow, Carys?' She picked up a colour chart.

Zach grabbed the chart off her and put it back on the stall. 'Look, Bethany, can the Carys makeover wait while you tell me what happened in the Chapter House?'

Bethany's eyes sparkled.

'Nothing much. There was this ancient rod that lit up, that's all.'

'Ancient rod that lit up? What are you gibbering about?'

Bethany scrunched up her nose in defiance. 'I'm not gibbering. Ask Carys.'

But Carys had wandered off. She was chatting to the owner of a jewellery stall.

Zach persisted. 'No, I'm asking *you,* Beth. So go on, tell me all about this ancient rod. You found it in a secret drawer, I suppose.'

Bethany told him how Carys had dislodged the stone.

'So you're saying that Carys happened to choose the seat with the artefact?'

'With the what?'

'The artefact. It's what archaeologists dig up.'

'Really? Anyway, the rod was incredible, Zach. It made the whole room light up, and when Carys held it, she saw her father. Her *dead* father. Then she fainted.'

Carys wandered back over to them. She was smiling.

'I've found out where I can get my nose pierced.'

Zach was horrified.

'You don't mean here, in the market?'

'No, of course not,' replied Carys, laughing.

She led them out of the market and back onto the Shambles.

'Are you having a stud or a ring?' asked Bethany.

'My mum's given me a ring.'

'Your *mum* has given you a nose ring?' Zach exclaimed. 'What kind of cool mother is that?'

'You should try living with her. She has her own reasons for giving me one.'

Zach was incredulous.

'What possible reason could a mother have for giving her daughter a nose ring?'

'She's cast some kind of spell over it,' said Carys, nonchalantly.

For the first time ever, because for once her audience was approving, Carys could feel a tingle of pride as she revealed her mother's weird ways – though it didn't make talk of spells any less ridiculous.

Zach was leaping around like a firecracker.

'A spell? Your mother cast a *spell?* And you live on *Merlin's* Farm? Carys, is there something you're not telling us? Wait a minute – what's your surname? Is it the same as Bethany's? Cadwallader?'

Zach was trotting backwards again, an action that not even Suzy could emulate, despite the dog's large repertoire of tricks.

'It sounds the same, but ours is the original spelling.' Carys spelled it out and then said the name in her soft, lilting accent: 'Cadwaladr.'

She made it sound like a rill bubbling down the Preseli Hills on a sunny day. It had a strange effect on Zach. He held his free hand high in the air and repeated the name in a long, drawn-out cry, oblivious of passers-by.

'CAD ... WAL ... AAA ... DDD ... ERRR'

The two girls dashed on ahead in case people guessed they were with the lunatic.

'What a character,' said Carys to Bethany as they sat down on an empty bench. 'I mean, is he for real?'

'Carys, I swear he's like this all the time. One minute he's talking like my dad, the next minute he's an absolute hoot!'

As Zach approached the two girls, he was snapping pictures with his mobile phone. He sat down and Suzy jumped onto his lap.

'Do you realise,' he asked Carys, pronouncing each word distinctly, 'whose illustrious surname you bear?'

'Yes,' she replied without enthusiasm.

'But I don't,' intervened Bethany. 'Whose, whose?'

'King Arthur was a Cadwaladr,' said Zach.

Carys looked unimpressed. 'So what?'

'So what?' echoed Zach, and then again, 'So *what?*'

Bethany giggled; a nervous giggle.

Carys persisted. 'Everybody round where I live claims to be descended from Arthur. What exactly are you saying, Zach?'

'I don't *exactly* know,' he replied, throwing his arms up in despair. 'But you belong to the Cadwaladrs of Merlin's Farm, and King Arthur was a Cadwaladr and he had a wizard –'

'Don't you see that these are *coincidences?*' cried Carys. 'It's chance, nothing more.'

'So you don't believe in magic at all?' asked Bethany, almost pleading. 'There's things happening all the time that we can't explain.'

'Because we can't explain something, that doesn't mean it's magic. All it means is we can't explain it.' Carys had clearly thought this question through many times.

Zach snapped his fingers and Suzy jumped off his lap. He stood up and began pacing up and down. 'That is true. But that needn't stop us from investigating it.' He stopped and turned to face the girls, holding his lapels like a professor. 'Everything in creation follows laws – we just haven't discovered the laws governing magic yet. Even magic has to make sense.'

Bethany smiled in Carys's direction, as if to say *I told you he's for real.*

Carys took out a black ribbon and tied back her hair. She was impressed, despite herself. She'd never heard magic talked about in such a down-to-earth manner.

Bethany went to speak but Zach got in first.

'Can I examine your ring, please, Carys?'

Carys fished out her silver nose ring and placed it on Zach's outstretched hand.

Zach turned it over gently in his palm, as if it were alive. 'I can't get over the fact that your mother cast a spell on this. It looks so … ordinary.'

'Thanks a lot,' said Carys, with mock indignation. 'I think it's beautiful.'

'I didn't mean that.'

'She's teasing, silly!' Bethany exclaimed.

Carys took the ring back and put it away. 'I'm looking forward to wearing it, but I'll never use it as Mum intended.'

'Oh, *I* would,' said Bethany, 'all the time. How does it work?'

'I'm quite sure it *doesn't* work, Beth, but Mum told me that if I'm in serious trouble, I'm supposed to hold the ring and repeat my middle name.'

'And then what happens?'

'Mum said help would arrive – as if by magic,' she added, laughing at the absurdity of it.

'Is your middle name supposed to have magic powers?' asked Zach.

'Of course not!' Carys was no longer finding it funny. 'It's my mother's middle name as well. It's a family name, passed down the female line, from mother to daughter.'

There was a silence.

'So, what *is* it?' asked Bethany.

'It's embarrassing, that's what it is!'

'No, but the name, what's the *name?*'

Carys adjusted her hair ribbon, tightening the bow.

'If you must know, it's Aranrhod.'

Zach looked puzzled. 'So?'

'In Welsh mythology, Aranrhod was the moon goddess. It means "silver wheel", see, like the moon?'

'What's embarrassing about that?' asked Bethany.

'How would *you* like to be named after a moon goddess? What's your middle name anyway?'

'I don't have one, but if I did, I'd want something like that – a star, maybe.'

Zach was even more in favour. 'Aranrhod is a fabulous name. It speaks to me of Welsh knights fighting on the strand for the love of a fair damsel, their swords glinting in the light of the moon goddess. But ho! What have we here?'

He jumped up and gave Suzy a hand signal. The dog stood on her hind legs while flailing her front paws like a boxer.

''Tis my sworn enemy, Sir Suzy Thomas, who dares challenge me in broad daylight.'

Zach began to swordfight with his dog.

'Have at you, mongrel cur!' he cried, throwing Suzy a treat. Then he sat down. When the girls had stopped laughing, he carried on.

'Bethany's right, Carys, your name isn't embarrassing at all.'

'Aah, but I haven't told you the awful part, the family legend that's *linked* to Aranrhod. The name is passed from generation to generation, right?' Carys's cynical tone indicated how little she believed all this. 'Well, the legend decrees that, one day, a bearer of the name will have to fight against a great evil.'

'It sounds like Pass The Parcel,' said Bethany, who had hung on Carys's every word.

Carys liked the playful image. 'It *is* like Pass The Parcel, Beth, you're right – and Mum believes that the music has stopped. *She* has to open the parcel. *She* has to fight the great evil. She's always believed it. All my life I've seen her waiting for instructions. And now she sees omens everywhere.'

'How far back does this Aranrhod legend go?' asked Zach.

'A long time, according to Mum. Why?'

'Wouldn't it be fabulous if it went all the way back to Merlin's time? Like Cadwaladr does.'

'Honestly, Zach,' said Bethany, 'why does everything have to reach back to Merlin?'

'It doesn't. But it would mean that Carys, who lives on Merlin's Farm, has legends about her surname *and* her middle name that go back to the old wizard. That would be cool.'

Carys was beginning to regret telling her friends about the legend. 'I wouldn't wish the legend of Aranrhod on any family. Because Mum believes she's the Chosen One, she's always assumed that I'll be in danger when the great evil comes. That's why ... that's why she's sent me to Worcester.' Carys tried one pocket and then the other, but failed to find a handkerchief to wipe her tear-filled eyes.

'If she hadn't,' said Bethany, handing Carys a tissue, 'we would never have met – so good has come out of the great evil!'

Carys smiled as she dried her eyes. She did like Bethany, despite her silliness.

'What about your father?' asked Zach.

Bethany began making frantic signs to Zach, shaking her head and mouthing the word 'No'.

Zach ignored her.

'Dad told me that your father had died, but nobody knows how.'

Bethany glared at Zach. 'You shouldn't ask her about that.'

Carys cleared her throat and put the tissue in her pocket. 'It's all right, Beth – really, it is.'

Carys meant it. After all the nonsense about magic rods and family legends, it would be a relief to talk about something that had really happened. *There's nothing more real than death,* she thought grimly.

'I could do with some help, though,' she added, patting her knee as an invitation to Suzy to sit on her lap. Suzy didn't budge, but looked at Zach and tilted her head. Zach winked and up she jumped onto Carys's lap, lying with her chin on her front paws.

Carys stroked the dog and spoke quietly but firmly. 'It's simple. Early one morning, about six months ago, my dad went up our hill to the place where the Stonehenge Bluestones came from. He had with him his dog and his shotgun. First, he shot Vala through the head, and then he shot himself through the heart.'

Chapter 10 · Talking Stones

It sounded like a newspaper report. But she'd managed it. Carys had described her father's death.

Nobody spoke.

It was too much for Bethany. Her eyes filled with tears. 'You shouldn't have asked her, I-I told you!'

Zach stared at the ground. 'I'm sorry, Carys – if I'd realised …'

'There's nothing to be sorry about,' said Carys. 'You didn't force me to tell you. And anyway, suicide isn't all that unusual amongst hill farmers.'

Reducing her father's death to a statistic in this way chilled the atmosphere even more.

'Yes, but, all the same …' Bethany was struggling to compose herself.

'I was angry at first,' said Carys. 'It felt like my father had deserted me. But then I looked at it from his point of view and began to wonder about the strain he must have been under, what with our water drying up and the price of sheep plummeting. So in the end it's been mostly sadness for me, a hole filled with sadness, always there, inside me.'

'What about your mother?' asked Zach. 'What with her illness and everything …'

'Mum's forebodings helped her in a way. An owl came to rest on the wall of our well the day before it happened, so she almost accepted the tragedy as part of the great evil she's expecting to arrive.'

Bethany was curious. 'An owl?'

'In olden times, owls were an ill omen in Wales – and they still are for my mother.'

There was another silence. This time it was Carys who spoke first.

'My brother Dylan took it the hardest. He feels betrayed.'

'What's he doing now?' asked Zach.

'A top job in London. He was head hunted by the Nash Institute, right after Dad died. So we've not seen a lot of Dylan.'

'What do they do?' asked Bethany.

Carys considered telling them about her nightmare and Dylan's boss, but she decided against it. 'Oh, they're trying to restore the earth's positive energy, or something.'

'Sounds a bit kooky,' said Zach.

Carys forced a laugh. 'That was my reaction. But it's well paid.'

Zach stood up and went some distance away. Suzy jumped down but knew not to follow him, and the girls took their cue from her. Zach looked as if he was counting on his fingers.

'That must have been so hard to talk about,' said Bethany to Carys. 'I'm surprised at Zach.'

'It's okay. He wasn't to know. And I do feel better now that I've told you everything.'

Zach made his way back.

'What were you counting on your fingers?' asked Bethany.

'Oh, nothing. It helps me to think. But I've come up blank.'

Carys stood up. 'Does that mean we've finished? I'm dying to get my nose done.'

Zach swept a loose lock of hair from his forehead. 'Do you mind if I give it a miss? I feel faint just thinking about it.'

Bethany rolled her eyes. 'Boys – honestly! Never mind, I'll come with you, Carys.'

'No, it's okay, I'd rather go on my own, thanks Beth.'

'But what if you get lost?'

'Beth, I won't get lost. But if I do I'll ring you, okay?'

'Yes, of course!' exclaimed Bethany, trying hard to hide her disappointment. 'See you back at the Palace, then.'

Carys laughed as she strode off down the Shambles. 'All right, Princess Bethany, I'll see you at the Palace!'

Zach stood staring after her. 'Can you imagine walking around with a ring in your nose that your mother has cast a spell over? It makes my sister's piercings seem totally boring.'

Bethany put on a long face. 'Talk about boring – Mum won't even let me wear make-up.' She bent down and stroked Suzy. 'I wish Carys had let me go with her.'

'She'll be okay. It only takes a second.'

'It's not that. It must be so hard for her – first her dad commits suicide and now she thinks her mum is going crazy. I thought *I* had problems.'

'Carys could be wrong, you know,' said Zach, as they began to wend their way home. 'Maybe her mother *isn't* going crazy. What if she's one of those Welsh wise women? After all, she lives on Merlin's Farm, and has a family name handed down from the moon goddess ...'

'No, not handed down from the moon goddess; named *after* her, silly!'

Zach began punctuating his remarks with leapfrogs over a line of bollards. Suzy kept pace with him, leaping over smaller, imaginary bollards. 'And remember this, Beth ...' (bollard) '... Carys is giving us ...' (bollard) '... a biased picture of her mother ...' (bollard) '... because she doesn't believe ...' (bollard) '... in magic.'

Bethany was running alongside Suzy. 'It's so frustrating. How can Carys *not* believe in magic after everything that happened with the rod last night –?'

Zach almost speared himself on the last bollard. He confronted Bethany.

'Will you *stop* it now with the magic rod thing?'

He wanted to go back over the bollards but Bethany stood in his way. Her face was flushed, with anger as much as from the running. 'I thought we were friends, Zach Thomas!'

Zach leant back against his bollard, puffing. 'Whoa, Beth, hold on. Of course we're friends, but the joke has gone on long enough, that's all.'

'I might tease you, Zach, but I would never lie to you. I'm telling you now: Carys and I *did* find an … art-arte … fact, and it *was* magic.'

'Okay, look,' said Zach, flopping down on the nearest bench, 'this is a stupid argument. When we get to your place, you can *show* me the artefact –'

'Yes, but –' intervened Bethany, sitting down next to him.

'But what?'

Bethany's aggression melted away. She stared at the ground.

'I *can't* show you the artefact.'

Zach guessed the problem immediately. 'Is it still in the Chapter House?'

Bethany nodded. She didn't look up.

Zach jumped up. 'Well, we'd better get this magic rod before somebody else does.' He walked purposefully away.

Bethany followed, dragging her feet. 'Thanks, Zach, but it's no use. Nobody's allowed in the Chapter House, so there's no way we can get the rod.'

Zach didn't turn round, but instead raised his voice. 'Of course we can get it – *silly!*'

Despite her glum mood, Bethany couldn't help laughing at Zach's imitation of her. She increased her pace, but Zach was breaking into a trot. 'Where did you leave it?' he shouted.

Bethany came alongside. 'It fell amongst all the builders' stuff. But I told you, we can't get *in.*'

In reply, Zach accelerated until the three of them were haring up the precinct, weaving in and out of benches and flowerbeds. Suzy was keeping up, but her leash was in danger of tripping up shoppers, so Zach swept her into his arms as he and Bethany raced at top speed, catching the pelican crossing on green.

But as they turned the last corner, breathing heavily, they saw Stephen. He was crossing from the Old Palace garden to the cathedral porch, as Carys and Bethany had done the night before, except Stephen didn't have to worry about being seen. His mission was not a secret one.

'Darn!' gasped Bethany, leaning on a bollard to get her breath. 'He'll be preparing for Evensong. We'll have to wait until tomorrow.'

'That's no good,' said Zach. 'The stonemason won't be there tomorrow, and I need him to let me in.'

'Well, look, Daddy will be occupied in the nave, so why don't we –'

'Of course, the south door!'

Off they ran again, Suzy getting another free ride. Round into the Close, through the massive, creaking door into the cloisters, and there they were, standing outside the Chapter House. Bethany looked around, recalling the previous night's events. *No,* she decided, *even in daylight, I don't like cloisters.*

'What do you want me to say?' she asked Zach.

'Nothing – you're not coming in. You really *would* be in trouble if you were caught in here a second time.'

Bethany knocked firmly on the door. 'Try keeping me out.'

Zach knew Beth well enough to realise it would be a waste of time arguing. 'All right, but you'll have to have Suzy – and not a word, from either of you.' Suzy had learned that barking was forbidden in the cathedral, so she took it as a reminder.

The door was opened by a man wearing an apron and holding a mallet in his hand. Various chisels were in a belt round his waist.

'Hello kids, I'm afraid this room isn't open for visitors,' he said.

'Hi. I'm Zach Thomas. You've met my father, Canon Thomas?'

'Yes, I know the Canon. You a message for me?'

'The thing is, he cleared out the Chapter House before you started work, but he's missing one of the candlesticks. He's worried in case it gets damaged or thrown out. I said I'd find it for him – we don't want him getting into trouble with the Dean, do we?'

'You better come in and look then. Who's your friend?'

Zach hesitated.

Bethany jumped in, smiling her sweetest smile. 'Oh! I'm not his friend. I'm Fran … his *sister.*'

Zach threw a brotherly glare at his new sister.

'So,' the man asked, 'what does it look like, this candlestick?'

It was then that Zach realised he hadn't the faintest idea what the rod looked like. He glanced at Bethany but she indicated that her lips had been sealed. Suzy crouched down with her chin on the floor and placed both front paws over her nose.

'It's difficult to describe,' muttered Zach.

'How big is it?'

'It's … pretty big,' Zach said, beginning to look among the scaffold poles.

'Let me 'elp,' offered the stonemason, moving towards Zach, who again looked appealingly at Bethany.

Her voice piped up at last.

'Will you have to replace *this* stone?' she asked, pointing to a stone over the door. The mason left Zach and came over to see which stone Bethany meant.

'Hmm, it don't look too bad from 'ere, but I won't know until I gets up close. This place is fair crumblin' to pieces. Only last night, the back of the Dean's seat fell away from the wall, just like that. The Dean was tellin' me 'ow 'is daughter was in 'ere with a friend, on some prank, when it broke. They were lucky not to be injured – and I'm lucky the stone 'ad clean breaks, so I can fix it.'

Bethany could feel her cheeks turning red. She quickly changed the subject. 'Do any other cathedrals have circular Chapter Houses?'

The stonemason took the bait.

'Yes, love, there's loads, but this was the first, see. That's why it's so special.'

That's not the only reason, thought Bethany.

By now, Zach was close to where Carys had fainted. He disappeared under a tarpaulin.

Bethany continued her diversionary tactic. 'Have you found any bits of the *Saxon* cathedral?'

'Funny you should ask that. The other side of that wall over there,' he said, pointing to the east section, where Zach was exploring under the tarpaulin, 'we uncovered the foundations of a curving wall –'

'How exciting!' exclaimed Bethany.

'So you like old buildings, then?'

'Ever since I was little. I would love to be a stonemason.'

Zach emerged from under the tarpaulin. Streaks of stone dust in his hair made him look prematurely grey. He grinned. 'And *I'm* going to be an archaeologist, digging up lost treasures.' He was clutching the rod.

Bethany rushed forward and took hold of it. 'Oh good, you've found it.' It was the first time she'd held the rod, and she was surprised how heavy it was. 'You'll never guess, Zach: they've found a wall belonging to the *Saxon* cathedral. And it was over there.' She pointed to where Zach had just come from.

Zach was brushing the dust from his clothes and hair. 'On the outside, I presume?'

'That's correct,' said the stonemason. 'The excavations were a few year ago now, the other side of the wall, there, behind the Dean's seat. I was tellin' your sister, the stone back o' the seat fell right off the wall last night.'

'Really?' said Zach. Seeing Bethany's worried expression, he added, with as much gravity as he could muster, 'It occurs to me that those Saxon excavations might have loosened that stone.'

The stonemason stood open-mouthed. 'Now why didn't I think o' that? Well I never!'

Bethany made a move towards the door. 'Thank you for letting us look for the candlestick. I'm dying to tell Daddy we've found it.'

The stonemason grunted.

'Huh, good job you did, too, 'cause I'd've chucked it in the skip right enough. Your brother did well to spot it in all this.'

Zach didn't mention that the rod had been glowing under the tarpaulin.

'Thanks a lot for your help, sir,' he said. 'My father will be pleased.'

At that moment, his father walked in.

Chapter 11   Strange Events

Zach snatched the rod off Bethany and held it up near his father's face. 'Dad, I told you the candlestick would still be here!'

Tom hesitated only for a moment.

'A-aah, well done, son. I was beginning to get ... a *bit* ... concerned.' He looked from his son to Bethany, and then to Suzy, who crept round the back of Bethany's legs.

He then turned to the stonemason.

'Everything okay, Ted? I hope they didn't get in your way?'

'Not in the least – your son and me 'ad a good chat about stones. Oh, an' if your daughter wants to come and watch us work sometime, she'd be welcome. I likes to encourage young 'uns interested in stonemasonry. It were always a man's trade, but nowadays ...'

'One of my daughters is thinking of stonemasonry as a career? That's news to me, Ted. But fathers are always the last to know.' He stared hard at Zach and managed a smile as he asked, 'Which of your sisters might that be, Zach?'

'Why *me*, silly Daddy – *Fran!*' cried Bethany, wrapping herself around Tom's arm and hanging onto it like she was his long-lost daughter.

'Ah, of course, *Fran!* That's why I can never find my hammer and chisels. Well, Ted, we'll leave you to it. Bye.'

Tom opened the door, ushered the trio out into the cloisters, and closed the door behind him. He was about to launch his enquiry when the door opened again, and Ted poked his head out.

'You can be sure I won't say a word about the candlestick to the Dean. No point you gettin' into trouble when no 'arm's been done. Bye, kids.' Then he shut the door, leaving Tom looking more confused.

'Right,' he said, 'you have thirty seconds to tell me: firstly, what *that* is, because we all know it isn't a candlestick; secondly, why Ted *thinks* it's a candlestick; thirdly, why he's not going to tell the Dean about it; and fourthly, why I've gained an extra daughter who is going to be a stonemasonette!'

For once, Zach was speechless.

Bethany took the rod off him and held it like a sword. 'It's simple.'

Zach's curiosity was as great as his father's as he wondered how Bethany was possibly going to explain everything – especially as he could see in her face that she was still working it out. But it was when the rod began to glow that Zach really thought they were dead.

Then, suddenly, he saw Bethany's eyes reflecting the rod's glow. She'd got it – whatever it was, she'd got it.

'Like I say, it's simple,' she repeated, only this time with feeling. 'This is a light sabre. It belongs to a friend of mine. He lent it to me so Carys and I could play with it on our midnight feast. Only we left it behind in the panic last night. It's expensive so I couldn't wait to get it back.'

The rod's light went off and Zach took up the story.

'We didn't want the stonemason to suspect that one of the girls from last night had returned to the scene of her crime –'

'So Zach told the mason that you'd left a candlestick behind when you cleared the room out, which is why he's not mentioning it to Stephen, so you won't get into trouble –'

'And … Fran?' asked Tom.

Zach pointed to Bethany. 'That was Beth's idea, so she wouldn't be implicated if the stonemason *did* happen to talk about our visit. Brilliant!'

Bethany was beaming. 'You see? I said it was simple.'

Tom strode vigorously towards the nave door, speaking as he went, with the trio trailing behind.

'*Simple?* On the contrary, I marvel at your ingenuity and cringe at your lack of fear. If the Dean had found you instead of me, the simple *truth* is you'd not be seeing each other all summer.'

As Tom opened the door, Bethany tugged on his cassock.

'So you're not going to tell Daddy, then?'

Tom turned and smiled wryly. 'How can I? I don't want him to know I was so irresponsible with a valuable Chapter House candlestick, do I?' He disappeared into the nave, with Zach chasing after him.

Zach returned a few moments later and signalled Bethany to follow him. She put Suzy on a tight leash. 'Where are we going?'

'The crypt. Dad's lent me his key. We need some privacy. I told Dad we wanted to play Star Wars amongst the pillars.'

'What did he say?'

'Beware the dark side of the Force!'

Unseen by those saying prayers in the chancel, the three of them padded up the south aisle towards the stairs that led down to the Norman crypt.

When they arrived, Zach placed the rod on a table, with the lettering face up. 'I can't be sure, but they look like Hebrew letters.' He took his phone out of his pocket.

'Who you calling?' asked Bethany.

'Nobody. I'm going to take some photos. I've had an idea. There's an antique shop in town that specialises in ancient artefacts. If we take some photos along –'

Zach started snapping away, being sure to get close-ups of the writing.

'They might identify it!' said Bethany. 'That's a super idea, but why don't we just take the rod?'

'Too risky. That might be the last we see of it. Even when we show them these photos, we mustn't let them suspect we've got this artefact in our possession. We'll have to invent a cover story.'

Bethany picked the rod up and held it close to her, like a queen holding her sceptre. 'You're right, this is *our* treasure.'

Zach was still taking pictures. 'Strictly, it belongs to you and Carys. Remember, I didn't even believe you'd found it.'

Bethany placed the rod gently back on the table. 'Well, if I'm honest, I have to say it's Carys's to keep, 'cause she found it. She led us into the cloisters, she bundled us into the Chapter House, and she chose the Dean's seat – in the dark as well.'

Zach was checking over the photos he'd snapped.

'This is strange. Look at this one, Beth.'

She peered at the tiny picture. 'Is this me?'

'It's the picture I took a moment ago. See, you're holding the rod.'

Bethany frowned. 'But where's the crypt? It looks like I'm standing on a hillside.'

'I know, it's weird.'

'Two pictures have merged, somehow,' said Bethany. 'I think you can do it on purpose if you know how.'

'Yes, but I can't recall ever taking a photo of a hillside.'

Bethany handed Zach his phone. 'Take another one of me. In fact, take two. One with the rod, and one without.'

'You mean –?'

'Try it.' She pulled a funny face for the first photo. Then she picked the rod up and posed for the second snap. Then they had a look at the results. The first one was normal. There was the funny face and the crypt in the background. But in the second one, Bethany was again standing on a hillside. But that wasn't all.

'Up there, near the top of the hill, above your right shoulder,' said Zach, 'isn't that a man and a dog climbing up the path?'

'Weren't they on the other photo?'

Zach flicked back and they studied the other photo of the hillside. No sign of them.

'What's going on?' asked Bethany.

Zach began pacing up and down. 'Beth, what if …?' He was running his fingers through his hair. 'What if that's Carys's dad and his dog, Vala?'

'That's ridiculous. They're both dead, for a start.'

'You were happy for *Carys* to see her dead father. Why's it so different now?'

'Because he's her father, that's why,' said Bethany, holding back tears. She snatched Zach's phone out of his hand and pointed to the almost invisible figures on the hillside. 'If that's what Carys saw last night, then she should have followed her father up that hill when she had the chance. Instead, she fainted.'

'Hold on, Beth, there's something wrong here. Why would her dad want Carys to follow him anyway? So that she could watch him commit suicide? No wonder she fainted.'

'Maybe he had a message for her before he died?'

Zach picked up the rod. 'Beth, until last night, this rod was buried in the wall of a twelfth century building. It's a weird way of delivering a message before you kill yourself. Much simpler to leave a suicide note.'

'Oh stop it, I can't talk about it any more, it's too awful.'

Zach was holding the rod like a sword, enjoying the feel of it in his hand.

'Wasn't that incredible,' he said, 'what the stonemason was saying? They excavated the foundations of a Saxon wall right behind where you found the rod.'

'So?' asked Bethany.

'So maybe when the Normans knocked that Saxon wall down, they used some of the stones to build the Chapter House.'

'So? I still don't see your point.'

'Well, maybe when the Saxons built *their* cathedral, they used some stones from pagan shrines that *they* had demolished …'

Using the rod, Zach graphically re-enacted every demolition.

Bethany laughed. 'I've just seen where this is leading. Merlin! Honestly, you're incredible. It's like the House that Zach Built. Merlin buries the rod in a pagan stone, which is used in the wall of a Saxon cathedral, and then used again in the Chapter House of *this* cathedral. It happens all the time.'

Zach was unbowed. He changed from demolition man to swordfighter. 'All I'm saying is, it *could* have happened like that. It could have been –'

'Please will you stop waving the rod around like that, Zach? You don't know what might happen!'

As Bethany seized the end of the rod, her mobile phone went off. She fished it out of her jeans and read the text message aloud: `'Piercing hurt like hell. See you at home. C.'`

Zach rubbed his nose and winced. 'I can safely say that piercing salons and tattoo parlours will never receive my custom. Let go of the rod, Beth, nothing's going to happen. It's not even glowing.'

But Bethany held on. With her other hand she tapped out a sympathetic reply to Carys. 'Zach, shall I tell her –?'

'Tell her what? That the rod has a message for her? I think she knows that.'

Zach pulled once more at the rod. 'Let *go,* Beth, I'm enjoying playing with it.'

Bethany held on tighter. 'Can't we at least tell her that the rod's message is still available?' Her thumb hovered over her phone's keypad.

'She wouldn't thank you, Beth. Carys will never follow her father up that hill – and who can blame her?'

Reluctantly, Bethany signed off and pressed Send. 'I wish we could get Carys's message *for* her.'

'Beth, is your end of the rod getting warm? Like, *very* warm?'

Zach changed hands. Bethany agreed and did likewise. She looked around, as if she weren't sure where she was.

'Za … ach! What's happening?' Her voice was distorted. She might have been speaking through a megaphone the wrong way round.

'Be … eth! I think we're moving!' Zach could have been speaking with treacle in his mouth.

Suzy started to bark in that way which says, 'I don't know what it's about, but it's exciting!' But instead of a small terrier, she sounded like a Great Dane. Zach grabbed her just in time …

A verger upstairs heard barking coming from the crypt and went down to investigate. But he couldn't find a dog anywhere. No dog, and no dog owners. The crypt was empty.

Chapter 12 Detective Work

'What happened?' whispered Bethany.

Zach looked around. 'I'd say you got your wish …'

They were standing in exactly the same position, each gripping an end of the rod. Zach was still holding onto Suzy, though she'd stopped barking – probably shocked into silence by the disappearance of the crypt.

Bethany let go of her end and sat down on a rock. She looked around. 'Can I ask a question?' In fact, Bethany knew the answer, but when you've been transported from a cathedral crypt on a Friday afternoon to a hillside in the dark, it's a question that has to be voiced: 'How did we get here?'

'Obviously the rod brought us here,' replied Zach, 'so I don't think we need to be scared.' Bethany had started shivering.

'I'm not scared. I'm shivering because I'm cold.'

Zach took off his jacket and helped Bethany put it on. 'And here, hold the rod close to you – it's still warm. I'll have Suzy.' He sat down next to Bethany and hugged Suzy to his chest. 'I owe you a huge apology.'

'What for?'

'For not believing you'd found a magic rod. Glowing like a light sabre was a neat party trick, but this – well, this is magic. Powerful magic. I'm sorry, but this *has* to be Merlin's doing.'

Bethany smiled and looked around again. 'It's getting lighter. We're on Carys's hillside, aren't we? The one in the photos?'

'I'm sure we are, yes. I'd say we're around about the spot where Carys's dad and Vala were in the photo. Think about it, Beth. Merlin must have known about wormholes and –'

'Frankly, Zach, I'm more concerned about what happens next. I'd rather not meet the ghost of Carys's dad, thank you very much.'

'I don't think he would be a ghost. We are probably in some kind of parallel universe. Einstein's Theory –'

A gunshot rang out.

It came from over the hill, a horrid sound, filling the empty morning air with an echo of death.

Suzy jumped and her ears pricked up. She struggled to free herself, but Zach didn't let go.

Bethany instinctively placed her hands over her ears to shut the sound out.

Then a dog started barking and growling. Suzy stopped struggling and froze.

Bethany bent her head to her knees, and began rocking back-wards and forwards.

A second shot rang out.

Bethany spoke.

'Za ... ach!'

Noticing that her voice was distorted, Zach put his hand on the rod. As the hillside began to swirl around like a carousel, he could just make out Bethany's twisted words:

'Is it okay to be scared now?'

There was a knock, and Helen popped her head round the door of Bethany's room. Bethany was wearing Zach's jacket. She and Zach were holding each end of the rod, staring at one another, rooted to the spot. Suzy was jumping up and trying to grab the rod, barking each time she failed. She stopped when the door opened.

'Is everything all right, Beth? Suzy barks so rarely, I was concerned.'

'Yes, everything's fine, Mum.' Bethany's voice sounded strained. 'We're … we're role-playing.'

Zach tried to explain Suzy's unusual behaviour. 'Suzy thought we were fighting – she doesn't like any kind of violence, do you, Suzy?'

Suzy went to bark in reply, thought better of it, and crept under the bed instead.

During this brief exchange, Bethany and Zach hadn't moved. They were both still firmly grasping the rod, as if their lives depended on it. Helen gave a little cough, went to go and then changed her mind.

'Oh, by the way, I didn't hear you come in. Have you found a secret door or something?'

A secret door? Could transportation by a magic rod count as entering through a secret door? Bethany and Zach exchanged glances, which was a mistake. It was as if a spell had been broken. They dropped onto the floor in an attempt to suppress their laughter; an attempt which failed.

Helen couldn't help laughing. 'You two, you're incredible when you get together. I hope you're finding room for Carys.'

'No problem, Mum, we had a great time up and down the Shambles. Didn't we, Zach?'

Duly prompted by Bethany, Zach went on at great length about how well they'd all got on.

'By the way, Mum,' said Bethany warily, 'try not to be too shocked when you see Carys, only she's had her nose pierced –'

Zach interrupted, 'Her mother gave her the ring!'

'It's nice of you to prepare me, Bethany, but in fact Carys told me about it this morning.'

'You didn't –?' began Bethany.

Helen smiled. 'No, I didn't express an opinion – I'm not her mother, after all.'

There was the sound of the front door banging shut.

Bethany jumped up. 'That'll be her.' She rushed past her mother through the open door.

'Are you staying for tea, Zach? A cold table as usual, I'm afraid, until we move into the Deanery, but you're more than welcome.'

Zach sat up and crossed his legs. 'I have things I need to do at home, and I'm not sure what's happening tonight, so can I –?'

'Hilda always leaves us far more than we need, so you're welcome any day, Zach – you don't have to book a table!'

Sounds of Bethany's high-pitched laughter drifted along the corridor and into the room.

Zach slipped the rod under the bed, next to Suzy. As he did so, Helen asked him what it was.

Zach hesitated. 'It's a … it's a light sabre – a surprise, for Carys …'

'How nice,' said Helen, in a tone that suggested otherwise.

Bethany and Carys walked in.

'Mum, what do you think?' asked Bethany, showing off her newly-pierced friend.

It was clear that Carys didn't want to be shown off. She flopped down onto the bed.

'I thought you were having a ring, Carys,' said Helen.

'Oh Mother,' cried Bethany, 'you have to wear a stud until it heals, you should know that!'

Helen did know that, but her question had allowed her to acknowledge the piercing without commenting on its appearance.

'Ah well,' she said, 'tea at the usual time.' And with that, she left.

As soon as she'd gone, Carys turned over so she was leaning on her elbow. 'Zach, Bethany was telling me how you and your new sister, Fran, retrieved the rod from the Chapter House. It's a good job your dad is such a sport.'

'He's terrific,' said Zach. He lay back down on the floor. Suzy came out of hiding and seated herself on his chest as if to say 'I'm keeping this one.'

'So where is it?' asked Carys.

'It's under the bed,' Zach replied. 'Helen asked me what it was.'

Bethany jumped up from her chair. 'What did you say?'

'It's all right. I stuck to your story that it's a light sabre.'

Bethany's eyes lit up with excitement. 'Did it glow again?'

'Did it glow *again?*' exclaimed Carys. 'What's been going on?'

Bethany took a running jump and landed on Carys, winding her and making her laugh at the same time. Bethany's face was close to Carys's as she blurted out, 'All kinds of things that you'd never believe but we hope you will because we think the rod had a message for you and we think maybe we've got it and we've been up a hillside and then we ended up here and my mum said –'

Here Bethany ran out of breath but she also had to laugh, which required more breath than talking, so she had no choice but to roll off Carys and off the bed and land with a thump next to Zach. Suzy looked down on her as if to compliment her on such a clever trick.

Zach took up the thread, laughing even before he spoke.

'Her mum said, "I didn't hear you come in." She didn't hear us come in!' he repeated, as though it was the funniest joke ever.

'You guys!' shouted Carys, who was trying not to catch their infectious laughter. 'What's happened to you?'

'The rod,' Zach shouted back, 'it's magic! When I was looking for it amongst all the scaffolding poles in the Chapter House, it glowed so I'd see it.'

'I didn't know that!' cried Bethany. 'And then, when Tom wanted to know what the rod was, it glowed again, which is when I called it a light sabre.'

'It was incredible,' said Zach. 'But to answer your question, Beth – no, it didn't glow when I told your mum it was a light sabre. I wonder why not?'

Bethany frowned. 'Maybe it was low on power after all it had done today.'

'You mean there's more?' asked Carys.

'I've already told you what happened,' Bethany reminded her. 'Weren't you listening?'

'Yes but –'

Bethany retrieved the rod from under the bed and held it in both hands above her as she lay on the floor.

'We were in the crypt –'

'The crypt?'

Zach took over the story. 'We'd gone to the crypt to study the rod in peace. Some weird things happened when I took pictures of it, then I started waving it round like a sword. This annoyed Beth, so she grabbed the other end, which is when your text came through. It was as if your text triggered something, for the rod began to feel warm, Suzy started barking, and –'

'And then –' said Bethany.

Zach interrupted. 'We ended up … *here!*'

'Yes, but, Zach, first we –'

'I know, I know, but I want Carys to absorb this first. We ended up *here*. With Suzy.'

'That's why Mum was here,' said Bethany. 'She heard Suzy barking and came to see if something was up.'

'Helen mentioned that she hadn't heard us come in,' Zach continued, 'and the reason why she hadn't heard us was because we hadn't come in through the door and up the stairs.'

Carys was puzzled. 'What do you mean?'

Bethany sounded smug as she announced, 'The rod had *transported* us here.'

There was silence.

Zach knocked Suzy off his chest and sat up. He looked Carys in the eye. 'You don't believe us, do you?'

'I'm trying to. I believe you aren't making it up, and that's a start.'

Bethany got up, removed Zach's jacket and placed it over the back of her chair. Then she sat down. She was getting down to business. 'There's more, Cass. The fact is, we didn't come *straight* here. At first we found ourselves near the top of a hill. It was early morning, and cold –'

'Which means we travelled through time as well, by the way,' whispered Zach, almost to himself. He drew Suzy towards him, and nodded to Bethany to go on.

'We heard a gunshot, a dog barked, we heard a second shot – and then … silence.' Bethany looked solemn.

'The next moment we were here, in Bethany's room,' said Zach. 'Now think about that for a moment.' He paused. 'I reckon the rod brought us here, rather than returning us to the crypt, in order to prove that we hadn't just had a vision or something. The rod wanted to make it clear that it *took* us there, to that hillside, in the same way that it brought us here. By magic transportation.'

'We reckon the rod took us where it tried to take *you* last night,' added Bethany. 'But it was all too sudden, too unexpected for you, so you fainted.'

Zach took his mobile phone from his pocket. 'That's why I think those photos were changed like that, Beth. They were a way of breaking you and me in gently. We became used to strange things happening, and we were shown the hillside before the rod took us there.'

'What hillside?' echoed Carys.

Zach flicked through the photos on his mobile phone. 'This hillside.'

Carys studied the photo which included the man and his dog.

'I was standing in the crypt when he took that,' said Bethany. 'It was weird.'

Bethany and Zach desperately wanted their friend to believe them. So much so that they didn't speak for two whole minutes, while Carys reflected. At last she spoke.

'Have you thought about what this means?'

'We haven't had a chance,' Bethany replied. 'As soon as we landed here, Mum was knocking on the door. Why, do *you* know what it means, Cass?'

'I think so, yes. Listen, when I held the rod in the Chapter House, you're right, Beth, I saw more than I wanted to, which is why I suppose I fainted. I saw what's on this photo, my father walking up the hill, with Vala, and with his gun under his arm. I knew I could follow him … but I-I knew what I would see. I didn't *want* to see that. Who or what would expect me to?'

Bethany's eyes were opening wider by the second.

Carys continued, 'Now, if what you say is true, you two have *heard* what I refused to *see*. If it's that important, there must be something we're missing, or that *I'm* missing.'

Carys paused.

'You said you heard a shot, then barking, then a second shot, right?'

'That's right,' replied Bethany. 'It was so scary!'

'Okay,' said Carys, 'the first thing to make clear is that my father and Vala both died instantly.' Carys was speaking in a businesslike way, to try and distance herself from the deep emotions evoked by the events she was recounting.

'Dad was shot through the heart and Vala, well, it was a clean shot to the head, poor thing.'

Zach ruffled Suzy's ears in case she'd understood.

'Now,' Carys continued, 'you say you heard a first shot, then some barking, then a second shot. You're sure about that sequence?'

'Yes,' Zach and Bethany declared with one voice.

'All right then, if the first shot you heard killed Dad, he couldn't have killed Vala ...'

'Oh, yes ...' Bethany agreed, as the logic sank in.

'But if the first shot killed *Vala,* he couldn't then have barked before the second shot.'

Carys sat up. 'So, let's assume you heard what really took place ...'

She paused.

'My father didn't commit suicide. He was murdered!'

Chapter 13   Deadly Danger

'They're closed,' said Carys, trying the door.

Bethany was peering through one of the windows. 'Are you sure this is the right place? I've never seen an antique shop with such small windows.'

'Zach said it was called Dredge's Emporium,' replied Carys, 'and that's what it says over the door, if you'd bothered to look.'

It had been a long day and much had happened, some of it disconcerting. Carys was still adjusting to the theory, for that's all it could be, that her father had been murdered. She couldn't think of anyone who would want to kill him, and yet it made more sense to her than suicide. But it was another burden to carry when she was already struggling with her friends' evidence for the existence of magic. It was difficult to explain Zach and Bethany's experiences with the rod in any other way, but Carys still found it all hard to swallow.

While Bethany and Carys had come to Dredge's with the photos of the rod, Zach was at home, researching his latest theory. He was still convinced that Merlin lay behind everything that had happened. In his mind, the trail led from Merlin's Farm where Carys lived, to the Chapter House where Carys found the rod, back to Merlin who had hidden it. The girls agreed that *somebody* must have hidden the rod, so they were happy for Zach to pursue his line of research.

'I can see someone in there, Cass. Don't stand there sulking, knock on the door or something.'

'I'm not sulking, and I tell you they're closed. I bet they live here and that's why you can see them.'

She came over to the window that Beth was using and elbowed her aside, so she could have a look through the small area that her friend had cleaned. They were so busy shoving each other to get the best view that they didn't hear the bell jingle or see Dredge come out of the shop.

'If you are that interested in my antiques, you'd better come inside.'

Both girls turned to face the dealer with expressions that mingled surprise with embarrassment. Bethany was first to recover.

'We thought you were closed.'

'I am always open to genuine seekers after truth. Come in, come in.'

Bethany went striding in but Carys hesitated.

She'd gone through a few doors in the past twenty-four hours – the Deanery garden, the cathedral, the cloisters, and the chapter house. On more than one occasion, she'd been surprised by what awaited her on the other side, so she could be forgiven for hesitating before crossing yet another strange threshold – strange in that it was new to her and also a bit weird. It looked dark inside the shop, and she could feel a blast of heat rushing out of the door. Furthermore, Mr Dredge was not the normal run of shopkeeper. That was a funny thing he'd called them – 'seekers after truth'; he was shabbily dressed, with a shawl around his shoulders that had holes where it had worn thin; and he walked with the aid of a cane that had a silver top in the form of a grotesque animal.

All of these observations went through Carys's mind in the instant that she hesitated. None of these alone would have been enough to make her pause, but taken together they formed a flash of intuition which produced a feeling of apprehension.

As soon as Bethany realised she was on her own with the old man, she ran back to Carys and pulled her into the shop. 'Come in will you – we haven't got all day!'

Carys shook off Bethany, walked in, and closed the door behind her with a bang. Without being invited, she plonked herself down in the first chair she came to, a faded wing chair. Bethany glared at her.

Carys glared back and then pulled a face. 'What's that *smell?*'

Before Bethany could change the subject, the old man responded. 'That, my dear, is the *past.*'

Dredge pirouetted with unexpected ease as he swung his cane round to include the whole shop.

'All of these objects have been around for a long time, some of them for centuries. During that time, the people who owned them experienced the pain of human existence, and *that* is what you can smell. That chair you're sitting in, for example.'

As he said this, he moved closer to Carys and leaned over her. He was so near that she could see traces of brown powder around his nostrils and feel the fringe of his shawl tickling her hand, which she quickly removed from the arm of the chair.

'Look, see how the right wing of the chair is more worn than the left. That side was closer to the fire as the owner fell asleep every night, in too much pain to go to bed.'

Dredge paused and stroked the arm of the chair, as if it were in need of solace.

'I wonder how many people *died* in this chair?'

He said 'died' as if it was a very long word indeed, making Carys squirm, as though an antique spring had burst through the upholstery. She wanted to get out of that horrid chair and leave the dark, smelly shop. But she was trapped by Dredge, who was obviously enjoying her discomfort. Carys turned her head and looked pleadingly at Bethany to rescue her.

At first, Bethany smiled the kind of smug smile that says 'Serves you right!' but then she relented. She went and sat at a dressing table on the other side of the shop and called out, with perfectly pitched contempt, 'But these are all just *things*, old objects that nobody wanted.'

Dredge straightened up and turned to face her.

'Things?' he shouted.

He took two or three strides towards Bethany, gliding along in a movement which dancers take years to master.

'You should never underestimate *things!*'

As if to demonstrate the wisdom of his advice, Dredge flicked back the head of the silver animal on top of his cane. With a grubby thumb and forefinger, he picked out a pinch of snuff which he applied to his nostrils with a resounding sniff.

He opened his mouth to continue his lecture and out came Radiohead's *Creep*. It was Bethany's mobile phone, signalling a text. She apologised to the shopkeeper, who still had his mouth open in astonishment, as if someone had opened a window and let a draught of air into his stuffy shop.

Bethany smiled. The text was from Carys, who had escaped from the chair and was perched on a kitchen stool. The message read:

`'Lunatic. Leave. Pls. Cx'`

Carys had her hands cupped round her phone in pleading supplication. Was she serious? Bethany hadn't known Carys long enough to be certain. Her thumb whizzed around her keypad.

`'Photos. Then leave. Promise. B.'`

This was not the first time they'd texted each other, but it was the first time Carys had added that little 'x'. Bethany added one herself and pressed Send. Then she took an envelope out of her pocket.

'What's this then?' Dredge muttered.

Bethany threw Carys a quick smile. They were proud of the cover story they'd prepared.

'We hope you can help us, sir,' she said. 'This summer two students at our school will be sent to help on a dig in Israel. We've all been given photos of an artefact and the first two students to identify it will be chosen to go. A friend told us you are an expert in this field.'

Bethany said all this as though she'd learned it by heart, which she had, but Dredge didn't notice. She was supposed to say 'archaeological dig', but hadn't pronounced it right once in rehearsals, so she missed the big word out.

Dredge took the envelope from her with a grunt of displeasure, as though it were a booby prize for the contest he'd lost. He took the photos out of the envelope, but instead of looking at them, he used them to point to the furniture piled high in his shop.

'Things,' he declared, 'are not always mere objects. Turn around on that seat, young lady, and look into the mirror, if you dare!'

Bethany was about to turn around and look, when Carys dashed across the room and shoved her aside.

'Let *me* – you always do everything!'

Bethany scowled but gave up her place; at least her friend was no longer nagging to leave. In fact, Carys was desperate to leave, more so now than ever, though she couldn't have explained why. She didn't understand the dealer's mumbo jumbo about 'things not being mere things' but she didn't really believe he was a lunatic either. From the moment Carys had entered the shop she'd felt uneasy, on edge, like she was walking down a badly lit corridor, with doors on either side, and she didn't know where they led. This is why she had decided to intervene now, although she didn't realise how much danger she faced.

The dealer stood behind her and waited for the mirror to begin working its magic. But it was he who was entranced as he looked at Carys's reflection. He was captivated by her sculpted face, sharp-edged, softened by an almost imperceptible down; a face that was the finished article, despite years of growing still ahead. Dredge was looking on features shaped by the beauty of the Preseli Hills but also carved out of terrible grief. This could be discerned most tellingly in the eyes: grey flecked with blue – tiny shards of bluestone lying in cool mountain pools.

Dredge shook himself free and spoke in a low, even voice.

'You are feeling an inconsolable sorrow, the sorrow of all the women who have begged that mirror to lie to them.'

After half a minute, Carys swivelled round on the seat and stood up. 'I'm not feeling anything. I'm sorry to spoil the game, but we

need to show you the photos and go home, or we'll be late for tea –
won't we Bethany?'

The old man was devastated. He stared hard at the mirror, trying
to discern what had gone wrong. He stared harder at Carys, as if
he should know her from somewhere. It was at this point that his
eyes focused on one of the photos in his hands. It almost finished
him. Dredge dropped down into the armchair that had nearly
swallowed Carys. Bethany expressed concern. Was he all right?
Even Carys, despite her earlier misgivings, joined in. Could they
get him anything?

'N-no, no, I get these … turns. But I'm fine now.'

Indeed he was. The colour had returned to his cheeks and there
was a burning light in his eyes.

'Now,' said the dealer, taking his time, 'let me get this straight.
You want me to identify th-this artefact?'

He laughed, as if mocking his own bizarre performance earlier
on. He tried to get up but started laughing again and fell back into
the chair. His attitude had changed. Carys threw a quizzical glance
at Bethany. Perhaps this man was a lunatic after all?

Dredge caught his breath and said, 'You know, this … object
is … familiar, and I should know what it is. After all, I am an
expert!'

He laughed again, but not in the same full-blooded way. This
was more of a nervous cackle. From walking all over them a few
moments ago, he was now walking on eggshells. He kept opening
his mouth, as if to say something, but then shutting it again. He
couldn't stop shifting his eyes from the photos to Carys and then
back to the photos again. The photographs resembled a poker
hand, the best hand he'd ever held. If a player with a brilliant hand
raises the stakes too high, he might scare them away. But if he acts
too casually, again he might lose them. At last Dredge spoke.

'If I help you to win, what's in it for me? I run a business, you
know, not a charity to help schoolchildren with their homework.'

'We don't have any money,' said Bethany.

'Does your teacher, er … does this … belong to … '

'Miss Wigglesbottom, yes,' said Bethany, avoiding eye contact
with Carys. 'The artefact is in her private collection. It's her

hobby. She spends all her holidays digging for artefacts.' She couldn't stop saying that word.

Carys had turned a spluttered laugh into a cough. *Miss Wigglesbottom?* How could Bethany say all this and keep a straight face? Carys glanced at a large, serious-looking book that was lying open nearby. She looked more closely, glad of the distraction, otherwise she might ruin everything by making Bethany laugh.

In all his time on this freezing earth, Dredge had never perspired. But as the possibility grew of possessing Aaron's Rod, the tension caused droplets to form on his upper lip. He wiped them off with the back of his hand and gazed at the brown smear of damp snuff that was left there.

'You can imagine, being a collector myself, how much I'd like to have … er, to hold this object, to be able to examine it … and maybe make an offer for it?'

'I'm sure that our teacher will be open to offers, yes.'

'So,' said Dredge, 'if I help you win, you will arrange for that to happen? Your teacher will bring the artefact to my shop?'

'Yes, no problem,' said Bethany, who was playing the same game as Dredge, but with the innocent cunning of a child. At this moment, she would have promised Dredge the Crown Jewels, to be delivered by the Queen herself, if it would persuade him to identify their rod – and she wouldn't have batted an eye.

Dredge invited Bethany to sit down at the same dining table that he had slid along in his session with Balimm the previous morning. Realising that Balimm could arrive for his return visit at any moment, Dredge sat down opposite Bethany and hurriedly laid out the photos. It was then that he saw what Carys was doing.

'Close that *book!*' he shouted. A look of sheer terror came over his face when Carys took one more lingering look. He jumped up, seized the nearest thing to hand, which happened to be one of the silver Georgian candlesticks, and hurled it in Carys's direction.

'Didn't you *hear* me, girl? I said *close* it!'

Dredge's throw was wild. The candlestick struck the stove and bounced into a box of picture frames. Carys closed the book carefully, as if it were made of glass. Then she stood quite still, not daring to move until she knew what Dredge was going to do next.

Dredge held his hands up, palms towards Carys, to assure her that he held no more missiles. He spoke softly. 'Come here, come here and sit down. That was most unfortunate, but you shouldn't have been looking in that book. It's a … special book. You didn't say anything that you read there, did you? I mean out loud – in even the tiniest whisper?'

Carys shook her head. She couldn't speak, he'd frightened her so much.

Seeing this, Dredge turned on the most persuasive charm that he could muster. 'I'm sorry I was so angry. I'm on edge because I have an important client coming to see me. Now, pay attention.' He held up one of the photos. 'I am absolutely certain that this is Aaron's Rod from the biblical legends.'

'Legends?' said Carys, taken aback by the ease with which he dismissed the Bible.

'Biblical legends, yes.'

Carys persisted. 'How can they be legends if you say this artefact is Aaron's Rod?'

'Because, my dear, objects survive, but the people who possess them pass away. Stories grow around the objects, as they do around places. The stories are passed from generation to generation, helping people to make sense of their pathetic lives. Sometimes people will die to preserve the honour of these stories, that's how important they are to human beings.'

Bethany rolled her eyes and sighed impatiently. 'Can we please get back to the rod? What are the markings?'

'Right, well, the markings may illustrate what I've been saying. They are Hebrew letters –'

Bethany smiled at Carys. 'We *thought* they might be Hebrew. What do they say?'

'Do you know the legend of the Ten Plagues?' asked Dredge.

'There you go again,' Carys protested. 'The Ten Plagues are not a legend. They are in the Bible, in Exodus. Aaron and Moses are trying to persuade Pharaoh to let the Israelites go – they use the rod to bring on various plagues.'

'Well, anyway,' continued Dredge, 'the rod was inscribed with the initial letters of those plagues.'

'Why did they do that?' asked Carys.

'I suppose because that is the rod's most famous legend, but there are many others. One says it was made on the sixth day of Creation out of a branch of the Tree of Life. Ridiculous! Another says that Joseph of Arimathea brought it to Britain with the Grail and other relics. It goes on and on. But however ridiculous, they're all interesting to antiquarians like me, because it's the legends and stories that make objects valuable, as much as their age.'

'Are there any legends about *Merlin* and the rod?'

As soon as Carys said it, she knew she'd made a mistake. Dredge almost levitated from his chair.

'Merlin? What can Merlin have to do with it? Why do you ask about Merlin?'

Dredge stood up and leant over Carys, as he had done earlier when she'd been in the armchair, only now his breath smelled of sewers. 'Tell me, girl, *tell* me! Why do you ask about Merlin?'

'I ... I don't know ... He was in my mind, I suppose – I saw his riddle in that book, and –'

'Riddle? You *saw* ... Merlin's ... *riddle?*'

Dredge dropped back onto his chair, his face the colour of the finest antique porcelain in his shop. His nose was twitching. He kept trying to ask a question of Carys, but was unable to voice it. It kept coming out as a squeak. After several attempts, he squeezed it out.

'Was it ... i-in silver i-ink?'

'Yes, but I promise I didn't say it out loud!'

Dredge was holding his throat with his fingers, as if he was choking on his own words. 'This cannot be happening. It is ... not ... *possible*. Merlin, you charlatan, not even you would use me like this. Th-that riddle was *mine!*'

His voice was so distorted now that neither girl could understand him. They were concerned that he might be having another attack.

Dredge looked across at the dressing table mirror which had failed to ensnare Carys. Then he stared at her face, as he had earlier. Then he looked at the book of spells and back to Carys. Then he glanced down at the photo of Aaron's Rod, and again at

Carys. But his face remained blank. Whatever answer he was after, he was not getting it. He stood up and again leaned over Carys.

'You come into my shop,' he spluttered, with many of his words lost to involuntary squeaks and grunts, 'dressed all in black, with your long black hair and skin as pale as the moon, with a silver stud piercing your nose – and eyes that are like windows into another world. You resist the power of my mirror, you read Merlin's riddle, and you possess a photo of Aaron's Rod. Who *are* you, girl?' He put his face so close to Carys's that it was all she could do to stop herself from retching. 'What … is … your … name?' His speech had become laboured now, as if he'd put body and soul into this last attempt to force Carys's identity out of her.

Carys felt her name being drawn out of her.

'Carys … Aranrhod … Cadwaladr,' she groaned. Then she stood up and began dragging herself and Bethany towards the door.

NOOOOOOOO …!

Dredge's scream was not of this earth. All of the edgy foreboding that Carys had been feeling ever since she paused on the shop's threshold, she now heard in that scream. It swirled around her, penetrated her being and came to rest as a hard knot of panic in her stomach.

… OOOOOOOOOOOOOO …!

She and Bethany had to get out, but the louder the scream grew, the harder it became for the girls to move towards the door.

… OOOOOOOOOOOOOOOOOOOOOO …!

It was as if they were struggling to escape from Hell itself.

'Dredge! Dredge!'

Someone was shouting out the dealer's name and hammering on the door outside. The screaming stopped dead, to be replaced by a sniveling sound, like a cornered rat might make. The resistance to their departure stopped and Carys was able to unlock the door. There, waiting to be let in, was a tall, bald man, dressed in a mustard and orange check suit.

Chapter 14 — Aaron's Rod

Balimm didn't wait for Carys and Bethany to clear the doorway before entering the shop himself, so he had to squeeze past them. It wasn't quite the collision on the station platform, for when she looked into the man's eyes Carys didn't fall down a black hole. But what she saw chilled her soul. It was like looking into a living death. Carys knew that she was a breath away from a being whose purpose was to empty creation of love and hope, of joy and faith, of peace and friendship – to destroy everything that made life worth living.

As for Bethany, she didn't see Balimm at all. From the moment that Dredge screamed, she'd closed her eyes and held onto Carys's hand until they were clear of the shop. They didn't stop running until they reached Zach's house.

Zach lived in the cathedral close. When the renovations to the Deanery were finished, Bethany and Carys would be Zach's neighbours, instead of being separated by the cathedral, as they were now.

On entering the hall, they were met by Suzy, barking madly. It was an old house, with not a perpendicular wall nor level floor to be seen. Not much of the walls or floors *could* be seen for all the books. They were everywhere.

As the girls climbed the stairs, Carys noticed that there were books piled against the wall on each step, forming a separate, literary staircase. A black cat overtook them, loping from book-step to book-step. It would be typical of Zach to have a well-read cat.

On the first landing, there was floor-to-ceiling shelving on the wall spaces between all the rooms. These shelves had overflowed onto the floor, so the family had to negotiate a path through Latin verse and Victorian gardening books on the way to their rooms.

Loud music was coming from one room – louder when the door opened and a girl poked her head out. She was about fifteen, with hair dyed blonde and wearing a red polka-dot bathrobe. She came out and shut the door behind her so she could hear herself speak.

She shouted, louder than she needed to, 'Hi, Beth!' And then, to Carys, 'You must be Carys. I'm Ruth. Do you want to come clubbing tonight? I know places where you'd get in easy.'

Carys politely declined.

Ruth squeezed past them to bang her fist on the bathroom door, using Robinson Crusoe and Teach Yourself Origami as stepping-stones. A teenage lad, wearing nothing but his underpants and an iPod, came out dancing with a towel over his arm. He danced his way between piles of National Geographics and disappeared into his room.

Carys and Bethany were now climbing onto a second landing.

'How many brothers and sisters does Zach have?' Carys asked.

'I'm not sure. I've met … four,' replied Bethany. 'You've met Ruth and that was Jerry with the iPod. At least I think it was. All the kids have names from the Old Testament.'

Carys simply adored the house.

Bethany laughed. 'Ours will be the same – you and I can have two bedrooms each.'

There were two doors off the second landing, plus a spiral staircase, which they had to climb to get to Zach's room – or rather his suite, for the whole loft had been converted. Two thirds of it formed a huge living space, while the other third included a dressing room where Zach's colourful clothes were kept, a toilet and a shower. Carys was surprised. She had expected Zach's room to be as exuberant and wacky as Zach himself, with computers and gadgets covering every surface. But there was not only an absence of gadgets, but an absence of surfaces!

A plain green carpet covered the floor, and the plasterboard walls erected under the eaves were all painted a shade of green, which set off the dark wood of the exposed beams. All the lighting was hidden. Zach was working on his laptop, swinging in a basket chair suspended from a beam. There were a couple of large beanbags, but the overall impression was of a monk's cell. Except there was no bed.

Carys flopped down on one of the beanbags. She had to know. 'Where's all your *stuff?*'

Zach took a remote control out of the green and black cowboy shirt he'd changed into. 'I prefer to live without clutter. It helps me to think clearly.' He pressed a button and the wall on his left slid open to allow a bed to trundle out from under the eaves. At the press of another button a desk appeared, with nothing on it but a large pad of paper and a jar of pens.

Carys couldn't believe her eyes. 'It's magic!'

Zach agreed. 'Merlin would have loved remote controls.'

Carys had to laugh when a slide show of gigantic photographs of herself and Bethany appeared on the wall at the far end, beamed from a hidden projector that had a wireless link to Zach's laptop. They were the pictures that Zach had snapped in the Shambles that afternoon.

Bethany raised her voice to be heard above the merriment. 'Guys, can we see these another time? We've got loads of business to get through.'

Zach looked duly penitent. 'Sorry, Beth, you're right – though *my* report won't take long.' He switched the projector off and returned the bed to its hiding place. 'I'm afraid I drew a blank on the Internet. Hardly anything about structures before the present cathedral. I think I was being too specific in my search. By the way, Beth, your mum invited me to tea, so we can continue the meeting at your place.'

Carys pointed to the paper and pens on the desk. 'Why doesn't Beth take notes?'

'That's a good idea,' Zach said, 'and I'll back them up on my computer.'

Bethany lay down on the floor with the pad of paper and jar of pens. 'Right. In the half an hour before tea, I propose we aim for a summary of what we know.' She sounded very businesslike. 'At the top, let's put that we have a magic rod. Are you happy with that, Carys?'

Carys buried herself more deeply in her beanbag. 'Why shouldn't I be?'

'Well, I thought you didn't believe in magic.'

'I didn't yesterday. But my mind is changing, almost by the minute. Call me crazy, but I'm beginning to go along with you guys.'

'For the ride?' asked Zach, tossing his hair back like a horse breaking into a gallop.

Carys smiled. 'No, Zach, not for the ride – it hasn't exactly been a *joy*ride so far, has it?'

Bethany disagreed. 'How can you say that, Cass? I've never *had* so much fun.'

Bethany was blessed with a memory that was good at editing out the bad parts.

Carys looked at Bethany, and then at Zach. She'd known them for such a short time, and yet she felt so close to them. She was not used to having friends she could be so honest with, who accepted her for what she was, including what her mother was, the whole package. And they were *fun* people.

'Oh, go on then,' she said, 'I'm in it for the ride as well!' She laughed without pulling her hair across her mouth.

'Was the rod's task to make Carys believe?' asked Bethany.

Carys sat up, a serious expression on her face. 'I don't think the rod has made me believe. It's been you two. *You've* done it.'

There was an awkward silence, broken by the squeaking of Bethany's felt tip as she vigorously underlined her notes. 'That's great. I feel we're getting somewhere. Now, I'd prefer you, Cass, to tell Zach what happened at Dredge's – if you can bear it. I'm not kidding, Zach, I had my eyes closed at the finish.'

'Why, what happened? Did you show him the photos?'

'We did,' said Carys, 'and I have to tell you that Beth was brilliant. She didn't bat an eyelid when she gave the dealer our cover story. He swallowed it whole.'

'What did he say about the artefact?'

Bethany rolled over and proclaimed to the ceiling, 'It's Aaron's Rod!'

'Aaron's Rod? From the Bible, you mean? And you believed him?'

Bethany rolled onto her front so she could look Zach in the eye. 'Zach, I'm telling you, if you'd been there, *you'd* have believed him. Dredge was –'

Carys interrupted. 'Hang on, Beth, I thought you wanted *me* to tell Zach what happened?'

Bethany mouthed a silent apology and went back to her notes.

But Zach wouldn't let Carys continue. He was adamant. 'I don't care what he was or what he did, the dealer was wrong. It's not Aaron's Rod.'

Carys was puzzled. 'What makes you so sure?'

'Easy. Beth, please draw me a rough outline of Aaron – you know, in his long robe and that.'

Bethany drew quite a good figure.

'Now give Aaron his rod.'

Bethany held her pen poised over the drawing for a moment and then slapped her free hand down hard. 'Of course!' she cried, as she drew a rod that was taller than Aaron.

Zach explained that Aaron's Rod would have been a long stick, like a shepherd's crook without the crook. 'Its main purpose was to fight off wild animals. A short rod like ours would be useless. You need length to keep the animal at bay, poke him and then give him a good whack.'

'How do you know all this?' inquired Carys.

Zach grinned. 'It's a common weapon in computer games. Anyway, did you ask Dredge about the markings? They may still help us.'

'They're –' Bethany began, before slapping a hand over her mouth and stifling a laugh.

Carys threw herself back onto her beanbag in mock despair.

Bethany was imploring. 'Please, Cass, just this bit and then I'll be quiet.' Then she added, before Carys could reply, 'Zach, they're Hebrew letters!'

Zach gave the thumbs-up sign. 'Well, at least Dredge got *some*thing right.'

Bethany called out, 'Okay, Carys, the floor is yours.'

Carys sat up. 'Thank you, Chair. Zach, Dredge told us that the markings are the initial letters of the Plagues.'

'Hang on, he's wrong again!' exclaimed Zach. 'There were *ten* plagues. There are never ten letters on our rod.' Zach fished out his mobile phone and showed both girls his original close-ups of the rod. They agreed there were only four letters.

Bethany was bitterly disappointed. 'Dredge was so *sure.*'

Zach was sorry that his dad had recommended *Dredge's Emporium.* 'We'll try a different shop tomorrow. Dredge must have been having fun with you.'

But Carys couldn't leave it there. 'There was nothing *fun* about Dredge. He was deadly serious. Everything you say makes sense, Zach – our rod is too short and it does only have four letters on it. But we're missing something here, we must be. Beth's right, he was *sure.* You weren't there, Zach – Dredge is no ordinary antique dealer …'

Carys asked Bethany to read her notes out. Maybe that would help. Carys patiently watched her friend put the top back on the pen she was using and place it next to the other pens in the jar. *Of course!*

Before Bethany could begin reading, Carys spoke urgently. 'Sorry, Beth, I don't need your notes after all, though I may need your excellent drawing of Aaron with his rod. Zach, can you get on the Internet?'

'Course. What are you after?'

'The Ark of the Covenant.'

'O … kay.' Zach tapped it into a search engine. 'There's loads – what do you want to know?'

'Its dimensions. I've had an idea, but I want some evidence before I say what it is.'

Zach soon found a site that gave the dimensions: 'The Ark was … 4ft x 2ft x 2ft. That's 1200mm x 600mm x 600mm. Look, there's a drawing. So what's your idea, Cass?'

'I happen to know, thanks to Pastor Lewis's course on the Book of Hebrews, that Aaron's Rod was kept in the Ark of the Covenant. I'm talking many centuries after Aaron died, when his rod had become a sacred relic.' Carys picked up Bethany's sketch of Aaron with his rod. 'Now, I want you to tell me how they kept *that* …' pointing to Aaron's Rod in the drawing '… in *that?*' pointing to the picture of the Ark on the website.

'They cut it – into – pieces,' said Zach, slowly. 'That's incredible! They cut up Aaron's Rod to keep it in the Ark … it'd be like chopping up Excalibur to fit it into your saddlebag.'

Carys pointed at Bethany. 'Make a note, will you, Beth? I must send a card to Pastor Lewis, thanking him for his course on Hebrews.'

Bethany was ecstatic. 'So Aaron's Rod *did* exist, and we've got a piece of it. Dredge was right, after all.'

Zach began shutting his laptop down. 'So what was the big deal with Dredge? You still haven't told me what happened that was so scary.'

Bethany went to speak, but Zach put a finger to his lips just in time.

'Dredge made me so mad,' said Carys, 'the way he insisted that everything that's recorded in the Bible is legend. He put the Plagues on a par with a legend that says Joseph of Arimathea brought the rod to Britain with the Holy Grail.'

Bethany's eyes widened, and she couldn't help butting in. 'He didn't like it when Cass contradicted him, but he only started ranting and raving when she asked him if there were any legends that would connect *Merlin* to the rod. He went berserk.'

Zach shot from his swinging basket seat and almost dropped his laptop as he danced a jig that conveyed both his excitement and his frustration. 'You asked him if there's a connection between

Merlin and the rod? After the way you've treated *me* whenever I've suggested it?'

Carys tried to keep a straight face. 'Of *course* there's a connection – that's what we've been telling you all along!'

Zach picked up a beanbag and threw it at Carys before trying to sit on her. After much hilarity, Bethany adjourned the meeting, to be continued in her room after tea.

'We've cut it fine,' shouted Carys, as the three of them whizzed down the spiral staircase. Zach leapt over the final spiral and landed neatly on his feet, which were couched in Native American moccasins.

Next they hurtled down the stairs to the first landing, to find Ruth blocking the way to the main stairs. She was dressed in two towels, one round her body, the other holding up her hair. She was resting one damp foot on Pilgrim's Progress.

Zach frowned and pointed to Ruth's foot. 'You'll get a bunion doing that.'

Ruth was not amused. 'Bunyan, bunion, I geddit, very funny. Have you got my hair drier?'

'Not guilty. Try Dave.'

Ruth didn't budge. She threatened her brother with her hair straighteners. 'If I find you've –'

Zach interrupted her. 'Rotten luck, getting a zit on your big night out.'

'What? Where?' she cried, running back to the bathroom, which was now occupied. 'Why does it always happen to *me?*'

They were halfway down the stairs when Suzy came bounding past them, using the book-steps. Unfortunately the Complete Works of Shakespeare made the pile on the bottom step top heavy, causing it to collapse. Suzy crashed into a basket of golf balls, sending them bouncing all over the hall. The girls were laughing so much, they nearly went flying as well.

Zach's mum, Annie, came out of the living room. She had a glass of white wine in her hand.

'What on earse –?'

'Maman, I've told you before,' Zach complained, 'the heavy volumes must always be at the *bottom* of the piles. Shakespeare sent Suzy flying. She might have hurt herself. She's not coming with us, by the way. Did you hear that, Suzy? Stay!'

Suzy looked crestfallen and climbed the stairs to see who else she could play with.

Annie was French, petite, with short hair coiffured to look tousled. She had a boyish face, with big brown eyes, which her neat nose and thin lips served to accentuate. Every feature was enhanced by expertly applied make-up. She wore faded blue jeans, a loose cream shirt hanging out, and open-toed slip-ons that revealed toes painted the same dark blue as her fingernails.

She kicked one of the golf balls across the hall. 'And 'oo eez going to pick up all zeez balls?' Her accent was pronounced, despite having lived in England for twenty years.

Carys and Bethany picked up a few balls, before Zach ushered them to the door.

'Sorry, Maman, we're late. I'm having tea at Beth's. I've told Daisy.'

The three of them ran across the cathedral close.

Carys was curious. 'Who's Daisy?'

'Our housekeeper.'

'You've got a *housekeeper?*'

'It's the only way Mum and Dad can work full-time and raise seven kids.'

'What does your mum do?' asked Bethany.

'She's an artist – Impressionist. She has a studio and gallery in town.'

'What does she paint?'

'Landscapes mainly. France a lot, of course, and *North* Pembrokeshire.'

Carys smiled at his emphasis. 'And whose are all the books?'

'They're Dad's. He's mad about books. Mum chains him up when it's the Hay Festival!'

The cathedral still hadn't been locked up for the night, so they were able to cut through the cloisters, across the nave and out through the main door. This time, unlike the previous night, there was no need to worry about being in public view as they ran between the front porch and the Palace garden gate. Considering how upset the girls had been by their visit to Dredge's, they were now in high spirits.

Chapter 15 — Pest Control

Balimm sat down at the dining table and summoned Dredge.

'One moment, give me a moment!' came the call from the back room.

It had to be Dredge, but it didn't sound like him. His voice wasn't that squeaky. At last he appeared. Gone were his cane and usual clothes. He was wearing a floor-length, loose-fitting, black robe. Neither did his features add up to the Dredge of old. For a start, he had whiskers. Not the whiskers sported by Edwardian gentlemen, but whiskers of the rodent variety. Also his ears, which he was trying to hide in a voluminous cloth cap, were distinctly rat-like. Balimm was shocked.

'Dredge! What has happened to you?'

The dealer was distressed. His enlarged front teeth made it difficult to speak clearly.

'F-forgive me, Balimm, but this has never h-happened to me before. I'm sure I shall recover soon. I am normally one hundred percent in control of my appearance, you know.'

'What triggered it? I heard you screaming …'

'Oh that!' He tried to sound unconcerned. 'It was those girls, pestering me to value some bauble. Worthless, but they wouldn't take no for an answer. And they hadn't even brought the thing with them. I had to value it from photographs. I'm not good with children. Th-they're different somehow, harder to read. They make me feel ill. I tried one of the girls on my mirror but she didn't bat an eye. In the end, I lost my temper and out came that scream.'

This account of the girls' visit was clever, because enough of it was true for Dredge to be able to put his whole self into the narration. But it was always going to be hard to deceive Balimm.

'Who were they? What were their names? The tall, dark one? I did not like the look she gave me, Dredge.'

Balimm's words made Dredge wince as he remembered looking into Carys's eyes in the mirror. He had suspected something then and should have acted upon his suspicion, used stronger magic to disarm her. Maybe if she'd been alone … but that brat with her kept up a barrage of distraction. Without doubt, they were a well-trained team.

'A couple of schoolgirls,' Dredge replied, 'teasing an old man for sport. And I let them get to me.'

Balimm felt uneasy. Dredge was not the demon he used to be, but still he should have swatted those girls away … with his tail?

Balimm saw with dismay that a rat's tail protruded from under Dredge's robe, growing as he watched. He felt dismay because Dredge had been a fine worker, promoting the spread of evil for hundreds of years and building a network of contacts that higher demons such as Balimm could draw upon with confidence. Now Dredge's useful days were over.

'Perhaps, you rat,' said Balimm – for it was pointless to call it Dredge any more – 'you are in this dreadful state out of fear? You have not found Aaron's Rod, and you were afraid of what I would do to you.'

The Dredge-rat jumped on this explanation.

'You're right. It was my fear of your anger which those girls latched onto.'

Balimm was growing weary of talking to a giant rat.

'The rod!' he barked. 'Tell me what you have!'

'I don't have the rod, as you guessed, but I have solved the riddle. *By a silver circle in a silver circle.* The first silver circle is the moon. So the rods are found by moonlight.'

'Excellent. Go on.'

'For the second half of the riddle, you must picture stone circles in the moonlight, the crystals in the granite sparkling like silver.'

'Of course. Stone circles – the obvious place for Merlin to have hidden them.'

For a moment, one brief moment, Balimm thought that that was it: problem solved. The rods were to be found by moonlight, in stone circles. Then he saw there was still a huge problem.

'Wait a minute. How do we know which circles?'

The rat was busy gnawing at the legs of a period bureau. It wasn't going to give the rod to Balimm, not now. With the rod's power, it might be able to recover human form.

It squeaked, 'I have helped you enough, Balimm. I have my own problems to attend to, as you will have noticed.'

Balimm was furious.

'Are you trying to tell me that this is all you have? I will find the rods in stone circles by moonlight?'

'Take the riddle to other Merlin experts if you will. They will tell you the same. Wizards are never specific. It's part of the game.'

'I have played these wizards' games long enough, and *you* have played with Balimm's patience once too often, rat!'

Balimm stood erect, feet apart. When it sensed what was afoot, the rat tried to run into the back room but it would no longer fit through the door. Out of Balimm's chest came a low groan, a sustained note of unbearable intensity.

The floor began to tremble, gently at first, and then more violently. The plates on the dresser crashed down, then the whole top section toppled over onto the dining table, sending the remaining candlestick flying. The walls were crumbling and falling inwards, bringing the ceiling down. Finally, the roof disintegrated and came crashing down. Balimm was untouched by any of this. But he hadn't finished.

He raised the pitch of the vibrations emanating from his chest. As Dredge had explained, every object in his shop was imbued with the pain of human existence that their owners had experienced, taking spirit form over the centuries but entombed within the physical objects.

Now Balimm's vibrations set them free and they were attracted to the rat's frightened spirit as to Gadarenes swine. Spirits of sorrow and mourning, of panic and disappointment, of fear and self-loathing swirled about the rubble before descending on the demon rat. As it writhed and squirmed in the broken treasures of the antique shop, everything began to sink as the quaking grew in intensity; sinking into the earth as if it were quicksand. The last item to go was the dressing table. Its mirror gave up its spirit of despair and broke into a thousand shards, all reflecting the dying gasp of the demon rat as it too slipped into the dissolving ground.

At last, everything was gone. Walls, roof, stove, floors, beams, windows, and all the antique items, the whole shop. It was as if it had never existed. The space between the shops on either side was now a piece of clear ground, earth that had been raked to a level smoothness.

Balimm stepped onto the pavement, and dirt trickled into the footprints he'd left until they were no longer there. He was walking away when he turned for one last look at his handiwork. He'd slipped up. In the centre of the plot there was something protruding, an object that had dared to withstand his power. He strode over to it. It was the corner of a rectangle of paper sticking out of the soil. He bent down and pulled at it. It was a photograph.

'So, the girls were pestering you to value some bauble? Worthless, was it? Dredge, you were, as I always thought, a double-crossing rat.'

Balimm slipped the photo of the rod into his pocket and walked away.

He should have been delighted, but he wasn't. Far from it. He didn't feel in control of events. More worrying was the knowledge that he'd lost control of himself. Killing Dredge had been enjoyable, but stupid. Dredge would be a difficult resource to replace. On the other hand, as a giant rat he would not have been much use.

It was hard to think what could have upset Dredge to the point where he had lost control like that. But then, what the rat had said about human children was right: they were dangerous. They lived in a storybook world, so telling stories came naturally to them.

And now two of these children had a piece of Aaron's Rod. Here, in Worcester. *By a silver circle in a silver circle.* According to Dredge's interpretation of the riddle, these girls had found the rod in a stone circle, by moonlight. How would they have known to do that?

He swore a demon oath under his breath. He had passed so close to them. When the tall girl had caught his eye, for a brief moment he had felt … disturbed. If he, Balimm, with all his power, had been disturbed by a passing glance, what chance did Dredge have? Balimm wasn't afraid at the idea of doing battle with these human children, but he was always glad to be forewarned.

All his thinking and walking had brought him to the cathedral roundabout, from where Carys had been so impressed by the building. Balimm was also impressed – no demon could fail to be. Unlike Carys, he despised all that the cathedral stood for: peace, love, hope, faith, all these things were Balimm's enemies. But this didn't mean he couldn't admire the cathedral, as a professional soldier might admire the design of the enemy's weaponry. He made his way round the crossing points until he was skirting the cathedral's grassy forecourt.

That was close enough for his comfort. He wouldn't have ventured inside, for he would have been overwhelmed by the centuries of loving thoughts, faithful prayers, and exchanges of fellowship that had soaked into the fabric of the cathedral. From where he was standing, he could feel it, almost touch it, and it sickened him.

He looked back to where he'd come from, to the shops and the human crowds, some beginning their Friday night binge drinking. He kept turning, back and forth, between the cathedral and the people. He smiled. Then his smile became a laugh, a laugh of scorn and spite. This was going to be so easy, destroying this world, removing its spirit. For however close to the cathedral most of these humans of Worcester passed, they did not see it as a spiritual reality that could revive their ailing souls. Instead they persisted in looking for salvation in material wealth. *It is not just the children who live in a fantasy world,* thought Balimm with grim satisfaction.

He turned to look at the cathedral one last time, as if saluting his enemy. From where he was now standing, he would have spied Carys and Bethany the previous night: creeping from the Old Palace garden gate to the cathedral door, bound for their midnight feast.

But as Balimm saluted his enemy this evening, who should he see but Carys, Bethany and Zach crossing in the other direction, from the cathedral door to the Palace garden gate. They had no reason to hide now. They were on their way to have tea at the Old Palace. And yes, they were in high spirits …

Chapter 16 Magic Topic

While they were lodging in the Old Palace, the Cadwalladers were having tea in the Palace Restaurant – in splendid isolation, since the restaurant was open to the public only at lunchtime. Every day, Hilda left them a cold platter.

This evening Stephen arrived late; he'd had a visitor.

'Who was it, dear?' asked Helen.

'Some professor. I told him to come back later. I will *not* have my family meal disrupted.'

It was Bethany's turn to say grace. She prayed, 'Thank you, God, for this food. Thank you for the magic things that happen to us. Amen.'

They all tucked in.

'My,' commented Stephen, 'you're all hungry today.'

They couldn't tell him that investigating magic was hard work.

Stephen passed more sandwiches down to his daughter. 'I was intrigued by your prayer, Beth. Tell us what "magic things" have happened to you today.'

Bethany looked round the table. Carys and Zach were staring hard at her.

'I didn't mean *real* magic,' she said. 'Fun things like making a new friend and the tricks that Suzy can do – you should have seen her sword fighting with Zach in the Shambles. *That* was magic.'

'And sucking the chocolate off chocolate fingers without biting into them,' said Zach, as he held aloft his third.

'Dad?'

'Yes, Bethany?'

'Do you believe in magic – real magic?'

'No, of course I don't.'

'Jesus did magic,' volunteered Zach.

'That wasn't magic, that was –'

Stephen paused. He took a bite of celery and crunched it noisily.

'Yes, darling, how *do* the miracles of Jesus differ from magic?' asked Helen, who enjoyed seeing her husband put on the spot occasionally.

'Well … people in those days –'

Stephen paused again, and took another bite.

'Yes, go on, Stephen … people in those days?'

'They *believed* in that kind of thing.'

Stephen's embarrassment had gone on long enough.

'I think we should leave Jesus out of this discussion,' Helen said. 'He was a very special case.'

She offered her husband some of his favourite cake, to make up for teasing him. Then she turned to her daughter. 'Since you raised it, Bethany, I'd be interested to know: do *you* believe in magic?'

'Yes, of course I do, silly!' was her unblinking reply.

'What about the rest of us?' inquired Helen, putting her own hand half way up. Zach put his hand all the way up. Stephen and Carys didn't respond. Bethany couldn't contain herself. She exclaimed, 'Carys!'

Carys ignored her and asked Helen why she had put her hand half way up.

'Well,' said Helen, 'I would believe in magic if it didn't break the laws of nature. Now, there may be another set of laws we don't know about. But since we don't know about those laws, that's why my hand goes part way up.'

134

'That's how *I* see it,' said Zach. 'Well, almost.'

Bethany couldn't rest. She had to pursue it. 'Carys, you *do* believe in magic. You *said!*'

'Darling, don't browbeat your friend,' said Stephen. 'Perhaps you misunderstood her.'

Carys came to Bethany's defence. 'It's okay, Stephen, Beth is right. The fact is I *do* believe ...'

Bethany beamed.

'... but I don't find it easy to admit it,' added Carys, smiling nervously.

Stephen cleared his throat. 'Don't worry, Carys, it's neither here nor there since there's no such thing.' He glanced at Helen and smiled.

Zach put his hand up. 'Stephen, can *I* ask you a question?'

'Is it about magic?'

'Sort of. It's about pagan shrines. Stone circles, that kind of thing.'

Stephen raised his eyebrows. 'Stone circles? I think this is one for your father, Zach, but since Tom's not here, I'll have a go.'

'Is it possible that the first Christian builders used the stones from pagan sites when they built their churches?'

'It's more than possible,' replied Stephen, thrilled that he knew the answer after all, 'we know they did. There's quite a famous church in Spain where you can see the pagan cup stones built into the wall. It was the obvious thing to do, when you think about it. Why waste good stones? Furthermore, in the process they were sanctifying the pagan sites –'

Helen interrupted. 'Like we took over their festivals, I suppose. I always think that was a bit mean.'

Carys caught Stephen's eye. 'Can *I* ask a question?'

'Of course,' Stephen replied, laughing, 'but don't feel you have to!'

'Mine is about Aaron's Rod.'

'Ah, sounds more like my field – but pass the cheese first, please. I'll need fortifying if this is going to be a biblical question.' Stephen chuckled as he cut himself a chunk of cheddar.

Carys dived in with her question. 'Why was Aaron's Rod so special?'

Stephen took a sip of tea.

'For a start,' he said, 'when Moses was bringing down the plagues on the Egyptians, Aaron used the rod to defeat Pharaoh's magicians.'

'So it was a magic rod!' Bethany declared, grinning from ear to ear.

'That's enough, Bethany,' said Helen sternly. 'No more magic questions today, thank you.'

Stephen continued, 'Then when Moses and Aaron were leading the Israelites across the desert, Moses used the rod to draw water from a rock. Also, the rod sprouted leaves and fruit overnight, during a test to see who should be Israel's first High Priest – that's when Aaron was appointed.'

There was a short silence, and then everybody spontaneously applauded and cheered.

'Did I pass?' Stephen asked as he stood up and took a bow.

Helen offered him another slice of cake and refilled his cup.

'No more cake for me, dear. I've a sermon to write and there's a programme I want to watch later. So, if you'll excuse me, everybody, I'll take my tea into the study. See you all later. Oh, and Helen, would you mind showing that professor up if he comes back? With any luck, he won't bother. I kind of got the impression he was after something – probably money.'

Chapter 17 — Timely Truth

The meeting had reconvened in Bethany's room. Zach and Beth were both on the floor – Zach with his laptop, Bethany kneeling in front of her notes. Carys was lying on the bed, upon one elbow. The rod was under the bed as usual. They'd all looked at it with renewed awe since agreeing that it was part of Aaron's Rod.

Zach was still curious about why Carys had inquired of Dredge if there were any legends connecting the rod with Merlin, when she'd never encouraged Zach's speculations in that direction.

Carys struggled to remember. 'I was sort of swept along by what was happening, I suppose. Dredge had screamed at me for daring to look at one of his books. I'd seen this riddle, written in the margin. I-I knew it was Merlin's riddle. Even more weird – I knew it was meant for me.'

'Merlin's riddle? Merlin *wrote* it in that book?' asked Zach, scarcely able to contain his excitement.

'Or it appeared by magic when the time was right,' replied Carys. 'I don't know how these things work, do I?'

'Okay, but what did the riddle say?'

'It was short. *By a silver circle in a silver circle.*'

Zach tapped it out on his keyboard. 'That is a fabulous riddle.'

'What do you mean?' asked Carys.

'Well, the repetition, it's beautiful. The two silver circles have different meanings. That's the riddle. We have to think of something different for each half.'

Bethany had written out the riddle in her notes. 'Will it tell us what we're supposed to do next?'

Carys was shaking her head. 'I can't see how.'

Zach grinned. 'That's why it's a riddle.' He got up and counted on his fingers as he paced the floor.

Bethany's face fell. 'I'm sorry, but I hate riddles.'

Zach stopped pacing. 'Forget it's a riddle, Beth. Just tell me – what does *a silver circle* suggest to you?'

Bethany drew a circle and wrote 'silver' next to it. Then she pondered. 'Well … what about the ring Carys's mum gave her?'

Zach didn't want to be hard on Bethany. 'That's good, Beth, really good. A silver ring is definitely a silver circle –'

Bethany knew what was coming. 'But –?'

'But, if I'm honest, I think it's *ever* so slightly too … obvious, if you see what I mean. When decoding a riddle, the idea is to look for meanings that are more hidden.'

'I told you I hate riddles, they're so silly!' said Bethany, pouting.

Carys had an idea. 'I suppose a hidden meaning for *a silver circle* would be Aranrhod – remember, I told you that Aranrhod means *silver wheel*? Well, a wheel is a circle.'

Zach dropped to the floor and typed: *by a silver circle = by an Aranrhod*. Then he typed his verdict, reading it out as he went: 'Considering everything that we've learned so far, it seems certain that *Aranrhod* is the meaning of the first half of the riddle.'

Zach stopped typing and addressed Carys directly. 'I'm glad it was your idea, Cass, not mine. It suggests your mother was right all along – about the name having a deep significance.'

Carys's head dropped onto the pillow. 'I-I know. I've been thinking about that. But a lot has happened. Especially at Dredge's Emporium. Our visit there changed everything for me.'

An air of gloom descended on the trio. It was as if the closer they got to understanding the events of the past twenty-four hours, especially the meaning of the rod and the riddle, the more serious were the implications.

Zach did his best to lift everyone's spirits. 'That's it, then, folks: according to a riddle written by Merlin many centuries ago, *something* has to be done by an Aranrhod. That wasn't so hard!'

But he wasn't fooling Bethany. 'Yes, thank you, Zach. But it doesn't help, does it, because we don't know *what* needs to be done, nor *where*. I don't get it, what's the point of sending a message in a riddle?'

Zach knelt down next to Bethany. He didn't like to see her so down. 'The point is, Beth, only the person it's intended for can understand a good riddle – and sometimes her friends, of course. Other people will be misled. It's actually a brilliant way to convey a secret message.'

Bethany threw her pen down wearily. 'Can we have a break from riddling? I want to hold the rod again – can I, *please?*'

The others agreed, so Bethany retrieved the rod and held it in front of her with both hands. The three of them stared. It was magnificent.

Zach whistled through his teeth. 'If it *is* Aaron's Rod, Cass has found what must be the most important biblical artefact after the Ark and the Grail –'

Bethany giggled. 'And your dad, and my mum, think it's a light sabre!'

Zach took the rod. 'I still can't get over the priests breaking it into pieces so it would fit in the Ark.' He scrutinised the ends. 'They did a good job; you'd never know.'

'That's because it's *magic*,' said Bethany.

Perhaps it was because they were holding the rod, or simply beholding it, but the atmosphere in the room had definitely brightened.

Bethany held her hand out to Zach for another turn, but he hadn't finished. 'Of course,' he continued, 'if they *hadn't* broken the rod into shorter lengths, it would have been too long for Merlin to hide inside a stone – a stone which would end up being built into our Chapter House wall.'

Carys reached out and took the rod. She lay on her back and held the rod at arms' length. 'I wonder … when Merlin hid this piece of Aaron's Rod, did he have the *other* pieces in his possession? And if he did, did he …?'

Carys's voice trailed away. A heavy silence descended as the awful but inevitable truth dawned.

Zach and Bethany waited. It had to be Carys to break this silence: 'How many are out there, Zach?'

'Well, we can guess quite accurately the length of the complete rod, and if we bear in mind that our piece holds four tenths of the –'

'How *many*, Zach?'

'Two.'

'Gosh, Carys,' whispered Bethany, 'so that's your mum's destiny, to find the three pieces of Aaron's Rod – well, two pieces, I suppose, since you've already found the first one.'

In the next silence that followed, Carys passed the rod back to Zach. They exchanged glances and understood. They waited for Bethany. She didn't keep them long.

'Oh *no!*'

Zach nodded. 'I'm afraid so, Beth. We have to conclude that *Carys* is the chosen Aranrhod –'

'Actually,' said Carys quietly, 'I'm relieved it's me and not Mum. I don't see how she could have coped. And I'm relieved that the waiting is over, the not knowing –'

Bethany interrupted. 'But there's still loads we don't know. For instance, the Chapter House must be the first silver circle because Carys found the first rod there – well, I can see it's a circle, but how is it a *silver* circle?'

'How about the moonlight shining in?' suggested Zach.

Bethany was indignant. 'What moonlight? Carys found the rod in pitch darkness.'

Carys was looking worried. 'Something else, Zach. You told us that Aaron used the rod as a weapon. Am I going to have to fight?'

'Judging from my vast experience in computer games, my answer to that would be negative. You are the Finder of the weapon, and it is someone else's role to be the Wielder.'

'Whose?'

'I think you know. But let me see if I can draw the threads together now that we're all agreed that Merlin is behind it all. Beth, you be Merlin. You sit here, cross-legged, on the desk, and try to look wise.'

Bethany climbed onto the desk and sat down. Then she twisted her face into her idea of wisdom.

'Knock, knock!'

'Oh no, not now, Bethany,' groaned Zach.

'Who's there?' responded Carys, who was glad for a bit of Bethany's silliness.

'Merlin.'

'Merlin who?'

'Merlin Brando!'

When Bethany had finished laughing, Zach gave her the rod. 'You'll have to imagine you've got the other two pieces. Now, Merlin, you have seen in your crystal ball –'

Bethany shook her head slowly. 'Get it right, young man: I use a crystal *pool* when I look into the future.'

'All right, you've seen in your crystal pool that one day a great evil will arise to threaten the whole world. It will be hundreds and hundreds of years in the future. For good to conquer this evil, the almighty power of Aaron's Rod will be needed. What do you, *Merlin*, do now?'

Bethany had no hesitation.

'I send King Arthur with the rod into the future.'

Carys laughed.

'Excuse me, Cass,' said Zach, 'you may laugh, but that would be the perfect solution. A mighty warrior with a fabulous weapon. But Arthur wouldn't travel well. He belongs to a different age. But his genes will travel comfortably through time. So Merlin, where would we find Arthur's courage, his strength of will, his upright character, today?'

Bethany had to think about this one, and then she twigged. 'In his descendants, of course. The Cadwaladrs of Merlin's Farm.'

'Correct. Now, Arthur has been sent through time via his genes, but how, O Merlin, will you send the rod pieces through time?'

'Hide them, silly!'

Zach didn't think Merlin would call anyone 'silly', but otherwise that was a good answer.

'And where do you hide the first piece?'

'That's easy. In the Chapter House of Worcester Cathedral.'

Zach took a deep breath and managed to keep his patience. 'The cathedral isn't built yet, O Merlin, so think again.'

'Oh silly me. In that case, I will hide it … in my favourite stone circle, on the banks of the river Severn, many days journey from my home.'

'Good, that's good. And the second? Where will you hide that?'

Bethany burst into a fit of giggles and declared that she didn't have the faintest idea, except that it would be in a silver circle.

'Never mind, let's carry on. I believe you've written a riddle to help identify the Finder?'

'That's right, she'll be an Aranrhod – a silver circle, get it?' Bethany drew a circle with her fingers and pointed upwards. 'The moon goddess allowed me to use her name. In *fact*,' added Bethany, getting animated, 'yes, in fact, I asked the moon goddess to *select* the first woman who would carry her name – that's brilliant!'

Zach objected, 'But you just made that up!'

'Makes no difference,' Bethany insisted, 'it's still brilliant.'

Carys chuckled at Zach's discomfiture. 'Come on, Zach, admit it, it's brilliant.'

Zach was outnumbered. 'All right, it's brilliant. So does *this* meet with your approval, O Wise One? The goddess's name, Aranrhod, which was bestowed on a woman *of the goddess's choice,* will be passed down the female line, while Arthur Cadwaladr's qualities will be passed down the male line.'

'That is my wise plan, yes, my son,' Bethany grunted, stroking an imaginary beard.

'So how will these descendants know when the music has stopped and it is they who must open the parcel?'

Bethany hesitated, and then dropped totally out of character. 'They'll just *know* – like Carys's mum knew.'

'Yes, but what made *her* know and not all the other Aranrhods who went before?'

Carys chimed in. 'Because she married my father.'

'Right!' Zach punched the air with one hand and thrust the other through his long hair. 'Merlin must have cast some kind of spell that kept the descendants of Cadwaladr and Aranrhod apart until the stirrings of the great evil, at which time that generation would meet and fall in love and unite the two legends.' He blew an imaginary trumpet fanfare: 'Tan-tarrah!'

Congratulating Bethany on a fine performance, Zach relieved her of the rod and slipped it back under the bed.

Bethany jumped down from the desk and went back to her pad of paper. 'So, Cass, shall I put that the Finder and the Wielder were meant to be your mum and ... oh dear, Cass, I'm sorry, I forgot.'

Carys sighed. 'Don't worry, Beth, you were right. Mum and Dad *were* meant to be the Finder and the Wielder. You know, I'm beginning to think that my father's murder wasn't foreseen by Merlin. I reckon it's messed up his grand design. No wonder my mum's been in such a state. She was convinced that it was up to her and Dad, but then her legendary Cadwaladr was taken from her.'

'It means we now have a motive for your father's murder,' said Zach.

'Yes, I know – to stop him being the Wielder. And it also means that *Dylan* may have to be the Wielder, which would be all right except he's working for the enemy.' Carys dropped her head.

'What do you mean?' asked Bethany. 'Didn't you say he has a good job at some Institute in London?'

'He does, but the professor who runs the place is –' She stopped.

'Is what?' prompted Zach.

Carys had to take a deep breath before she could continue. 'For a while now,' she said, 'I've been having nightmares. There was always this tall, bald man, wearing a multi-coloured suit. Each time I've had the dream, I'm closer to him. Yesterday morning, before my mum woke me, I bumped into him. He was getting off the train at Foregate Street.'

'Foregate Street!' Zach exclaimed. 'So you think he's here?'

Carys nodded. 'When I opened the shop door this afternoon to escape from Dredge's, there he was.'

Bethany put her hands over her eyes.

Carys continued, 'When I looked into his eyes, I knew for certain that I was *this* close to pure evil.' She indicated the distance between her finger and thumb. 'And this evil being is Dylan's boss.'

Bethany let her hands slide down her face, revealing eyes like saucers.

There was a knock on the door and Helen walked in.

She was holding a photograph of the rod.

Chapter 18 Lost Property

When the Professor called back, Helen showed him to Stephen's study. Stephen stood up to welcome his visitor. 'Ah, come and sit down, Professor ... Nash,' said Stephen, reading from Balimm's visiting card.

'I am disturbing you – Sunday's sermon?' asked Balimm.

'Yes, for my sins,' replied Stephen. 'I fear my sermons will strike the cathedral faithful as terribly plain.'

'Plain or fancy, the Church is fighting a losing battle against the forces of evil. Would you not agree?'

Stephen chuckled. 'How would you like to write my sermon for me, Professor? It sounds like you'd have more to say than me at the moment.'

'I would have a lot to say, but I suspect far too heretical for your pulpit.'

'My dear sir, the only good things to come out of the Church are the work of lay people or heretics. Now, if I remember from your card, you're the founder of the Institute for the Resurrection –'

Balimm flinched, and quickly corrected Stephen: 'For the *Restoration* of the Earth's Spiritual Energy, yes, that is correct. Is the Earth going to forgive the way humans have mistreated her?'

Clergy meet all kinds of people. Often they simply knock on the door, as this professor had done, and expect a sympathetic hearing. In Sheffield it had been tramps who used to call at Stephen's vicarage. Deaneries obviously got a higher class of caller.

'This is excellent material for my sermon,' enthused Stephen. 'Yes, I agree, Professor, we can't have too much energy … er, being … what was it? Restored? Yes, excellent idea. Now, how much do I … do people donate?'

'Donate?' Balimm laughed, a hollow laugh. He must do his business and get out. The girls had come into this building. The rod could not be far away.

'No, no,' he continued, 'I am not after your money. I was in your cathedral yesterday …'

Try as Balimm might, the word 'praying' wouldn't come out. He paraphrased: '… having a quiet moment.'

Stephen was forced to reassess his first impressions of this man.

Balimm went on, 'I left my hat on the pew, which is of no consequence – I would forget my head if it were not screwed on tight, as the saying goes.'

'I know the feeling well, Professor.'

'But I also left this … which is of far greater consequence.'

Balimm took the photo of the rod from his pocket and handed it to Stephen. He leaned forward. 'I am offering a reward of … ten thousand pounds for its recovery.'

Stephen's eyebrows almost touched his receding hairline. Such a sum would help the Chapter House Restoration Fund, it would indeed. He was curious. 'Why is it so valuable, Professor?'

'Well, in commercial terms, I suppose it is not that valuable. But, as I explained earlier, I founded my Institute in order to put back some of the spiritual energy that has been removed by human vandalism. This artefact, part of a sacred candlestick, was robbed from a grave in Syria.'

Stephen shook his head. 'Monstrous.'

'I am building a small museum – more of a shrine – where this and other stolen artefacts from the region can be restored. That is partly what I mean by restoration of the earth's spiritual energy.'

Stephen's face was glowing. 'I would gladly donate money from my own pocket to such a worthy cause, and here you are, offering money to *me* if I can recover this artefact. There's enough material here for *ten* sermons. I assure you, Professor,' he said, giving the photo back, 'that if I trace your property, no reward will be necessary.'

Balimm refused the photograph. 'Hold onto it for identification purposes, and I shall insist you keep the reward. I know how much building work costs. And don't worry, I have my own personal fortune which, like my many oil wells, will never run dry.'

The figure he'd quoted was high, but Balimm had found, from long experience of corrupting humans, that the easiest way was through large amounts of money. There were always fewer awkward questions. The voice of conscience was more easily silenced.

Stephen was assuring his departing guest that he would look into it straight away, when there was a knock on the door and Helen popped her head round.

'Oh, you're going – I was wondering if you'd like a cup of tea or coffee?'

'That's kind of you, darling, but the Professor is leaving. Professor Nash is offering a substantial reward for the recovery of his property, which he left on a pew in the cathedral yesterday.'

Helen's expression didn't hold out much hope. 'Unless it was an umbrella, Professor, it may well have gone bye-bye. I hope it wasn't your laptop?'

Stephen intervened. 'No, darling, much more valuable. It was this artefact ...' He passed the photo to Helen. 'The Professor is intent on restoring it to the Syrian grave from which it was robbed.'

Helen recognised the rod. 'Hmm, I may be able to throw some light on this. If you can hold on, Professor?'

Balimm was more than happy to wait, confident that the prize was within his grasp.

Helen went to Bethany's room.

She knocked, went in and closed the door.

Chapter 19 Sorry Ha

Helen held up the photo of the rod, like a lawyer showing a piece of evidence to the jury. Bethany sat back on her heels and scratched at some marks on her jeans, avoiding her mother's eyes. Carys became like a rag doll on the bed, one arm hanging limply to the floor. She had a good idea what was coming.

Zach tried to bluff it out. He jumped up from the floor, offered Helen a chair and took the photo from her. 'Oh good, you've found it. I hate losing photos. I can replace them but they're expensive.'

'Nice try, Zach,' said Helen, 'but we all know it's not the photograph but the object *in* the photograph which concerns us. It's an artefact of some kind. An absent-minded professor left it on a pew in the cathedral yesterday. He's with Stephen now, and he's offered the cathedral a substantial sum if he can get it back. I recognised it, of course, as your light sabre. But I didn't say that you had it, because I knew it must be a misunderstanding. So I've come quietly to ask for it back. Please?'

Carys spoke, staring at the ceiling. 'This professor, is he tall, bald, and wearing a colourful suit?'

'Why yes, he is. Do you know him, Carys?'

Zach caught Carys's eye and shook his head.

'Only in passing,' she replied, with the faintest of smiles.

'Look,' Helen continued, in a conciliatory tone, 'I realise that this thing has given you hours of fun, and I've been thrilled to see you all so happy. It's been a misunderstanding, like I say. You didn't realise what the thing was.'

'You're right, Helen,' said Zach, 'we thought it was a broken candlestick. It was perfect for a light sabre.'

Helen laughed. 'A magic one, of course.'

While they were talking, Bethany had become more bent forward until her forehead was touching her knees. She was like a jack-in-the-box, with the lid squashing her emotions down. All might have been fine, if Helen hadn't laughed at the idea of the rod being magic.

'It *was* magic!' she cried.

Her voice was muffled by her contorted position.

'Yes, I know, darling,' said Helen, innocently rubbing salt into the wound, 'it was magic for me too, to see you all being so entertained.'

That was it. The lid jumped open and Bethany sprang bolt upright. Tears flowed hot and furious.

'No!' she shouted. 'It really was *magic* – it did magic … *things!*' She spat out the word. 'We need the rod to fight against a great evil – and now evil will win!'

Bethany's eyes were clamped shut, her fists clenched. Carys came and knelt in front of her friend and put her long arms around her, to stifle the flames of her burning pain. Carys knew her friend's pain, because she was feeling it too.

Zach was counting wildly on his fingers, but there was no obvious escape plan.

Helen, meanwhile, was dumbfounded.

'Bethany, I haven't seen you this distressed since you were little. I'm so sorry, but we have to return the artefact to the Professor. We have no choice.'

Zach reached under the bed and retrieved the rod. He passed it to Carys, who held it reverently. *Dredge was right,* she thought, *we should never underestimate 'things'.*

Zach took it back and handed it to Helen.

'Bethany was right about evil winning,' he said. 'I'm afraid an evil man has deceived you.'

Helen sighed. 'I don't have time to join in your game, much as I'd love to.'

She held out her hand. 'And the Professor's photo, please, Zach.'

Zach took it out of his pocket, but didn't hand it over. 'Seriously, Helen, this photo is mine.'

'Zach, come on, the Professor brought it with him.'

'I don't care, it's my photo – oh, never mind, here …' and he gave it to Helen.

Helen went out of the door and then leant back in.

'I hate to see you all so upset. I'll try and make it up to you, I promise.'

Then she left.

A few seconds later, Zach ran out of the door. He caught up with Helen along the corridor.

'What *is* it Zach?' she snapped. 'Be quick – and no more games.'

Zach flipped through the photos stored on his mobile phone. In a few seconds he'd found the original of the photo in Helen's hand. 'There, look, this proves it's my photo. I took it in the crypt earlier today.'

Helen compared the photo in her hand with the electronic original, and had to agree they were identical. 'But I don't see what difference it makes, Zach. Maybe you dropped it in town.'

'Yes, maybe I did, but what if the Professor were to say he *took* the photo? Would that make you question the rest of his story?'

'Perhaps, a little,' replied Helen. 'But I'm not prepared to ask him –'

'No, no, of course not,' interrupted Zach. 'But when you give the rod to the Professor, simply make some casual comment about the quality of the photo – how he must have a great camera, something like that. And see what he says. Will you do that?'

'Well, if the opportunity arises, I'll try – and Zach, I'm sorry I didn't believe you.'

Zach raced back to Bethany's room. Carys was sitting on one of the office swivel chairs and Bethany was standing behind her, weaving her hair into one large plait.

Zach laughed. 'I always know when my sisters are upset – they do each other's hair.'

'Hair therapy,' said Carys, smiling, 'you should try it. It works.'

'What did you chase after Mum for?' asked Bethany.

'I'll tell you later. Clutching at straws.'

They heard Balimm being led by Helen down the stairs to the front door.

Then the door banged shut.

Bethany was heartbroken. 'There goes my dream of an exciting summer.'

To Carys, it was more the sound of a door slamming on her scepticism and unbelief.

Zach rushed to the window to see the enemy for himself, albeit from behind, as Balimm crossed the car park to the main entrance. Zach called the girls to the window.

'Look at him. He's loving it.'

Balimm was indeed. He was holding the rod aloft like a torch. But Balimm intended using it to spread darkness, not light.

Bethany looked inconsolable. 'We've failed. We let the rod down.'

Zach disagreed. 'We didn't let the *rod* down, Beth. Look at it now.'

'I don't believe it – it's glowing. The traitor!'

'More to the point, look at the Professor …' said Carys.

Balimm was beginning to glow too. It was like watching a battery being charged.

Carys nodded. 'It's as I suspected. He and Dredge aren't human. A lot about our visit to that shop falls into place. I don't think we'll ever know the danger Beth and I were in.'

'And yet,' said Zach, 'you *had* to go there, to get Merlin's riddle.'

Bethany was still troubled. 'How can the rod *do* that, change sides like that?'

Zach did his best to reassure her. 'Beth, it's just a rod. Like the stones your dad was talking about at tea were just stones. One minute they're part of a pagan shrine, the next moment they're part of a Christian church. Even when objects like Aaron's Rod are loaded with spiritual power, what's important is what you do with them. Good old Merlin used his magic powers to programme the rod to respond to the chosen Aranrhod and her friends. Now this evil creature is going to use his powers to make the rod achieve *his* ends.'

The bluestone flecks in Carys's eyes were coalescing in the evening light, giving her gaze a steely hue. Her jaw was set. She looked like her mother always looked when she saw her imaginary foe coming over the horizon.

'We must stop him. Agreed?'

Bethany and Zach responded: 'Agreed!' The two of them left the window and returned to their places on the floor – Bethany to her notepad and Zach to his laptop.

Carys continued watching Balimm until he disappeared from sight. A bird fell from a tree that Balimm had walked under, and some leaves turned brown and drifted down to cover it like a pall. Carys's eyes brimmed with large, salty tears. She whispered two words:

'Sorry, Ma ...'

Part Three

Living Legends

moon goddess, being beaten...We'll finish the riddle," and then we must work out...

"You meant it, didn't you Cass?" asked Zach. "What...Carys left the window and joined her friends on the floor. "We must stop it." "in." "Yes," insisted Carys. "I may be a lovely-dovey

Chapter 20 Under Attack

'You meant it, didn't you, Cass?' asked Zach.

'Meant what?' Carys left the window and joined her friends on the floor.

'We must stop him.'

'Yes,' insisted Carys. 'I may be a lovey-dovey moon goddess but I hate being beaten. We'll finish the riddle, and then we must work out a plan of action.'

Bethany and Zach exchanged glances. This was a different Carys. She was no longer mucking in or offering suggestions; she was giving orders.

Bethany was looking glum. 'We don't stand much chance now the Professor has the rod.'

'I know it's hard, Bethany, but we must try not to talk like that,' said Carys. 'For a start, he only has one rod and we think there may be others. And secondly, we've got something the Professor will never have: each other. Now, where had we reached?'

Zach consulted his notes. 'We'd agreed that the task had to skip a generation because of your dad's death, Carys, making you the Finder and Dylan the Wielder – which is when you told us about Dylan's boss being Professor Nash, the inhuman creature who now possesses rod Number One. Are we clear on that?'

Bethany put her hand up. 'Not clear.'

'Why not?'

'Two reasons. First, if Carys's dad was killed to stop him being the Wielder, why is Dylan still alive? Second, what's so special about wielding anyway? We've all wielded the rod and we even saw the enemy wielding it. Sorry to be so thick.'

The ensuing silence was broken by a knock on the door. It was Helen. 'I've brought some ice cream for you all. I'm sorry about what happened.'

Carys passed round the bowls.

'It wasn't your fault, Mum,' said Bethany, tucking into chocolate and vanilla scoops, 'and I'm sorry I shouted at you. I was upset.'

'Thank you, Beth.'

Zach caught Helen's eye. 'Did you …?'

'I did. I remarked how clear the photo was and that he must have a good camera, and he said he needed one in his work. Then he threw the photo in the waste paper basket, saying he didn't need it any more. So here it is, Zach, back to its rightful owner.'

'What's this?' asked Carys.

'I set a trap for the Professor,' Zach explained, 'to see if he'd claim that my photo of the rod was his. And he did. It's only a little lie, but I hoped it would sow a seed of doubt in Helen's mind about the Professor.'

'And has it?' asked Carys, glancing at Helen.

'Well, it's a strange thing to do, but then he's a strange man – I mean, those clothes! And Stephen has told me about his Institute. Something about restoring the earth's spiritual energy. He's an eccentric.' Helen gathered up the cartons, moved towards the door and added, 'But he's donated a large cheque to the cathedral, so …' She shrugged her shoulders. 'Anyway, Beth, if you need anything, I'll be in the Great Hall, watching the news.'

When Helen had gone, Carys tried to answer Bethany's questions.

'Dylan told me that the Professor has a special job lined up for him, so I presume that's why he's still alive. The Professor is protecting him, at least until he's done the special job. But I can't imagine what that might be, and I take your point about wielding not being special.'

Zach was busy on his finger-counting. 'Hold on, hold on, we're forgetting something – we've only wielded a *piece* of Aaron's Rod. Won't the complete rod be something else entirely? The complete rod might need special wielding. What do you think?'

Zach didn't wait for an answer, but dropped to the floor to tap all that into his notes. Carys saw that Bethany wasn't taking notes any longer, but was doodling stone circles and magic rods. She looked exhausted, and no wonder. What a day it had been. What a twenty-four hours …

Carys knelt down by her. 'Beth, why don't you go and have a quiet time with your mum?'

'What about you two?'

'We'll work on the riddle and then call it a day.'

'Okay. If you're sure …'

Carys crouched down. 'Want a piggy-back?'

'I'm too heavy, silly!'

'Try me …'

Along the corridor, Carys pretended that Bethany was too heavy and began to stagger, much to Bethany's amusement.

'Your plait's coming undone, sorry,' said Bethany.

'Not your fault. My hair's too fine for plaiting. It always slips out.'

'Cass?'

'Yes Beth?'

'Are you going to stay for ever? I hope you do …'

At that point they reached the Great Hall.

Helen greeted them. 'Oh, hello! Meeting over?'

'Almost. I'm delivering one tired daughter for a quiet time with her mum.'

Carys deposited Bethany on Helen's lap.

'Oh goody,' said Helen. 'Are you joining us Carys?'

'Zach and I –'

'Sit down a moment, there was an interesting item in the news headlines.'

Carys sat down.

Then Helen called out, 'Stephen!'

Stephen poked his head round the study door. 'What is it, love? You know –'

'Come and see this. Funny goings-on around stone circles. Here, look.'

The news item was about a phenomenon that had been reported by a farmer in Worcestershire.

'Mr Sykes is convinced that a whining sound is affecting his animals,' said the newsreader. 'The farmer has traced the sound to a local stone circle. Alan Shooter is there now.'

Alan Shooter appeared onscreen, leaning on a gate, as the farmer brought his cows in for milking.

'So Alan, what's going on?' asked the newsreader.

'Well, George, Mr Sykes is correct. The sound originates in a stone circle not far from here. And he –'

'Sorry to interrupt you, Alan, but we can't hear the sound this end. Has it stopped?'

The reporter spoke over a distant camera shot of Neolithic stones silhouetted against the sky.

'No, it's worse if anything, George, but our microphones aren't picking it up for some reason.'

The newsreader was curious. 'What *kind* of sound is it, Alan?'

The picture began jumping and the reporter's voice faltered. 'It's … eerie. It gets inside you somehow, deep … inside you. Sorry, George, I'm handing back … tired … batteries –'

The screen went blank.

'I'm sorry, but we seem to have lost Alan for the moment. Whatever this phenomenon turns out to be, one thing is certain: it is spreading rapidly. Our Scotland correspondent, Andrew Rooke, is waiting for us at Glandarr. Andy, what's the latest there?'

Andrew Rooke's voice could be heard over pictures of a beautiful Scottish glen.

'Well, George, as you know, Glandarr is one of the quietest spots in the British Isles. The loudest sound to be heard in this glen,' – the picture changed to library shots of the workings of a whisky distillery – 'is the gurgling of whisky as it flows through the famous Glandarr Distillery, and, of course,' – the picture changed to a close-up of Rooke standing with someone outside a pub – 'the singing that emanates from the Golden Fleece here, when the locals have downed a few drams. I have the landlord with me now, Robbie McPherson. We can all hear that awful whining sound, Robbie. Where's it coming from, d'ye know?'

The landlord was a big man, with a white beard and long ginger hair that blew in the wind. He had craggy features, and bulbous eyes that stared as if they'd just beheld what no mortal eyes should see.

'Aye, it's a-coming from the Standing Stone of Glandarr.'

'And what do you think is causing it? Have you any idea?'

The landlord crouched over the microphone as if intending to bite it off. 'Some reckon it's a wind that blows off the North Sea every hundred years, warning of a hard winter ahead.' He shifted from one foot to the other, and seemed to look behind him without turning his head. 'Some say it's the souls of all the fishermen who've drowned off these shores, a-wailing 'cause they can no longer sip a glass of Glandarr whisky.'

'Thank you, Robbie,' said the reporter as he turned to face the camera. 'George, they even claim that this weird sound is lowering the alcohol content in the whisky. In the interests of science I'm going to test this theory and it may take –'

The screen went blank for a second time.

'Apologies for the abrupt ending to Robbie's report. If I didn't know any better, I'd say the sound of the stones is affecting our equipment. Apparently, this sound has been detected coming from ancient stones in other countries. In Carnack, in Southern Brittany, evening tours of the famous Neolithic sites have had to be cancelled. In a moment, I'll be talking to the Minister for the Environment, Judy Fallows, for the Government's reaction. But first, some other news.'

Carys ran to fetch Zach. She found him working on the riddle.

'Carys, I still can't figure out why the Chapter House is a *silver* circle. I've been –'

'Zach, listen will you?'

He kept still. 'What's that weird sound?'

'It's the Professor, I'm sure of it. He's using the rod to do something with Neolithic stones. It's on the news.'

They ran to the Great Hall in time to see Judy Fallows reassuring everyone not to panic. The sound was not a danger to human health. It could be due to changes in the earth's magnetic field, caused by heavy sunspot activity. That's why it was affecting batteries. Government scientists were also working on a theory that global warming was heating the stones and so releasing trapped carbon dioxide. As the gas escaped, it was vibrating molecules in the stone. People should keep away –'

Helen laughed. 'Surprise, surprise – they're blaming it on global warming.'

Carys spoke in solemn tones. 'The Professor is doing this.'

Zach threw her looks like daggers.

But Carys persisted. 'Stephen, that candlestick, which Professor Nash claimed was his, is in fact part of Aaron's Rod. Bethany and I found it in the Chapter House last night. It has enormous powers and –'

Helen waved a hand dismissively in Stephen's direction. 'Darling, take no notice. It's all part of an elaborate role-playing game that has kept the three of them amused for hours.'

'But Helen –'

Helen turned to Carys and used her strictest tone. 'It's not a good time for this, Carys. I happen to think there's more to this weird noise than the government is letting on. I wouldn't mind betting that all of these stones are within shouting distance of mobile phone masts. Stephen, I wonder if my parents are all right?'

Stephen handed his phone to Helen, reminded everyone he had to finish his sermon, and retired to his study. Zach and Carys went back to Bethany's room.

Zach rounded on Carys. 'That was so *stupid* of you, Cass.'

'No it wasn't. We can't save the world on our own, you know.'

'I don't mean that. I mean it's obvious they wouldn't believe you. You found Aaron's Rod in the Chapter House? It has enormous powers? Thank goodness Helen latched onto the idea that we've been playing a game.'

Carys's head dropped. 'I suppose you're right. I'm –'

Zach's mobile phone rang.

'Dad? Dad? Is that you? Speak up, you're very faint ... no, Helen's using it ... where are you?'

Zach started madly pressing keys. 'The line's gone dead, Cass. What shall we do? Dad sounds like he's in trouble somewhere.'

'Run and tell Stephen,' said Carys, already halfway along the corridor.

'Where are you going?' shouted Zach from the top of the stairs as Carys was opening the front door.

'The Chapter House, of course – hurry!'

As soon as Carys was inside the cathedral, she heard Suzy barking.

'I'm coming!' Carys yelled.

The terrible sound of the stones was much stronger here. She picked up a bible from one of the pews as she raced through the nave. Carys dived into the Chapter House, to find Tom on his hands and knees, gasping for breath. Carys made straight for *her* seat, the Dean's seat, opposite the door. The summer sun was still high enough in the Western sky to spotlight her through the windows. She sat down and began reading from the bible.

'In the beginning, when God made ...'

'Good Gracious!' exclaimed Stephen, as he and Zach arrived, followed by Helen and Bethany.

Although the attack had lessened on Tom from the moment Carys had started reading Genesis, there were still enough negative forces swirling round the Chapter House to cause Stephen problems as he went to the aid of his canon.

'No, Stephen, over here!' yelled Carys. 'Leave him – come and read!'

Stephen was sufficiently convinced by the spiritual nature of what was happening to believe Carys this time. This was more than role-playing.

'Here, this is your seat, what's left of it,' Carys said to Stephen, who was beginning to look ill. 'Read anything. Out loud.'

Stephen took the bible off Carys and sat down, being careful not to lean back. Carys addressed the others. 'The rest of you, come and sit down and *pray*. If you can't pray, think about good things.'

Helen sat down next to Stephen. She was suffering so much under the barrage of negative forces that she found it impossible to pray or even to think good thoughts. Worry for the plight of the world was weighing her down and bringing her close to despair. She broke down in tears.

Bethany gripped her mother's hand. 'Think about all the fun we've had since moving to Worcester. That's what I'm doing.' It was never hard for Bethany to think nice thoughts.

Suzy wasn't affected either. She was going from person to person, waiting for someone to suggest a game. In the end, she went and sat by Tom, who by now was sitting cross-legged on the floor, meditating. Zach and Carys were at Stephen's right hand, also managing to pray.

The evening sun had moved north of west as it neared the horizon, casting a pink glow over the group. They looked like survivors from a future holocaust, meeting in a bombed out church.

It took almost an hour for the eerie sound to disappear.

'Do you know why this is called the Chapter House?' asked Tom, his affability recovered along with his strength. 'Because the monks used to meet here every day, to read a chapter from the bible and discuss the day's business. It strikes me now as an admirable tradition.'

'Except we'll be discussing the *night's* business,' declared Carys. 'This is too urgent to leave 'til the morning.'

'Carys, I must thank you,' said Tom. 'You knew what was required.'

Carys smiled. 'I am, after all, my mother's daughter. It's only taken me thirteen years to realise it. Stephen, this is a temporary lull. It'll begin again, but stronger. You need to set up a rota, straight away. How many seats in here?'

'Very biblical – twelve each side of me. Twenty-five in all.'

'If we can keep all twenty-five seats filled, it'll be easier. Try and get a hundred volunteers, so nobody has to be in here longer than fifteen minutes every hour. Keep *your* seat occupied by your strongest people, spiritually speaking. Your seat is like the keystone in this place. It's where we found Aaron's Rod.'

'Which is why there's no back to my seat,' observed Stephen.

'We didn't pull it off, honestly,' Bethany protested. 'It fell away all by itself!'

'And what made you think it was Aaron's Rod?' asked Helen. 'It's unlikely, don't you think?'

'Totally,' admitted Carys. 'We had no idea what it was. Not until we took some photos to Dredge's Emporium in town.'

Tom was impressed. 'You went to Dredge's? He's the best. A bit weird, mind, but the older the stuff, the more he knows.'

Carys snorted. 'A *bit* weird? You're telling me. But he identified it straight away.'

Zach had retrieved the photos on his mobile phone and was showing his father the close-ups he'd taken of the Hebrew letters, which Tom confirmed were plague initials.

'What we didn't know was that the dealer was trying to get the rod for the Professor,' said Zach.

'The Professor arrived as we were leaving,' said Carys. 'He squeezed past me and it was like skirting the edge of a black hole. I knew he was evil.'

Helen put two and two together.

'And *that's* when you mislaid the photograph. Only a little lie, Zach, but I should have listened. To think he nearly bought us off for a mere ten grand ...'

Stephen reached inside his pocket and pulled out a cheque. Wistfully, he tore it up. 'I should have known. Not even billionaires throw their money around like that. Restoration of the Earth's Spiritual Energy indeed – the tramps in Sheffield had better stories. Why didn't we recognise him for what he was?'

'Don't be hard on yourselves,' said Tom. 'Evil is brilliant at disguising itself – it's the only way it can survive. In a fair fight it loses every time.'

Stephen moved towards the door. 'Come on Tom, we need to get this rota going before the enemy returns. I'll need your help choosing the right people.'

Helen was concerned. 'The volunteers will need feeding, but I'm not authorised to use the kitchen.'

'Ring Hilda,' suggested Stephen. 'She'll help, I'm sure.'

'What about –?'

Carys ushered her to the door. 'We'll be fine. You get on. The first volunteers will be along soon.'

Helen was reassured.

Not long after Helen had gone, Carys had a phone call. It was Dylan, on the edge of the city, wanting directions. He had urgent business to discuss.

Chapter 21 Ley Lies

Carys sat down wearily on the Dean's seat. 'Dylan is the last person I need to see right now.'

'Do you think the Professor has sent him?' asked Bethany.

'I bet he has – in case we've found another rod,' Zach replied.

'Then we must throw him off the scent,' said Carys, with steel in her voice.

Zach sat down next to Carys. Like her, he was tired; physically, but also mentally – too tired even to count on his fingers. He managed a faint smile. 'I admire your determination, Cass, but I would like to point out that we haven't got a scent to throw him off.'

'No, but I bet Merlin has …' muttered Carys, almost to herself.

Bethany heard her. 'What do you mean?' she asked, sitting down on the other side of Carys.

'Nothing,' replied Carys. 'Forget it. It would sound silly.'

Zach laughed. 'Since when has that stopped any of *us* three speaking?'

Bethany giggled. 'Zach's right, Cass. If you don't tell us, I may be forced to dig out a joke.'

That was enough to convince Carys.

'Well, it's just that I feel a desperate need to go home and see Mum tonight.'

'Tonight?' echoed Zach.

'Yes, tonight.'

Bethany laid her hand on Carys's. 'That's not silly, Cass. It's only natural after all that's happened.'

'Yes, but I'm thinking that maybe I'm feeling this need so strongly because I'm *meant* to go.'

Zach tossed his hair back off his face. 'Gotcha. Merlin planned for you to go home tonight so that you'd find the next rod. Well, Carys, you know how keen I've been for Merlin connections, but even I find that idea slightly silly. As Beth says, it's only natural you'd want see your mum as soon as possible – though I can't see it happening tonight.'

Bethany was bursting to say what she thought. 'It's a *very* silly idea, because whether Carys goes home or not, she won't find the next rod – for the simple reason that she doesn't know where it is.'

Carys raised her voice. 'I didn't know where the first rod was but I *found* it, didn't I?'

'Yes, but you didn't have the riddle then,' countered Bethany. 'I thought the riddle was your signpost telling you where to look next?'

'Well, the riddle's no use if we can't solve it, is it?' said Carys, annoyed by Bethany's persistence.

'But we won't find another rod until we *have* solved it!'

Zach intervened. 'Bethany, a signpost points a direction, but you still have to find the destination yourself. In other words, the riddle is a clue, not the answer. Although I don't think Merlin has anything to do with Carys's wanting to go home, I'm in favour of letting her follow her instincts. Remember, we do believe that she is the Aranrhod, the Finder, the riddle's first *silver circle*. Agreed?'

'I suppose so,' Bethany replied. 'Except Carys chose the correct seat out of *twenty-five* last night. Is she going to carry on having that kind of luck?'

'Right now,' said Carys, 'we're going round in tired circles and Dylan will be here any minute. Somehow I want to squeeze information out of him, while he's getting misleading information out of *me* – and I haven't the faintest idea how to do that. I wish *you* could talk to him, Zach, but I'm sure Dylan won't speak to anyone but me.'

Zach pulled a face. 'I've got that devious kind of mind, you mean ...'

'Well, that was clever, the trap you laid for the Professor with the photo.'

Zach was beginning to sift ideas through his fingers. 'Would you mind if I secretly listened in?'

Carys was encouraged. 'That's a good idea. At least I'd feel I wasn't on my own.'

'Dylan's coming to the cathedral, right? Talk to him in the north choir stalls and I can hide behind you in the north aisle. I'll hear you from there, and hopefully I'll get an idea how we can throw him off the track and buy us some time.' Zach turned at the door. 'This isn't going to be easy for you, Cass. I'll be right behind you. Good luck.'

'Thanks Zach. Now Bethany, you'll be on your own here 'til the first volunteers arrive. Can you face that?'

'Of course,' replied Bethany bravely. She looked around. 'Can Suzy stay with me?'

Carys laughed. 'Suzy *has* to stay with you.'

'And what do you want me to do?'

Carys thought for a moment. 'You should ... play with Suzy. But if the sound of the stones returns, or if you feel strange in any way, you must come and tell me. Promise?'

Bethany promised and knelt down to ruffle Suzy's ears.

*

'Carys?'

'Up here Dyl!'

Carys was standing on the chancel steps, waving.

Dylan ran up the centre aisle. *Here's a man with a mission,* thought Carys.

They embraced, and Carys made sure they sat down in the north choir stalls.

'What are you doing back in Worcester already?' asked Carys.

Dylan could hardly contain his enthusiasm.

'Things are taking off, sis. The Professor says my special task isn't far off now.'

'That's marvellous. He must be a clever man – well, I suppose he *is* a professor.'

'It's amazing, you meeting him –'

'We didn't meet properly, Dyl –'

'No, but he says you helped him. He didn't go into details, but it's a fantastic feeling, Cass, that we're on the same team. He'd like you to work for him when you finish school. Wouldn't *that* be something?'

'I'll think about it, Dyl. At least now I understand what the Professor is trying to do. He explained it to Bethany's dad, about –'

'Putting back into the earth the spiritual energy we've taken out and squandered,' interrupted Dylan.

Carys laid a playful punch on her brother's shoulder. 'Wow! You know a lot more about it than yesterday – I'm impressed.'

'I've had a couple of sessions with the Prof. He's brought me up to scratch, so I'll be ready.'

Ready for what? thought Carys.

Although she didn't feel it at all, Carys made a great effort to appear proud and keen. 'I think it's brilliant how the Professor is using the stone circles –'

'I know. Thing is, I never realised how many there are in this country – and all over the world. But to go global, he needs more power. About these rods, Carys –'

'What I didn't understand, Dyl, when Stephen explained it to me, was how the Professor distributed his ... er, *treatment* ... so quickly. He'd had the rod a couple of hours, if that, and there were stones being affected in southern Brittany.'

'I don't blame you, not getting it. I'd never heard of ley lines either.'

'What are they?'

Dylan laughed. 'It makes a change, me knowing more about something than you, sis. Ley lines are straight lines of spiritual

170

force that link all these ancient sites. They form a kind of national grid – well, they did when people knew how to use them. The Prof knew they'd still work once he had the power. So, Carys, about these rods –'

Carys wondered if Dylan knew the rods added up to form Aaron's Rod.

'Can you tell me what these rods are, Dyl? Where's their power come from?'

Dylan hesitated.

He knows about Aaron's Rod, Carys thought, *but he's not allowed to tell me.*

'The rods are a power source from an ancient civilisation,' explained Dylan. 'Does that make sense?'

'It'll do,' answered Carys with a smile.

'So you've found more of these power rods, then, love?'

'How many more does the Professor want?' asked Carys. She wondered if Zach had had any ideas yet, for she didn't know how much longer she could pretend to support the Professor's work.

'He says there are two more rods,' Dylan replied. 'Since you had one, he reckoned it was worth asking if you had the others, or at least knew where they might be.'

So we were right, there are three rods. She was delighted to have secured information from Dylan without giving him anything, but she didn't think she could –

The church door banged shut.

'Carys! Carys! I've done it!'

It was Zach. He'd left the building and then re-entered. He raced up the nave, and shouted, 'Where are you?'

'Up here, Zach, with my brother!'

Zach ran up the chancel steps.

'Why all the excitement?' asked Carys, dying to know what Zach had come up with.

'I know where the other rods are. Hi, Dylan, I'm Zach.'

'Hi, Zach.' Dylan's face lit up. 'You've found the other rods, you say?'

'Well,' said Zach, 'it was simple in the end.'

Yes, Zach, and keep *it simple. Don't overplay your hand.*

171

'In the attic, where we found the first rod, Carys, I found an old map of ley lines. I'm not certain what they are …'

Brilliant, Zach, leave something for Dylan to contribute.

Dylan was beaming with pride. 'They're lines of spiritual force that link Neolithic sites.'

'Well,' continued Zach, 'there are masses of these lines converging on Worcester – right through the Old Palace, in fact. And the only other place that compares is Stonehenge.'

'Oh no! Really?' cried Carys. 'That's incredible. But how are we going to get near it?'

Dylan was already halfway down the nave.

'Aren't you staying for supper?' Carys called out.

'Too busy, Cass. Thanks for your help – hurry up and finish school!'

And he was gone.

Carys had won but it felt more like she'd lost. 'I hope Dylan will forgive me when he finds out.'

'Remember, Carys,' said Zach, 'you're fighting the Professor. If Dylan gets hurt in the crossfire, that's not your fault.'

The first volunteers were arriving.

Carys took Zach aside. 'When the volunteers are settled, can you bring Bethany home? Our only hope of getting to Mum's tonight is if your dad drives us. Would he do that, do you think?'

'He would if you asked him, after what you did tonight – which was incredible, by the way. Dad was so impressed that you knew what to do.'

'Should Beth come with us? It might be dangerous.'

Zach didn't hesitate. 'We wouldn't be the same team without her. She says silly things that turn out to be brilliant – or do I mean the other way round? Anyway, we don't know where the danger lies, do we? As things stand at the moment, I'd say Worcester is a more dangerous place to be than North Pembrokeshire.'

Carys agreed. 'You're right, Zach – the Professor knows we're here, for one thing. I think we should go as soon as possible, while we have the advantage and the enemy is busy digging up Stonehenge!'

Chapter 22 Trust Suzy

Tom agreed to drive. Stephen and Helen were actually keen for Bethany to go – they agreed with Zach's assessment that Worcester was the more dangerous place to be. Also, they had been reassured by Carys's reaction to the attack in the Chapter House.

So the party set off at about eleven. Tom, Carys, Zach, Bethany – and Suzy, who insisted on going.

Carys hadn't been able to warn Branwen directly of their coming, there being no phone in the farmhouse. But she had rung Mrs Jones and asked her to pop along and say that Branwen should expect them about 3am. Bethany fell asleep almost as soon as they crossed the Severn. It was mild enough for Tom to have the sun-roof open, re-named the 'moon-roof' by Zach, who stayed awake until the Welsh border.

It was a beautiful night, one of those mild summer nights when the moon and the clouds and a whole universe of stars are there for no other reason than to decorate the sky. Carys stared at the moon, which was almost full. Maybe Aranrhod, the moon goddess, could answer her questions.

Would she find another rod? Was this her destiny? Does everybody have a destiny? What was her brother's destiny? It had to be something to do with the rods, that was clear. But Dylan wasn't the Finder, that was Aranrhod's destiny. He was the Wielder, but what did that mean? Maybe Carys wasn't meant to know yet. At least they had the jump on him, though she still felt guilty at deceiving her brother like that.

Had her father been murdered? Was that the significance of what her friends had heard when the rod transported them to that hillside? Carys was surprised how little difference it made to her feelings about her father's death. He was still dead.

Once Zach had fallen asleep, Tom switched on the radio for the news. The damage caused by the sound of the stones had levelled off, but things were worse than when they'd left Worcester. Within a certain range of the stones, birds fell from the sky and animals lay down, too weak to feed. People were similarly affected; and so the plague of extreme fatigue returned, but more widespread than before. Planes landing at airports in proximity to a stone circle were being diverted after some had had to make emergency landings.

The damaging sound wasn't only emanating from Neolithic sites. Most medieval cathedrals and ancient churches, even in the middle of cities, were emitting the sound – those whose builders had incorporated pagan stones into their structure.

The Samaritans were being swamped with calls, as people's reservoirs of hope were being drained. But there were few signs of panic, since panic required energy. Evacuation orders had been issued for areas where there was a concentration of Neolithic settlements, but many people feared leaving their homes. There had been some looting, but also tales of thieves falling asleep as they escaped with their loot.

There was an increase in UFO sightings, which was to be expected since many people weren't convinced by the Government's vague scientific explanations. Some wanted the army to be sent in to blow up the stones, but this presented many

174

logistical problems – especially if it meant blowing up cathedrals. In any case, English Heritage wouldn't hear of it.

Carys was most interested in an item about Stonehenge. Druids had tried to congregate at Stonehenge but were unable to get near it. The site wasn't producing the whining sound like other stone circles, but there was some kind of force field around it. There were people in lab coats inside the famous monument digging holes. Lots of holes. Weary police had repeatedly failed to penetrate the ancient site in order to stop them.

Carys wondered how deep the Professor would get his workers to dig in their search for the rods. That was such a clever idea of Zach's to trick the Professor by laying a false trail to Stonehenge.

Carys used up the last of her battery ringing Stephen. She wanted to know how the volunteers were getting on. Stephen reported that it was sorting out the spiritual oaks from the reeds. But he was proud that they were mitigating the ill effects of the sound of the stones in their area.

Stephen had told the bishop, who'd spread the word. Volunteers to pray and read from scripture were recruited in other parts of the country, but these groups found it difficult to make the initial penetration of the stone circles. Single standing stones were easier to attack. Stephen realised it had been the prompt action of Carys that had allowed them to penetrate the Chapter House. He'd been amazed to learn from her that the room was effectively a stone circle built into the cathedral.

The campaign of prayer and bible reading had undoubtedly lessened the sound of the stones across the country, but Carys also reckoned that the Professor had reached the limit of his power. This explained his frantic attempts at Stonehenge to find the other two rods. She understood more than ever that she was involved in a race against time.

Carys had learned a curious fact from her conversation with Stephen. On the basis of 'know your enemy', he had sent a couple of volunteers to *Dredge's Emporium*, to encourage the dealer to tell them all he knew about the Professor. But the shop had disappeared. Where the shop had been was now a plot of dirt. People in neighbouring shops had never heard of Dredge and swore that the plot had been vacant for as long as they could remember.

This news was more evidence for Carys that neither the Professor nor Dredge were human. It was comforting to know that it wasn't members of the human race who were being so evil; and it strengthened her to know that she and her two friends, along with many other people, had held their own against these demonic forces. But for how much longer?

When Carys explained about the shop to Tom and told him her conclusions, she expected him to laugh and dismiss the idea of demons – but no, he didn't. Instead, Tom wondered if the hard lesson to be learned from all this was how blind we'd become to spiritual realities.

As they approached her home valley, Carys began to feel as nervous as when she and Dylan had driven into Worcester. Why should she feel nervous about returning home less than forty-eight hours after leaving? She realised it was because she had changed. She would never have believed it possible that a person could change so much in so short a time. This was largely due to the extreme nature of her experiences. It was also due to the friends she'd made. It was time to wake them.

Tom had made good progress because the roads were empty – people had been advised to stay in their homes until this weird sound of the stones ceased. So it wasn't yet two-thirty when the car rounded the last bend. Merlin's Farm should have come into sight, but the niche where the farmhouse nestled in the hills was shrouded in darkness.

On the journey, the whining sound from ancient stones had never left them, but it hadn't been strong except when they skirted Carmarthen – reputed to be Merlin's birthplace. However, the closer they got to Carys's home, the louder and stronger the sound became.

Tom chuckled. 'This must be a very Neolithic area.'

At last, Carys made out the outlines of the house. 'I can't understand why there are no lights on.'

Tom tried to reassure her. 'Carys, it's two-thirty in the morning. Your mother's in bed.'

'She should be expecting us. And we always keep a light on over the front door,' Carys insisted. 'It's an important tradition out here.'

'What, you mean as a beacon for the lost?' asked Tom.

'I suppose so, yes,' replied Carys. 'I've never really thought about why we do it. But we do – always.'

'I've just thought,' said Tom, 'it'll be the sound of the stones draining the electricity supply.'

'Yes, but we keep a good supply of candles. We're used to power cuts round here. But then we place a candle in the window. I'm worried, Tom.'

Tom drove into the farmyard. Then he turned the car round and drove it back out again. He parked the car so he was facing down the long drive. He was parked, Carys noticed, a stone's throw from the well.

'Why haven't you parked in the yard?'

'A trick from my student days. The battery will go flat while we're here. This way I can roll down the hill and jump-start the engine.'

They all bundled out, Zach and Bethany wiping the sleep from their eyes.

'Is this your home, Cass?' Bethany was eager to see where her new friend lived.

'Yes, Beth, this is my home. And this … is my front door.' Carys turned the knob and walked into the door, because it didn't open.

Tom joked, 'Where I come from we *open* doors, rather than try to walk through them.'

Carys didn't laugh. 'Where I come from, doors are never locked. There *is* something wrong. There has to be.'

Zach set off running. 'I'll check all the windows in case –'

Carys shouted after him, 'Zach, it's okay – I know a way in!'

She led everyone round to the right side of the house.

'This kitchen window has a broken catch. We keep it closed by wedging some cardboard in it. Here …'

Zach asked his dad to lift him up to the window. When he'd climbed in, Tom passed him a torch he'd brought from the car. The batteries were fading fast.

'The hall is straight ahead,' Carys told him.

Zach tried switching on some lights, but they weren't working. The others made their way back to the front door, which Zach had already opened.

'The key was in the lock,' he said. He didn't point out the significance of this. He didn't need to. There was a note on the mat. It was from Mrs Jones, warning Branwen of their projected arrival time.

Everyone gathered in the hall.

'What happens now?' asked Bethany.

'We conduct a thorough search,' answered Carys. 'If Mum has been overcome ...' Her voice faltered.

Zach came to her rescue. 'Beth and I will do upstairs.'

Bethany looked up the darkened stairs. 'Can we take Suzy? How many rooms are there, Cass?'

'Three. My bedroom is to the left, Dylan's room and the bathroom to the right, over the kitchen.'

Under protest, Tom agreed to search the kitchen, while Carys did the living room and her mum's bedroom. They both knew this was the most likely place for Branwen to be, but Carys insisted. She wanted to be alone when she found her mum.

But they didn't find Branwen anywhere.

'What I find most worrying,' said Carys when they were all back in the hall, 'is that Mum didn't leave a note saying where she's gone.'

'Maybe she was in a hurry,' suggested Tom.

'Or she didn't want to leave a trail for ... you know ...' Zach's voice faded away.

'Where's Suzy?' asked Bethany.

They all tumbled into the kitchen to see Suzy scratching at a door at the far end.

'The basement!' cried Carys.

'I'm sorry, I assumed it was the larder,' said Tom.

'It is, kind of. It's where Mum keeps all her preserves and stuff. She won't be down there.'

Zach opened the door. 'Sorry, Cass, but my vote is with Suzy.' The dog scampered down the steps into the blackness. Everybody followed.

Suzy was wrong. There was no sign of Branwen.

Tom shone his fading torch around the well-stocked shelves lining the walls. 'How did you know your mum wouldn't be here, Carys? She might have been getting some provisions.'

'The door was closed. When Mum comes down here for something, she always leaves the door open.'

They all started back up the steps. Except Suzy. The dog refused to budge. Zach went to the top of the steps. No reaction. 'Come on, Suzy, let's find some *food.*' Food usually did the trick, but not this time.

The others had reached the far end of the kitchen by now. Zach called out to them. 'Wait a minute – I've had an idea. Come back down the basement.'

When they were all surrounded by tins and jars again, Zach made his point.

'Seeing you all at the far end of the kitchen, I realised why Suzy was staying here. She knows where Branwen is. And I'm pretty sure I do as well. Look around you again.'

They looked, in the dying light of the torch.

'I've got it!' exclaimed Bethany. 'The basement is under the kitchen –'

'But it's not as big!' interrupted Tom. 'Well done, Suzy.'

Carys was amazed. 'How come I've never noticed that before and I've lived here all my life?'

'We all accept our surroundings without question,' answered Tom. 'You had no reason to notice it.'

'But if there is a secret room, Mum would have heard us by now. Unless –'

'Don't let's jump to conclusions, Cass,' said Zach.

'This tin won't move.' It was Bethany. While everyone had been talking, Bethany had been busy. 'I've been moving tins and jars out of the way. I was feeling for a door handle. But this tin won't move. Here, Tom, you try.'

Tom pulled on the tin. A whole section of shelving slid forwards out of the basement. They all squeezed through into another room. A room lit by candles.

At the far end, Branwen was seated at a table. She had her back to them. She was well wrapped up against air that felt damp and chilly. To her right was a pair of silver scales, in which she was weighing a yellow powder. To her left was a leather-bound book, open at the recipe for whatever it was she was concocting. Branwen pushed back her chair and swivelled round to face her visitors. She clicked her tongue against her teeth and spoke in a firm but clouded voice.

'Well now, it took you long enough to find me.'

Chapter 23 — Compare Notes

'*Mother!* What are you *playing* at? We've scoured the whole house looking for you!' Carys didn't know where to put herself, she was so angry. She paced the floor and waved her arms about. 'I was worried sick – you might have called out or something.'

Branwen pointed to the secret door 'Stop shouting, close the door, and then I'll answer you.'

This wasn't how Carys had visualised the homecoming. She had imagined that her mother would be weakened by the sound of the stones, afraid and lonely. She had pictured running to embrace Branwen and telling her how sorry she was for having misjudged her all these years. As it was, Branwen was safe, hidden in her own secret den. Carys had misjudged her mother yet again.

When Tom had slid the door back into place, Branwen whispered, 'Now, listen.'

They listened.

Bethany was the first to notice. 'The whining, it's stopped.'

Branwen took Bethany's hand and drew her closer. 'Well done. It's always harder, I think, to notice what's *not* there, than what *is*. But the silence occurs only in this room, I'm afraid.'

'So this room is soundproof?'

'Yes, Bethany, but more importantly, it's everything *else* proof.'

Bethany was intrigued. 'How did you know my name? Did you magic it?'

'I certainly did not. The first lesson in magic is don't waste it. But no, who else could you be? And is the curious cleric your father?'

Tom was going round the room checking out row upon row of books, some of which looked ancient. He came across to Branwen. 'Please excuse my manners, but I am an avid bibliophile. Some of these titles I have read about, but thought they were the stuff of legend. Hare's Book of Crystalline Geometry, for example, is referred to by Da Vinci as a classic text in spiritual architecture, and yet no copy has ever turned up.'

'If we survive,' said Branwen, 'you will be welcome to come and read them all.'

'We *shall* survive, and so I cordially accept your invitation. I am Zach's father. Canon Roland Thomas, at your service, but everyone calls me Tom.'

'I'm pleased to meet you, Tom. My name is Branwen Aranrhod Cadwaladr, but everyone calls me crazy!' At this, Branwen laughed so heartily that she started coughing. She signalled to Carys to pass her a glass of cloudy liquid. When she could speak again, she was wheezing.

Carys frowned. 'You're sounding chesty, Mum.'

'I'm all right,' insisted Branwen. 'My chest is the least of your problems.'

She began scratching Suzy's chin. 'And who are *you*?' Suzy had been sitting by Branwen's chair the whole time, waiting to be introduced.

'She's Suzy,' said Tom. 'She's the clever one who found you. Say hello, Suzy.'

Suzy lifted her paw and Branwen shook it. 'It's a good job you came, then, isn't it, Suzy?' She took something from the table and gave it to the dog. 'That's for finding me.'

Zach had finished going round the room reading the labels on dozens of jars and bottles that contained coloured powders and liquids. Some had objects in the liquid, and one or two of these objects might have been moving, but he didn't linger long enough to make certain. There were also jars of herbs, all labelled in small, meticulous writing.

Branwen saw him scanning her desktop. 'Zach, you won't find a crystal ball on my desk.'

Zach was embarrassed. 'Well, I –'

'I wear it around my neck.' She pulled out from amongst her clothing a small chunk of polished bluestone granite attached to a silver chain.

'But I thought it had to be a glass ball,' said Bethany, nestling the stone in her hand.

'It can be a ball, of course, but anything will do if it helps you to concentrate. Even an old stick,' Branwen added, squeezing Bethany's hand around the stone.

Branwen addressed Tom. 'I suggest you stay here with me, out of reach of the sound of the stones, while the others go and see what food and drink they can find upstairs. They'll need to keep their strength up for what lies ahead.'

Tom drew back the secret door. After Zach and Bethany had gone through with Suzy, Carys stayed back.

'Mum, is it something about us three, or are children not harmed by the sound of the stones?'

'I'm afraid children *are* harmed, though it takes longer. Children are physically more vulnerable but, for some reason, this makes your spirits stronger. You don't despair so readily. It's as if you haven't fully accepted reality yet – life is still a game.'

Tom laughed. 'Then I should be immune, because I haven't accepted life's reality either!'

'You're only joking,' said Branwen, 'but there's something in that. It's how come wizards get to be so old as they play their game of life.'

'That would explain why Beth has been the *least* affected,' suggested Carys.

'I'm sure you're right,' agreed Branwen, 'but you do need to feed her!'

When Tom had closed the door behind Carys, he turned to Branwen.

'What about animals? Should I have kept Suzy down here?'

'I don't think so, Tom. Most animals, when they get ill, lie down and die. But dogs have something about them. Suzy is almost like a human child.'

Carys, Zach, and Bethany were sitting round the kitchen table. Carys had found some bread, cheese, apple juice and chocolate biscuits – even a bag of dry dog food that she hadn't had the heart to throw away after Vala died. It was still dark outside, but the moon and a solitary candle made the room light enough for their needs.

'Your mother is great,' said Bethany.

Zach agreed. 'And what about all those jars and bottles? I didn't understand half the labels.'

Carys wasn't listening. She couldn't get over how her mother had changed. Branwen was no longer dithering, no longer fearful, because the hour had come at last. Carys mumbled, almost to herself, 'I bet she knows I'm the rod Finder.'

Zach heard her. 'Your mum seems to know a lot of things.'

Bethany pointed out that she hadn't known everybody's name.

Zach licked the chocolate off one of the biscuits. 'Perhaps your mum knew all along it was going to be you, Cass. Maybe that's why she sent you to Worcester.'

Carys didn't like that idea.

'If she'd known that much, she could have told me what to look for and how to find it. No, I think she sees only vaguely into the future – like I did in my dreams.'

'Do you think she knows how your dad died?' asked Bethany.

'I don't know *what* she knows,' Carys replied edgily. She was tired of being questioned – and Bethany had touched a nerve.

Carys went on, 'To be honest, I'm confused. I thought *I* was the prophesied Aranrhod, and now I find my mother is running the war from her bunker.'

Zach intervened. 'I don't think it's quite like that.'

184

'Oh, don't you?' snapped Carys. 'And how would *you* know what it's like? You haven't had this 'responsibility' hanging over your whole life like a shroud. Remember, Zach, I didn't *ask* to be an Aranrhod!'

She ran out of the kitchen as tears began to flow. Down the corridor, up the stairs she ran, and threw herself onto her bed, her own bed, the bed she'd cried herself to sleep in so many times in the last six months. But the one thing she *couldn't* do now was fall asleep. She had to find the next rod before the Professor did. And what was going to happen to Dylan? So many unanswered questions, so many dangers, known and unknown. She was only thirteen – how was she supposed to cope with it all?

There was a knock on her door. It was Branwen. Bethany had alerted her.

'I'm sorry I wasn't upstairs when you arrived, love, but I had to stay where I was protected.'

Carys pulled herself up until she was seated on her pillow, knees drawn to her chin.

'And *I'm* sorry I shouted at you, Mum. It was a shock, finding you in a room I didn't realise existed! And how come you were expecting me?' Tears made Carys's voice sound snuffly.

Branwen sat down on the bed. 'I knew that when you found the rod and lost it to Balimm, your thoughts would turn to me.'

'Who's Balimm?'

'He's Professor Nash. Dylan's employer. Balimm is a highly ranked demon. He commands hundreds of legions. But he has ideas above his station. Balimm wants to rule the world, and more. But to do that, he has to destroy it first – destroy it from our viewpoint, at any rate.'

'How do you know all this?'

'Well, not because I'm clever, that's a fact. It's all out there ...'

Branwen made a vague gesture towards the ceiling.

'... common knowledge in the circles I move in.'

Carys was beginning to feel better. If her mother had spoken before in this down-to-earth way about her magical abilities, maybe things would have been different. But then, if they *had* been different, they might have been different in other ways as well, like not meeting Bethany and Zach.

Branwen continued, 'We knew that Balimm had set his sights on getting hold of Aaron's Rod to power his ambitious plans. So we reckoned that Aranrhod's task would be to find it first.'

'*We* reckoned? Who's *we?*'

'Nobody in their right mind works alone in this business. It's far too dangerous. You did the right thing, making those friends downstairs.'

'I don't deserve them, Ma. They've been so patient with me.'

'Which is what they're being right now. You're very lucky.'

Carys leaned across to her bedside table and picked up the little music box. She wasn't sure if she should raise the subject of her father's death. She opened the box. As she watched the tiny ballerina dance in the moonbeams coming through the skylight, Carys knew she had to.

'Mum, I think the Professor – Balimm – murdered Dad.'

'Who told you that?'

'Is it true?'

'Come closer girl … here, next to me.'

Carys moved down and sat on the bed next to her mum.

Branwen took the music box off her and closed the lid. The music stopped.

'You're much further along than I expected.'

'So you knew? And you didn't tell us?'

Branwen took Carys's hand in hers. 'Ever since your father died, I've been dreading this. I hope you'll forgive me, but think for a moment. Can you imagine what Dylan's reaction would have been? Would he have understood that Balimm is a demon? Would you? You would now, of course – but then? I don't think so. You would both have assumed that I was crazed with grief. Even worse, you might have insisted on a murder investigation, when there was no evidence and everything pointed to suicide.'

Carys thought back to how sceptical she'd been about her mother's fears and premonitions.

'You're right, Mum. We wouldn't have believed you. But why was Dad killed? Did he refuse to find Aaron's Rod for Balimm?'

'No, no. Balimm had uncovered the legend which says that Aaron's Rod can be drawn from the stone it's buried in only by a direct descendant of Arthur Cadwaladr. Bryn wouldn't promise to do that. Your father knew Balimm's intentions.'

Carys threw her head back. 'So that's what wielding the rod means! Drawing it out of stone. Was it Merlin who buried it, like he did with Arthur's sword?'

'The fact is, love, Aaron's Rod *was* Arthur's sword. It was the weapon he withdrew from the stone and used in his battles. It became the famed Excalibur in legend.'

'You know, Mum, after everything I've learned, that actually makes sense.'

Branwen shook her head in disbelief. 'Carys, how on earth did you discover so much in so short a time? Your powers must be accelerating.'

Carys couldn't help but laugh at this idea. 'No, Mum, I'm sorry to disappoint you, but it's nothing to do with my powers. It's my new friends. We've worked everything out together.'

Carys laughed again as she pictured their meetings. 'We know an idea is brewing in Zach's mind when he starts counting on his fingers – he's incredible. And Bethany, well, she calls everyone "silly" while telling the silliest jokes you've ever heard, and then she'll blurt out something that turns out to be spot on – she's amazing.'

'In these times, friends are like an extra layer of armour. I'm so pleased for you, love. If Dyl had had such friends after Bryn died, perhaps he wouldn't –'

Carys interrupted Branwen before she recalled those painful times. Better to keep her mind on the task in hand. 'Mum, do you think Dyl knows what his special task will be?'

'He may do – if Balimm has persuaded him it's for a good cause. I would think that Balimm learned from Bryn that Cadwaladrs can't be corrupted, but he knows that anybody can be fooled. Mind you, that goes for Balimm as well, as you've discovered. I'm afraid your father was hasty in saying no, but that was Bryn, straight up and down, like his name ...'

Branwen stood up. 'I must get back to my hole. I'm beginning to feel the effect of the sound.'

Carys knew that the sound of the stones wasn't the cause of the tears falling down her mother's cheeks, glittering in the moonlight like silver beads. She stood up and held her mother close to her. 'Mum, how have you carried these burdens all by yourself?'

'It's been hard, but I had you – and Dylan, until Bryn died.'

'But you *didn't* have me.' Carys tightened her embrace. 'I didn't believe in you.'

'No, but you never stopped loving me. That was enough. And I knew that the reckoning was coming soon.'

They moved towards the door.

'Did you know it would be me?' asked Carys.

'No, I didn't. Though when you told me about your nightmare on Thursday morning … well, I almost made you stay home.'

Carys laughed. '*That's* why you were so glad when Dylan offered to drive me.'

Branwen smiled her crooked smile. 'That's right, at least you wouldn't bump into Balimm on the station platform. But deep down I knew that the chosen Aranrhod, whoever she was, wouldn't be able to avoid her destiny by changing her plans. It would have found us out.'

'As it did,' said Carys, stepping into the corridor.

Branwen took her arm and stopped her.

'Would you have preferred it to be me?' she asked, looking deep into Carys's eyes.

Carys didn't hesitate.

'No, I'm glad it's me.'

Branwen leaned forward and kissed her daughter's cheek. 'That's good. Now go.'

Carys rushed downstairs, feeling a weight had been lifted from her shoulders. She found her friends poring over one of those framed aerial photos of the farm, taken from a helicopter.

'Sorry I was rotten to you, Zach. You and Beth, well, you're the best friends anybody could have.'

Zach smiled. 'Forget it. So what is our plan of action? Dylan's dug up half of Wiltshire by now. Time is a-pressing.'

He went to hang the photo back on the wall, when Carys stopped him and pointed to something in the picture.

'It's a circle, guys, the well is a circle …'

She sat down with a thump.

Zach gently, almost reverently, laid the framed photo back on the table.

'You mean the second rod is …?'

Bethany wasn't so sure. 'Wait a minute, everyone, the riddle, remember? The well's a circle all right, but there's no way it's silver.'

Carys reminded Bethany that they still hadn't figured out any silver link with the Chapter House, but they'd found the first rod there.

At that moment, Branwen was walking through on her way to rejoin Tom in the basement. She winked at Zach. 'I hope your father hasn't messed with any of my ingredients.'

'Mum, before you go down, can you think of a connection between our well and silver?'

'What do you mean, love?'

'I found this riddle –'

'Oh no, not a riddle …'

'We think Merlin meant her to find it,' said Bethany.

'I'm sure he did, love. Merlin adored riddles. And he was fond of silver when everyone else was into gold. But my advice would be: don't put too much store by a Merlin riddle. He was a rascal, you know. Loved nothing better than to tease his clients with riddles, instead of telling them the remedy straight out. I bet he's cackling right now at you struggling with his silver whatnots – wells, did you say?'

And Branwen passed on through. Carys returned the photograph to the wall and sat down.

'If it's any help …'

Carys looked up to see that her mother had reappeared at the basement door.

'… there is a folk tradition in well-building of putting a silver coin between every layer of stones. Supposed to make the water run silvery smooth and clear. When our well ran dry, Bryn was sorely tempted to dismantle it. The well had stopped working, so he reckoned he had the right to reclaim any silver that was there. But I persuaded him it would be churlish. Anyway, that just occurred to me, if it's any use?'

Branwen shut the door and went back down to her den.

'That's got to be it!' cried Zach.

'The well is a silver circle!' exclaimed Bethany.

Carys put her head in her hands.

Zach shushed Bethany and came round to speak to Carys.

'What's wrong, Cass? Don't you agree?'

'Yes, I agree. The second rod is surely down our well. But don't expect me to be happy about it.'

'Why on earth not?' asked Bethany.

'Three reasons. Firstly, because in my worst nightmare I fell down that well. Secondly, it's like a black hole, waiting to suck me into nothingness – and thirdly, it's teeming with rats as big as cats!'

Chapter 24 — Black Hole

Tom offered to help. He would lower Carys down the well, then go back to the safety of Branwen's den. After half an hour, he would return and check on progress. He and Zach looked for some suitable rope in the outbuildings, while Bethany helped Branwen attach a torch to a baseball cap. Branwen gave them some batteries from a stock that she kept in her den for emergencies.

Carys fashioned a harness at one end of the rope and they tied the other end to a fence post.

'How are you feeling about this?' asked Tom.

'Not good,' replied Carys. 'In fact, I'm terrified. But then I picture myself holding another piece of the rod and I feel better.'

'How deep is the well?' asked Bethany.

'That's a point,' said Carys. 'Do we know if the rope's long enough?'

Tom laughed. 'If the well is deeper than the length of this rope, it would be easier to start from Australia!'

Zach adopted a familiar pose, hands grasping his lapels. 'Judging from its inconvenient location outside the farmyard, this is an artesian well. Artesian wells like this don't have to be deep. They intercept underground streams flowing down a hillside, and these can be quite near the surface.'

'So why is this well dry?' asked Bethany, who was dropping stones down and counting.

'I suppose the stream got diverted,' said Carys, as she climbed onto the rim of the well. 'The earth is always shifting under our feet, you know.'

Even in the moonlight it was impossible to see much deeper than a couple of metres.

'It's a black hole,' murmured Carys.

Zach tried to reassure her. 'This is real, Cass, not some awful dream. In real life, you're in control.'

'At the slightest problem,' said Tom, 'shout and we'll pull you up. But get a move on, I'm beginning to feel drowsy. You don't want me fainting when you're half way down.'

Carys shifted round, lowered her legs over and began the descent.

The batteries in her baseball cap torch were so precious that Carys decided to keep them for when she was searching for the rod. Soon she was being lowered in total blackness. She looked up and could barely make out, against a dull, moonlit sky, the silhouettes of Zach and Bethany peering over the edge. Carys kept shouting that she was all right, though this wasn't her idea of a good time. She had to keep pushing herself away from the wall to avoid rubbing against it, which was awkward and unpleasant.

'The wall is wet!' she shouted. 'And the air is getting colder!'

She hadn't bargained for the damp and the cold. To say a well was dry only meant it no longer intercepted the underground stream or aquifer. There was always bound to be moisture working its way down the hillside, seeping through the soil, squeezing through tiny holes in the porous cement which held the wall of the well together. *What if the wall decides to collapse while I'm down here? I'll be buried alive!* She told herself not to be silly, that wells had survived intact for centuries – hadn't they?

Something else she hadn't foreseen was the smell – of staleness, of disuse, common in rooms that have been shut up for a long period. But with an extra layer of damp earth.

Perfect conditions for rats! What shall I do if I feel a giant rat brush against my leg? What if it bites me? What if there are dozens of them?

By now, Carys was longing to be back on the surface, breathing the air, feeling the wind on her face, seeing life flourish all around her – even rodent life. She'd seen many rats around the farm but that was different. It was the thought of being trapped in a confined space with them. One thought kept repeating inside her head: *this is like a tomb.* She began to shiver.

Carys was still descending. Would the rope be long enough after all? She hadn't dreamt the well would be this deep. But Zach had only said artesian wells didn't *have* to be deep.

At last, she hit the bottom. The rope went slack. She tried to shout up that she was okay, but her teeth were chattering so much from the cold, and her jaw was so tense from fear, that she could hardly open her mouth. All she managed was a strangulated cry. She heard her friends shouting from the top but couldn't make out the words.

Some light would make her feel better. Carys switched on her head lamp. Nothing happened. The batteries had run down even without being used. She was on the verge of bursting into tears and curling up in a ball when anger took over.

I will not cry. I will not give in. This is all Balimm's fault and I will not let that evil creature win. I found one rod in the dark – I can find another!

Carys kicked at the wall in fury. Her foot hit thin air. She lost her balance and fell onto her backside. Her outstretched hands helped to break her fall. Her right hand landed on … something. She had gardening gloves on but as she wrapped her hand around the object, she could feel that it was solid, about thirty centimetres long. *It's not the rod, too short and misshapen for that.* Without warning, a picture came into her mind: Dylan teasing her by throwing dead rats in her direction. Stiff rats. About thirty centimetres –

Carys jumped to her feet, too frozen with cold and terror even to scream. Her breathing was fast and shallow as she pressed her back against the wall and tried, with all her might, to calm herself. *Carys Aranrhod, what are you doing? Afraid of a dead rat? Dead is good. Dead means rats don't live down here. They die!*

Although the idea of walking on a carpet of dead rats wasn't brilliant, Carys gradually regained her composure and courage. She tried to work out how her angry foot could have struck thin air. She found the answer: a large hole at the base of the wall, either the entry or exit point for the water in the days before the well dried up. This discovery wasn't a great comfort, as Carys now imagined hordes of rats swimming through the well on the current. *The well is dry now, Carys, and the rats are dead. Remember why you came down this black hole. You're Aranrhod, the Finder – so get finding.*

Wasting no more time, Carys worked her way round the wall, feeling for loose stones. After a while she took her gloves off. She didn't want anything between her hands and the rod. She had done three full circles, passing her bag on the ground at each circuit, when she began thinking she should have started higher. Or maybe lower, since Merlin would have been shorter than her. Her fingers were getting cold. They were numb at the tips where she was scraping along the mortar between the bricks. She had no idea how much time had passed. She tried to work faster.

Carys was in the middle of her fourth circuit. Was she imagining it, or was the wall in front of her lighter than a moment ago? Were the batteries in her torch reviving? Was the sound of the stones weakening?

Then she realised that it was growing lighter all around her, not just in front.

Was dawn breaking? No, nothing but blackness above her. It was then that she remembered. Carys swung round and there it was, as it had been in the Chapter House.

Light was forcing its way round the edges of a stone, sending out pinpoint rays. These were slowly merging to form tiny beams. These beams got larger as the light removed more of the cement.

Patterns were thrown on the wall opposite like some space-age graffiti.

This time Carys was enjoying the experience far more. She knew what was happening. In the Chapter House she had been amazed, but she'd also been mystified. She had never felt afraid, but certainly apprehensive about what would happen next. And when she had seen her father, she had been too shocked and overcome to follow.

Now Carys stood in the way of the light and enjoyed seeing the patterns land on her. She took delight in wondering about the source of the light. Where did it originate? Was it the light that God 'let be' in the beginning? Light that was able to create, to forge, to melt – stubborn hearts as well as stubborn stone?

The stone dropped to the ground.

Carys smiled at Merlin's trickery. Now, for the second time in a little over forty-eight hours, Carys drew out of its hiding-place a section of Aaron's Rod.

WHAM!

The light flooded the bottom of the well and then shot up, up and into the night sky, a sharp-edged column of light with no end.

Carys savoured the moment. She felt confident again. She felt loved. She felt warm! Aaron's Rod found by a silver circle, in a silver circle. Found by an Aranrhod in a well.

This time she knew what she was doing. This time she was Carys Aranrhod finding Aaron's Rod. She was neither ashamed of her past nor afraid of her future. She accepted her destiny. Happy with it. Proud of it.

And when Carys held the rod in both hands and found herself racing Vala down a hillside at sunrise, with her father waiting at the bottom to declare her the winner even though the dog was way ahead, she didn't faint. Instead she accepted the experience as a precious gift.

The light went out.

But just before blackness descended, Carys saw on the ground her doll, the one thrown into the well by Dylan all those years ago. The dead rat had been her doll. Wait until she could tell Dylan!

She roared with laughter at the idea of sending Dylan down the well to recover the doll after all these years.

Carys tugged on the rope a few times. No need to shout. Bethany and Zach would know by the light that she had found the second rod.

Her ascent was slow but smooth – too smooth. Even if Tom had fully recovered his strength, he couldn't pull her up as smoothly as this. Carys didn't like it. Also, Bethany and Zach were too quiet. They should be partying. Perhaps they'd been overcome and had to go and recover with Mum? Perhaps Tom was too weak to pull her up, so he'd attached the rope to the car – but wouldn't she hear the engine?

When Carys's head came above the rim of the well, all became clear.

Balimm was standing a short distance from the well, holding the rope in his right hand and the first rod in his left. Bethany was hugging Suzy to herself, close to Zach. The whole area of the well was surrounded by what could only be described as weird creatures.

Bethany saw Carys taking in the situation. 'They're demons,' she explained.

'Don't worry,' said Carys, 'help will be arriving soon.'

Balimm smiled in the twisted, sardonic way that demons always smile at the misfortune of others.

'Help? I do not think so, Miss … Carys? What a charming name …'

'It's from *caru*, meaning *to love*.' Carys was never more delighted by her name than now. 'Love is something you've never experienced, Mr Balimm.'

Balimm flinched at the double-barrelled firing of that dreadful word.

'You are the girl who turned Dredge back into a giant rat. He underestimated you. As you can see by the troops I have brought along, I do not intend to make the same mistake.'

'How did you know I was here?' asked Carys.

'The light, of course – the whole universe knows you are here.'

'But you were at Stonehenge …'

'Indeed I was, but journey time is cut when you travel by rod. Don't worry, I have left Dylan digging. He will find the final piece

196

of Aaron's Rod at Stonehenge. Preseli, Worcester and Stonehenge form a remarkable triangle of forces – the mountain, the river and the plain. And Stonehenge is the prince of stone circles, after all, and in part built with stone from this very mountain. It all fits together well. The rat was right, the rods are to be found in stone circles, by moonlight. So, I predict Dylan will find the last rod before this moonlit night is over. He will draw it from the stone and I will become ruler of a delightfully dead world.'

Carys couldn't believe how wrong Balimm was – stone circles by moonlight! Dredge must have given Balimm this false information to get the rods for himself. *This is why evil never wins in the long run, because there is no cooperation. Every creature is out for itself. Balimm, for all his power, can trust no one and be sure of nothing.* She almost felt sorry for the demon: loveless, isolated and, in the end, rather stupid.

But it was Balimm's power that counted now.

'I must go,' he said, 'so I will take that.'

Balimm pointed the first rod at Carys. The second rod sprang out of her bag and joined with the first.

The double-length rod was impressive. Balimm held it aloft in his left hand and it glowed along its length, so that the initial letters of eight plagues stood out against the light. And as had happened when Balimm had walked away with the first rod, his whole body began to glow, as he absorbed some of the rod's power.

'I must go and distribute more power amongst my legions,' he declared. 'But I shall be back. Victory is sweeter, I find, if I can share it with the losers. Not the fruits, you understand, just the victory. My demons will keep you here until I return with the complete Aaron's Rod. Then I shall be unstoppable. I look forward to demonstrating some of my new powers.'

'But the stones!' Carys called out. Her arms and legs were tiring as she clung to the rope. 'The sound will get stronger …'

'Oh dear,' said Balimm, 'you're right. I'd forgotten about that, and there are so *many* stone circles around here, the ill effects must be strong already. So perhaps I was wrong and I shall *not* see you again. But, for my sake, do try to … hang on.'

He was gone, and the rope he'd been holding fell to the ground.

Chapter 25 · Star Riders

'Help me!' cried Carys as she grabbed the rim of the well with both hands. Zach rushed to help her clamber out.

Carys tore the harness off and threw the rope to the ground. 'That makes me so *mad*. After all I went through down that … that *rat hole!* I was sure we'd be able to keep this rod out of Balimm's clutches.'

'Is Balimm the Professor?' asked Zach.

'Yes, I'm sorry, Zach – Mum filled me in on a few things. Mainly confirming what we already knew. I did learn one important detail which was puzzling us: Dylan's special task is to draw the final rod from stone –'

'So it *is* like Arthur and Excalibur, then!'

Carys smiled. 'More than even you could have guessed, Zach.'

'What do you mean?'

'I'll explain later.' Carys relished the thought of telling her friend that Aaron's Rod and Excalibur were one and the same. 'How's Bethany?'

'She's a star. We've been swapping corny jokes. Look at her now.'

Bethany was practising tricks with Suzy, and telling the dog corny jokes.

Carys shouted over to Beth, 'Keep up the good work, Beth – yes, and you, Suzy!'

Zach consulted his watch. 'Dad will be here in ten minutes, to check on us.'

Carys slumped onto the ground, her back against the well. 'I don't see any way out of this. Your dad's great, Zach, but he can't fight all these demons. And I don't want Mum involved either.'

'*Your mum!*' exclaimed Zach. 'The ring – we've forgotten about your nose ring!'

Carys looked up in surprise. 'You're not serious, are you?'

'Why not? I thought you were supposed to use it when you're in serious trouble?' Zach surveyed the scene. 'I think this qualifies, don't you?'

Carys fished out the ring. 'Take a good look, Zach. It's an ordinary silver ring. It's a ring my mother bought in a shop in Carmarthen and then muttered a few words over.'

'I thought you *believed* in your mother now?'

'What's that supposed to mean? She was right about lots of things, but –'

'But what?'

'I don't think she foresaw *this* kind of trouble. She had in mind that I'd be lost, or maybe have a sprained ankle or something. Honestly, Zach, look at the ring again, and then look at the mess we're in.'

Zach inspected the ring from all angles. Then he breathed on it and rubbed it on his jacket. 'I was hoping a genie would appear,' he said, forcing a laugh. But Carys wasn't paying any attention. She was staring at the ground, her head in her hands. Zach sat down beside her.

'Carys, I think you're being affected by the stones. This is not the Carys I've got to know in the past two days. I've seen you go against your natural instincts to win through; I've seen you swallow your pride and ignore your fear – nobody else could have gone down that well like you did.'

Carys lifted her head. Her face was dirty from the descent down the well. She wiped some tears away with the back of her hand and smeared the dirt across her cheeks. Then she took her ring back and looked at it wistfully. 'Thanks, Zach, but all that was following my destiny as Finder. It was planned out by Merlin, you know that.'

'Yes, but Carys, you still had to do it. You've become more than Merlin's rod Finder. You've become our leader. You've made plans and given orders that Merlin couldn't have foreseen. And you've become our friend.'

Carys thrust the ring back into her pocket. 'That's not fair. You know how much I value our friendship. But I'm not Superwoman. I had a task to perform, and I've done it. End of story.'

Zach got up and tossed his hair back. He stood in front of Carys, arms folded, feet apart.

'I hate to say this, Cass, but you *haven't* performed your task. You've found two pieces of Aaron's Rod. What about the third and final piece? Don't you think you should finish the job? The story can't end here. It just can't.'

'But Zach, what's the point? If I did find the third rod, Balimm would only pinch it off us and then he'd have the complete rod. So maybe it's better if the story does end like this.'

Zach crouched down so he was level with her, eye to eye. 'Cass, listen: you don't know what will happen when you finish your task. You ... you might sprout wings and fly to the moon to meet the original Aranrhod. You and Dylan might be proclaimed King and Queen of Fairyland. A thousand angels might descend and knock Balimm and his demons off this planet. Don't you see? Your task is to find the three rods that make up Aaron's Rod, not to speculate what might happen afterwards. Right?'

'Well ...' replied Carys. It wasn't exactly enthusiastic agreement, but it was better than outright denial. Zach was getting somewhere.

He held out his hand. 'Give me the ring again ... now, what it boils down to is this. This is no longer an ordinary ring because *you* are no longer an ordinary person. Repeat your name over and over and help will arrive. It's *got* to, otherwise your task can't be completed.'

Zach offered his hand to Carys to help her up. 'Trust me.'

Carys didn't take it. 'Trust you?'

He still held it out. 'All right, don't trust me. Trust yourself. Trust your mother. Trust the ring. It will work.'

Finally, Carys took his hand and stood up. 'Okay, I'll try.'

Zach placed the ring in her right hand and squeezed her fist around it. 'There is no try. Only *do*.'

Carys saw Bethany playing with Suzy. She saw Zach's expression, half pleading, half confident. They were both depending on her. Perhaps the world too. She couldn't let them down.

Carys held the ring between her palms. She repeated 'Aranrhod' over and over again, visualizing the name being passed down the generations, carrying its powerful intent. Carys pictured it finally landing in her family, like an owl on the well wall, an omen of a life that would be ended, and a sign of lives that would be changed forever.

When nothing had happened after a few minutes, Zach told her to stop and thanked her for trying. Carys now felt terrible to have been proven right. She glanced up to say how sorry she was, but Zach had gone over to see if Bethany needed a rest.

As Carys looked over in that direction, she noticed something odd about the demon circle. There was a definite bulge around where Bethany and Suzy were. Like as if the demons … were … keeping their distance?

'Bethany!' Carys called out. 'Get up close to a demon and tell one of your silliest jokes – go on, I dare you.'

'I don't think it'll laugh,' answered Bethany. 'They're a miserable bunch.'

'No, but *you'll* laugh,' Carys insisted. 'Go on, try the one you can almost see through.'

So Bethany approached the demon and recited, 'Doctor, doctor, people keep ignoring me. *Next please!*' and then she laughed hysterically.

Carys was watching the demon's reactions carefully, to register the slightest movement. But she didn't need to be so watchful, for the demon took a step back! Not a few millimetres, but a whole step. And it didn't retire gracefully, as if to say this kind of humour

202

wasn't its style, but it *jumped* back. It reminded Carys of livestock back home getting a shock from an electric fence. And the way the demon edged forwards again was exactly what the farm animals did, until they learned to steer clear of those fences.

'And another!' called out Carys.

Bethany had spotted the effect her joke had had on the demon, and could see where it might lead, so she put everything into her next joke: 'Doctor, doctor, I think I'm a snooker ball. *Come to the front of the cue!*' More crazy laughter from Bethany. The demon had the same electrified reaction. So even when it was expecting it, the demon couldn't help but move back. An involuntary reflex. A weakness.

At that moment, Tom's voice spoke in the darkness, nearby. 'What do you want me to do?'

'Wait a mo!' cried Carys. From the direction his voice had come, she worked out that Tom was hiding behind his car. She called Bethany and Zach together.

'Bethany, your jokes are giving these demons a headache.'

Bethany giggled. 'I'm not offended.'

'I need you to tell a joke marathon to a small section of this circle of demons, the ones with their backs to the car. We'll support you as best we can. Zach will do tricks with Suzy, and I'll try to laugh as much as I can, but the jokes are losing a *bit* of their appeal for me.'

'Oh, don't worry, I could tell Knock-Knock and Doctor-Doctor jokes all day,' said Bethany, 'and I find them even funnier when nobody laughs. Doctor, doctor, I think I'm a curtain. *You do look drawn!*' And she was off again, bent double at the sheer, wanton silliness of it.

Carys gave her a hug. 'You're our secret weapon, Beth. Get into position, concentrating your fire on those four there. Okay? Are you ready? The joke marathon begins … now!'

And so, perhaps for the first time in history, a little girl told silly jokes to an audience of demons in order to escape their evil clutches. When Carys reckoned the demons were distracted, she called out to Tom to crawl into the car from his side and be ready to roll.

Bethany was outstanding, and her jokes truly awful. Carys oversaw the campaign, like her father's sheepdog, Vala. She directed Bethany, Zach and Suzy to the next point of attack until a small section of the circle of demons had retreated against the car. Since they couldn't go further back, they had to go sideways, so Carys was able to manoeuvre a split and open the car door. Before the demons saw the danger, everyone dived in and slammed the door shut.

Tom let the brake off. 'Here's hoping.'

When the car was rolling down the drive, Tom shoved it into first gear and gently let the clutch out. The engine jolted, then spluttered into life … then faded away.

The demons gave chase, but not all were well designed for horizontal movement. Even those with what could loosely be termed 'legs' weren't greatly adept at putting one in front of the other. Some of the demons resorted to rolling down the hill, while others took large leaps through the air. One did a clever series of cartwheels, while some smaller demons enlisted big ones to hurl them through the air like hammers.

And so there were a few who managed to reach the car once it had stopped. They clambered over the roof, and pulled at the wing mirrors and windscreen wipers, like monkeys in a demonic safari park.

Tom tried twice more to jump-start the car, without success. There was enough slope left for one more attempt.

'It's now or never,' said Tom. 'Fingers crossed.'

The engine caught, sputtered and fluttered, then caught more convincingly – to everyone's joy they were accelerating up the hill on the other side. The sun had crept above the horizon, turning the sky ahead of them the palest of azures, while strips of clouds lingering from the night were glowing pink and fresh. It made everyone feel better, but they weren't shaking off the demons, who were attacking the car ever more vigorously.

Then the engine began to putter and splutter again.

'It's not the battery,' said Tom.

'It must be the petrol,' said Carys.

'No, there's plenty.'

'I don't mean that. I mean the petrol is losing its … energy.'

They rolled to a stop, with a hill behind them and a hill in front. They were stuck.

Tom leaned back against the headrest. 'I don't think I could have driven for much longer anyway. I don't feel too good.'

'Hey, Cass,' said Zach, in a sombre voice, 'I'm sorry I forced you to use the ring. That was mean of me.'

'Thanks Zach. I'm only sorry I couldn't make it work.'

The slower demons had arrived by now. The horde were all over the car, covering the windows, making it pitch dark inside. The demons were shaking the car and thumping the glass. It wouldn't be long before they either broke through or tipped the car over.

There was a deathly hush inside the vehicle, broken only by Tom's laboured breathing. Bethany didn't feel like telling any more jokes. Even if she did, there were far too many demons to fight off. Worst of all, they couldn't move. This was the end.

'What ring?'

This question was asked by Tom. Curiosity had beaten his exhaustion.

'Branwen gave Carys a magic ring for when she was in trouble,' explained Zach.

'But nothing happened when she tried it,' said Bethany.

'What was supposed to happen?' asked Tom.

Carys thumped the dashboard with her fist. 'If I'd made it work, *help* would have arrived.'

There was a loud bang and a squeal. A shaft of sunlight, fresh from sunrise, came in through the rear window. Tom looked in the rear-view mirror.

'Help … like the cavalry, you mean?'

There were two more bangs and light came shooting through one of the side windows. The canon, three children and a dog looked out on a scene to challenge the senses of all sensible people. It was indeed the cavalry. Four horses, to be exact, and riders. But how to begin to describe them?

The horses were somewhat larger than life, magnificent stallions with shiny coats, and tails that almost reached the ground.

Their hooves were silver, glinting rose-red as they caught the rays of the sun. They had no bit, bridle or saddle, for their riders rode bareback and held onto their steeds' long, flowing manes.

Their riders were children, two boys and two girls, varying in age from younger than Bethany to older than Carys. They were dressed in white tunics, loosely draped and sleeveless, with capes coloured to match their horses: white, red, black, and grey.

They were armed. One of the boys had a lance, with which he speared the demons and threw them high in the air. One of the girls had a bow and arrows, with which she pierced the demons. The second boy had a long-handled mace which he wielded like a polo stick, to boot the demons. The second girl had an endless supply of nets, with which she bagged the hapless demons and hung them from tree branches. They would be collected later, along with the weapons.

The red-caped boy dismounted and approached the car. He opened the door and shook Tom's hand.

I'M TERRIBLY SORRY WE'RE LATE.

'Who *are* you? Seeing your horses, I thought –'

WE'RE STAR RIDERS. MY NAME IS ALDEBARAN. WE HEARD THAT BRANWEN'S DAUGHTER WAS IN SERIOUS TROUBLE.

He looked across at Carys.

THAT MUST BE YOU. CARYS, ISN'T IT? YOU WILL RIDE WITH CAPELLA, SHE'S ON PROCYON, THE WHITE HORSE. SHE'LL PULL YOU UP, DON'T WORRY.

Carys walked over to the white horse, in a daze – not because of the exotic nature of her rescuers but because her rescue call had worked. She had successfully 'magicked' the ring.

Aldebaran opened the rear passenger door and a little girl and a dog jumped out.

'Hello, I'm Bethany and this is Suzy. We'd like to ride on the black horse, please, with the other girl. What's her name?'

THE GIRL'S NAME IS ELECTRA, AND HER HORSE IS CALLED MIRA.

Bethany picked up Suzy and went running over to the black horse.

'Hello, Electra! I wish *I'd* been named after the stars …'

Zach jumped out. 'Thanks for rescuing us. I think my dad may have a couple of questions for you. I assume the grey is mine?'

THAT'S REGULUS, RIDDEN BY SIRIUS.

Zach ran over and was hoisted up by a strong arm.

'How do I stay on?' asked Zach.

TRUST REGULUS. HE WON'T LET YOU FALL.

Tom squeezed himself out of the car. 'I can't help but notice the colour of your horses. It might be a coincidence, of course …'

I KNOW WHAT YOU'RE THINKING. ST JOHN'S APOCALYPSE. END OF THE WORLD AND ALL THAT. BY THE WAY, OUR LATE ARRIVAL WAS NOT OUR FAULT. RIGEL WAS SUPPOSED TO BE MINE ALL AFTERNOON BUT DAD WAS CALLED OUT – YET ANOTHER WAR. YOU'RE LUCKY HE MADE IT BACK IN TIME. WELL, ONLY JUST, BY THE LOOKS OF THINGS WHEN WE ARRIVED HERE. PRETTY CLOSE CALL, I'D SAY.

Capella shouted across to Aldebaran, CARYS WANTS WORCESTER. DO WE KNOW IT?

Aldebaran replied, RIGEL REMEMBERS THE BATTLE OF WORCESTER, 1651, YES, OF COURSE – FOLLOW ME!

And off they flew into the sunrise.

Chapter 26 — Number Ten

'Darling, it's five o'clock. You've had a good two hours. You need to get back over to the Chapter House. Stephen! Your coffee will be cold.'

Helen drew back the curtains in their temporary bedroom in the Old Palace.

'I shall miss this when we move, morning coffee looking out over the river.'

'I feel dreadful,' Stephen mumbled, sipping his coffee.

'Don't complain. At least we're still on our feet.'

'Why, what's happening?'

'It's awful,' Helen answered. 'Everybody's too weak and dispirited to do anything. People are giving up without a fight. Sitting around like zombies.'

Stephen hurried to get dressed. 'Zombies? Are you sure? I don't understand, love. I thought prayer rotas like ours were happening all over the country. I thought we were winning.'

'I wouldn't say that even here we are winning, exactly,' said Helen. 'We're holding our own – just. But the national campaign of prayers and bible reading isn't proving to be so effective when the volunteers aren't inside the stone circle like ours are. We're lucky. If we hadn't penetrated the Chapter House when we did and established a foothold, we'd be in the same position as the rest of the country.'

'Any word from Beth?'

'How can there be, dear?'

'Oh, blast, yes, batteries – I didn't realise how much we depended on them. Life before batteries … how on earth did we manage?'

'I don't know, I'm sure …'

Helen picked up a pair of binoculars. 'I keep meaning to ask Hilda if those are Welsh hills or the Malverns? Hold on … Good Heavens! Darling, what's that bit in Revelation …?'

'What bit?'

'About the four horses …'

'Chapter Six, I think. The Four Horsemen of the Apocalypse – wonderfully poetic imagery.'

'So it's not real then, dear?'

'Apocalyptic visions are never real, though they may point to certain truths … Famine, Plague, War … the Antichrist is it, on the white horse?'

'No, I believe it's Carys. Bethany is on the black one – oh look, she's waving!'

Stephen was at the window in time to see the horses disappear over the roof. He dashed out of the room, across the corridor and into Bethany's room. He looked down at the children and Tom dismounting, along with the four Star Riders. Stephen opened the window and shouted down to them.

'Bethany, what do you think the bishop will say if he hears that the Four Horsemen of the Apocalypse are parked in the Old Palace car park – and that the Antichrist has taken his parking place?'

'Okay, Daddy, we'll send them into the garden.'

Stephen ran back to his bedroom to finish dressing. He could hear Helen letting them all in downstairs. They were seated in the Great Hall when Stephen loped in, hitching up his invisible gown.

He was muttering, 'Chapter Six ... or was it Chapter Eight? I should've taken the Book of Revelation more seriously.'

Bethany rushed to meet him. 'Daddy, you are silly. This isn't the Antichrist. It's Capella. And that's Electra, Sirius and Aldebaran. I wish you'd named *me* after a star.'

'How –?' asked Stephen.

Tom shook his head. 'Don't ask. Just believe.'

'But who –?'

Carys tried to explain. 'These are Star Riders –'

'But the horses ... the colours ...'

Carys continued, 'Yes, they are those horses, but these are the *children* of the Four Horsemen of the Apocalypse.'

'They rescued us from Balimm's horde of demons,' added Tom.

'Balimm is your Professor,' explained Bethany, with a trace of smugness.

YES, WE KNOW BALIMM OF OLD, said Aldebaran.

HE IS POWERFUL, said Capella.

HE MUST NOT GET HIS HANDS ON THE COMPLETE AARON'S ROD, said Electra.

IF HE DOES, THIS PLANET IS FINISHED, said Sirius.

Stephen sank into a chair. 'Well, thank you for those encouraging words.'

Helen took his hand and pulled him back to his feet. 'Sorry, Stephen, we must go to the Chapter House. You're due to take over from Alan and yours is the key seat, remember. I don't like the look of the river. And there's a few birds on the ground. I think we may be in danger of losing our privileged status. You're going to have to pray your hardest.'

Stephen let himself be dragged towards the door. He turned and looked back at the strange scene. 'Look after the children, Tom!'

Tom laughed. 'The last people you need to worry about are these children. Now go!'

Helen and Stephen left, and Tom was soon deep in conversation with the Star Riders.

Bethany was curled up inside an armchair many times too big for her. She'd fallen asleep, hugging Suzy to her chest like a well-worn teddy bear.

'Cass,' Zach whispered, 'what's the news nationwide – any idea?'

Carys nodded. 'Helen filled me in. It's not good. The country has ground to a halt. The Government's declared a state of emergency. They've closed all airports. There's no broadcasting or telephones. I didn't tell Helen, but it's going to get a lot worse. We haven't even felt the full impact of the second rod yet.'

'Next time we'll be better prepared,' said Zach.

Carys was not impressed. 'So will Balimm. He's already a lot more powerful now that he possesses two rods – and he's going to be extra careful when he learns that we've friends in high places.'

The front door banged. They heard what Helen was saying when she was halfway up the stairs. It was more bad news. 'The volunteers are down to a few minutes before collapsing. It's looking bad, I'm afraid. We're going to have to increase the number of bible readers –'

'That's not going to work,' said Carys. 'People can't keep on and on praying and reading. The fact is, we've been too narrow in our response.'

'What … do you … mean?' gasped Helen. She was leaning on the marble mantlepiece, getting her breath.

'Well, the stones are drawing the spirit out of people, but the human spirit thrives on more than religious writings and prayers.'

'So?'

Carys wondered where to begin. 'You still don't know what happened to us in Wales, and the details don't matter. But when we were held captive by some demon guards, we escaped by deploying a secret weapon – your daughter.'

'Really? What did she do?'

'Like I say, the details don't matter, but if we devised a new strategy, using what we learned last night, could we spread it nationwide?'

Helen's face fell. '*We* couldn't, I'm afraid. The Government can communicate nationwide, through its emergency channels, but the problem would be getting them to believe you. After all, Stephen and I didn't believe you. The Government is still clinging to its theories about global warming and the rest.'

'I'm afraid Helen is right,' said Tom. He had wandered over with his new friends and listened in to the last part of the conversation. 'Without hard evidence, all our explanations and theories are mumbo-jumbo. We're sunk, I'm afraid.'

'I'm not so sure,' said Carys. 'Aldebaran, I've a small favour to ask before you head back home. And Helen, I know she's sleeping peacefully, but can you wake our secret weapon, please?'

*

The private secretary knocked and was ushered into the Prime Minister's office.

'P-Prime Minister, there is ... someone, er, that is, a person, a young person ... in fact, a girl ... who wishes to speak with you.'

'Good grief, man,' said the Prime Minister, 'sixty million people wish to speak with me. I thought the phones were down?'

'Er, no, that is, she's at the d-door – the, ah, little girl.'

'Talk sense, will you? There's a whole battalion guarding this –'

'Excuse me, Prime Minister, sir,' declared a high-ranking army officer, who walked in without knocking, 'there's a young lady to see you. She says it's urgent.'

'So I've been told, brigadier, so I've been told. And how did one little girl penetrate all your defences, tell me that?'

'She's not alone, Prime Minister. Bethany has with her a large canon, his son, Zach, a friend from Wales called ...' – and here the brigadier consulted his notes – '... Carys Aranrhod Cadwaladr – oh, and a small dog called Suzy.'

'Another crazy sect who want to convince me that the Apocalypse is nigh – and you let them *through?*'

'We couldn't stop them, sir, you see –'

'Stand aside. I will show you how to deal with unsolicited callers ...'

The Prime Minister went and opened the front door himself. There on the doorstep was Bethany. Behind her, hovering a metre above the cobbles of Downing Street, were the Four Horses of The Apocalypse. On their backs were what looked like extras from a

Greek tragedy – along with a large canon, a boy, a girl, and a mongrel dog.

When the Prime Minister came round, his tone was much calmer. He addressed the little girl almost reverently.

'No, no, you were right to come to me, if you think you have found a way of … how did you put it?'

'It's simple,' said Bethany. 'We've found a way of neutralising the negatively polarised flow of energy which has been reversed by means of thousands of demons using the power of Aaron's Rod to induce the spirits of the Neolithic stones to bend to their will.'

'Did you get all that? Did you *get* it?'

The Prime Minister was addressing his top scientific advisors, who were frantically scribbling.

'Every word, Prime Minister, but it's mumbo-jumbo.'

'Listen to me, you clowns. Those horses out there are *not* mumbo-jumbo, so this little girl's words are not mumbo-jumbo either – is that clear?'

'To be fair,' said Bethany, 'it's simpler to understand when you've experienced it, as I have. I would like to tell you what happened last night, if I may?'

During the next ten minutes, Downing Street staff were amazed to hear peals of laughter ringing out from the PM's office. At one point they swore they heard the Prime Minister *giggling*.

When they emerged, the Prime Minister and Bethany both had damp cheeks and a rosy glow about them. Bethany turned on the doorstep. 'Now you promise, cross your heart, that you will do everything, word for word as I told you? No spin?'

'I promise. Cross my heart and hope to lose the next election!'

'Because if you don't, my friends' horses will come back. It will be their fathers riding them next time – and you know what that means. So goodbye, Mr PM!'

The Prime Minister watched as Electra hauled Bethany on board. The four horses rose above the rooftops and galloped away with the sun on their backs. The Prime Minister waved goodbye and picked up a telephone.

'I need the Archbishop of Canterbury. Now. You have? Good. Shame it's not a video line because his face will be – *Archbishop? I must be brief because of the power situation, you understand? So we have no time for any argy-bargy. I have a new strategy to deal with the sound of the stones. I have it from an impeccable source, and it has been tried and tested.*

'This is what you must do. First, in all your ancient cathedrals and churches, you must organise children's parties and games ... yes, that IS what I said, parties and games. Get hold of joke books and encourage the children to swap jokes. Yes, in the cathedrals and churches. And oh yes, dogs. If a child has a pet dog, get them to take it to the party ... I realise they are houses of God, but I'm sure God loves children and their dogs as much as we do. No argy-bargy, remember?

'Second, we need some parish Pied Pipers, maybe teenagers who still have some energy? They are to lead groups of young children into the stone circles and ... yes, Archbishop, you're getting the hang of it now, they should have a party, with games and jokes. No, not in the next field. I said inside the stone circles ... yes, I know no one has penetrated the circles but has anybody let a child try? I agree, I wouldn't have let MY children near them either. But I'm told they don't feel the effect as badly. Yes, hide-and-seek round the stones, lots of fun and laughter. And dogs.

'Archbishop, I need you to believe in this. That's the spirit – the Church might WELL find a new direction. Stranger things have happened – much stranger. What? Yes, of course keep the rotas of prayer and bible reading going. This is to be in addition to present efforts. An all-out offensive. Think of it as sending in the cavalry. If we survive, that is how I shall remember today.'

A staff member passed a note to the PM.

'Oh, and I've got you a text, should you need it. Matthew 18:3. "Unless you change and become as little –" oh, you know it, yes, well ... onwards and upwards. Bye, Archbishop.'

He put the phone down and threw himself back in his chair. His staff leaned forwards, on the edges of their seats.

'The old boy's going to do it!'

Everyone in the room burst into applause.

Chapter 27   Mulled Mullein

Carys had asked Capella and her friends to drop them all at the farm. Then it was time to say goodbye. As the Star Riders were mounting their steeds, Bethany asked them a question that had been bothering her. 'Are you real?'

The four equestrian children laughed, scattering stardust from their hair.

THE CURTAIN SEPARATING REALITY FROM LEGEND IS THIN ... said Aldebaran, climbing onto blood-red Rigel,

... THIN AS A BUTTERFLY'S GOSSAMER WING ... said Capella, as she mounted snow white Procyon.

... BUT A FLUTTERING BUTTERFLY WING ... said Electra, leaping onto coal black Mira,

... CAUSES HURRICANES TO BLOW IN DISTANT LANDS, said Sirius, hauling himself up by Regulus's pale grey mane.

Zach finished a frantic bout of finger-counting and asked, 'So you're less than real but more than a legend?'

IF YOU SAY SO! said Aldebaran, laughing.

LEGENDS AND APOCALYPTIC VISIONS ... said Capella with a smile,

... AREN'T LAWS TO BE OBEYED ... said Electra, tying back her golden hair with a black ribbon,

... BUT STORIES TO BE TOLD AND RE-TOLD, said Sirius, kicking his heels into Regulus's side.

The four horses had lifted from the ground and were already some distance away when Carys called out, 'Wait!'

Keeping in formation, they swung round.

Carys shouted, 'What if the story is changed in the telling?'

As they swept past, each added their own final words.

THAT IS THE STORYTELLER'S PRIVILEGE ... said Aldebaran,

... BUT IF THE NEW STORY CONTAINS NO TRUTHS ... said Capella,

... THAT SPEAK TO PEOPLE'S HEARTS ... said Electra,

... THEN THE STORY WILL NOT LAST, said Sirius.

In a flash, the Star Riders were gone. The quiet valley crackled with faint echoes of their parting words. The thin air shimmered with traces of silvery light from the horses' hooves. 'I shall miss you!' cried Bethany. Then she turned with the others and walked up to the farm gate.

The farm looked different in the daylight, much friendlier, turning the events of the night into a distant dream. But the rope which had lowered Carys down the well was still lying limp on the ground, a chilling reminder of how real those events had been.

They piled into the house, and Carys ran on ahead to see her mother.

Branwen was ill. Trying to speak made her cough, and once she coughed it took her a long time to stop. She also had a slight fever. Doctors were out of the question. There was no transport and Branwen wouldn't have allowed it anyway.

Branwen pointed to a large book open on her table, and the empty glass next to it. Then she pointed to the scales and a pestle and mortar next to them. Carys saw the recipe for the herbal remedy that Branwen wanted brewing, as the others were squeezing through the secret door.

'Mum's not well,' Carys told them. 'It's not the sound of the stones, it's a bronchial attack. She gets them on and off. But it's a bad one. Mum needs us to make an infusion of mullein.'

Carys read aloud from the book: 'Mullein – infusion good for bronchitis. Pour a cup of boiling water onto one or two teaspoons of the dried leaves or flowers and allow to infuse for about twelve minutes. This should be drunk three times a day.'

Everyone was instructed to search the shelves for a herbal jar marked 'Mullein'. Zach soon found it, but the jar was empty. Branwen indicated that mullein grew up the hill.

'Does anybody know what this plant looks like?' asked Carys.

Nobody did.

Tom came forward and spoke to Branwen.

'I wonder, do you happen to have a copy of The Cyclopedia of Herbs & Medicinal Plants?'

Branwen nodded, and once again they all searched. Carys began to get a feeling that she'd had before, one that she was now beginning to recognise. A feeling that something important was about to happen. It was the strangest feeling, because she had no idea at all what the event might be.

'Got it.'

Zach had scored again. He couldn't reach the book, so his dad lifted it down with loving care. 'An earlier edition than mine, I see. Oh, and I say, full colour illustrations. Beautiful.'

He found the entry for Mullein and laid the book out on a table for all to see.

An easily grown biennial plant
with white, hairy, velvety leaves
with long, dense spikes of yellow flowers.
The wool was once used for lamp-wicks.
Grows to 3ft.

A coloured drawing of the plant had been included, plus a list of alternative names:

Bullock's Lungwort
Woollen Blanket Herb
Shepherd's Club
Aaron's Rod

Bethany shouted out, 'Look - Aaron's Rod! Mullein is also called Aaron's Rod!'

'And you can see why,' said Tom. 'It really does look like a wooden rod that's sprouted leaves and flowers. I would never have believed it.'

Deep within Carys, an upsurge of delight took her breath away and signalled the fulfilment of her premonition.

'Right,' she announced, 'I'm staying with Mum and I think the hill will be too much for Tom, so it's down to Zach, Beth and Suzy to fetch the mullein. We only need the leaves, so mind you don't damage the rods. I'll need them to help me find the final piece of Aaron's Rod.'

Zach raised his hand to speak. 'Surely you don't think that this plant called Aaron's Rod has anything to do with *our* Aaron's Rod, do you?'

'I don't think, I know,' replied Carys.

'But what about Merlin's riddle?' asked Bethany. 'Where's the silver circle?'

'Right now, Beth, I'd rather trust my Finder's instinct than play games with Merlin. We don't have time.'

The mullein hunters set off. There had been no sign of Balimm, but Tom refused to let Zach and Beth go up the hill alone. He insisted on escorting them, joking that he could always roll back down the hill if the sound of the stones became too strong.

Left alone with Branwen, Carys had time to think.

She had no doubt that the national 'silly jokes strategy' would reduce the sound of the stones where it was implemented, but she also knew there would be large gaps. And the negative flow would get worse as Balimm deployed his additional power supply. But it must be giving Balimm something to think about. She chuckled as she told Branwen the effect that Bethany had had on the demon guards.

What about Aaron's Rod, the medicinal plant? The drawing in the book showed it looking indeed like a rod sprouting leaves and flowers, as the original Aaron's Rod was reputed to have done. How was she going to know which plant was marking the spot?

And how could the same plant have survived on the same spot for hundreds of years? As always, the clue raised more questions than answers.

The front door of the farmhouse banged shut.

Carys froze. Had the gang forgotten something? Had Tom had to give up so soon? When nobody announced themselves, Carys knew: *Balimm is back.* What should she do? The secret door was wide open. She could close it and hide with her mother. But that would leave the others to face Balimm without her, and she couldn't allow that. So she raced out, closed the door behind her, and dashed up the steps two at a time to face her enemy. She had no plan, but at least this time she wouldn't be hanging onto a rope at the top of a well. She picked up a broom and a bread knife on her way through the kitchen, and then put them down again. They would be no use against Balimm. And anyway, she was the Finder, and Zach had told her that the Finder doesn't have to fight.

She heard a creaking floorboard above her. He was upstairs, maybe searching for clues. She decided to make a run for it. She had no idea what powers Balimm possessed, whether he could fly or shoot missiles or fireballs from the rod, but she felt she'd have a better chance of surviving once she was running outside, rather than being trapped in the house with him. So she scooted along the corridor to the hall.

BANG!

The crash occurred at the blind corner where the corridor met the bottom step of the stairs. Carys hit the floor with a thud.

Chapter 28 Carys Decides

Carys lay with her face to the floor. She wasn't hurt, but she didn't want to get up. She felt nothing but despair. *We can't escape our destiny. We may run but it will find us out in the end. My nightmare collision with Balimm has happened after all. Not on a station platform but in my own home.*

'Hi sis. That was quite a tackle. Are you hurt, love?'

'*Dylan!*' Carys shouted with anger fuelled by relief. 'You might have called out!'

Dylan helped Carys to her feet. 'How's Ma? Is she all right?'

'Sh-she's fine. She's … staying with Mrs Jones until life returns to normal.'

Carys walked on into the living room, away from the kitchen.

Dylan followed.

'That was a mean trick, Cass, sending us to Stonehenge. You made me look a right fool in front of the Professor.'

'But he's not a professor. He's … he's …'

Carys stopped. It was useless. It would serve no purpose to say Nash was a demon.

'… he's an evil man.'

'That's rubbish, Carys, and you know it. He's a saint, more like. He knows where we've all been going wrong.'

Carys didn't sit down. She needed to remain on her feet, to keep her mind sharp.

Dylan continued, 'Professor Nash says we've forgotten the link between physical and spiritual energy. Our ancestors understood this link and nurtured it. They found refreshment at the spiritual fountains which they created with their stone circles. It's all so wonderfully obvious.'

'Y-you sound different, Dyl.'

'The Professor doesn't want anything to interfere with his plans … nor any*one*.'

That was a threat. Carys had never seen Dylan threaten a fly, let alone his own sister. She would have to be careful, though she was sure he would never harm her. She mustn't be afraid to challenge him. 'So how do you explain the *negative* effects that your treatment of the stones is having on people – *and* on things like petrol?'

'Simple, love. The Professor is detoxing the earth. Drawing out the poisons, so that creation can begin again with a clean slate. Detox is always painful. Headaches, tiredness – classic symptoms of detox. But they don't last. People are going to feel so much better when the process is complete. And the *earth* has been suffering so much already that she won't mind a bit more pain if it's putting things right.'

'Dylan, I hate to say this, but you've been brainwashed.'

Dylan wasn't listening. He was in full flow.

'We've been tearing the earth to pieces, ripping out the coal and minerals, sucking out the oil and gas, all for our physical gratification, with no regard to the damage we've caused to the earth's spirit. When our ancestors chopped down a tree, they apologised to it. That's what we've lost, that spiritual connection.'

'You're spouting gobbledygook,' insisted Carys. 'The earth isn't a living being.'

'You'll thank the Professor when we're through. Harmony restored, creation in balance, the lion will sit down with the lamb. It'll be Eden, sis, a return to Eden.'

Dylan was sounding more evangelical than Pastor Lewis.

'Who will run this new, refreshed planet?' Carys asked. 'The Prof?'

'Well, he isn't going to want people to return to their old ways. But they'll thank him, because they'll be happy again.'

Carys hardly recognised her brother by now. It was scary. But she had to ask the most difficult question of all. 'And you, Dyl, what's he promised you? A seat at his right hand?'

'Nobody can expect him to run a whole planet by himself. I'll have an important role, yes – but I'll have earned it. Without me the project couldn't happen, not fully. I'm dying to tell you all about it, but I'm sworn to secrecy.'

Dylan knew what his task would be; Carys could see it in his eyes. Balimm must have woven a web of lies that included Dylan's ability to withdraw Aaron's Rod from its stone. Maybe he'd even explained away their father's suicide as a lack of courage. Certainly, Balimm wouldn't have allowed Dylan to talk to his sister again without blocking off all the angles that she might use to disarm him. But it was possible he'd forgotten one …

'Don't you think it's strange, Dylan, that this mighty professor, with an army of workers and limitless funds at his disposal, needs me, your little sister, to supply him with the power he needs? I know where the third precious rod lies hidden, but you don't. I wonder what your Prof thinks about that? '

Dylan's front weakened. He was no longer Professor Nash's right hand man, self-assured and confident. He was Dyl, Carys's brother. He collapsed onto a chair and ran a hand through his bouncing hair.

'Don't sis, it's not fair. I've always been second to you. Ever since you could talk, you've made me look ordinary.'

Carys was burning up inside, feeling her brother's pain, unspoken all these years.

'Dylan, I –'

'I know you never meant it, Cass. The point is, this is my chance to be somebody, to be a success – yes, to be rich, and why not? Tell me the location of the third rod and everything will work out. I'll look after you and Mum, you know I will.'

Carys was in a dilemma now, and she could see why Balimm had sent Dylan again rather than face her himself. The demon understood humanity enough to know the power of blood ties. He was banking on the fact that Carys would be unwilling to hurt her brother, no matter how high the stakes.

'I need time to think about this, Dyl. I promise, no more tricks. For what it's worth, I hated deceiving you about Stonehenge and I hope one day you'll forgive me. Walk with me to the old tree and I'll give you my decision.'

Carys's mention of the old tree, the hub of many of their childhood games, softened Dylan's stance enough to allow him to trust her. So he walked with her. She was determined to stay outwardly calm, but inside, her emotions were churning and her thoughts racing.

Was it right to make such an important decision alone? Shouldn't she wait and have a meeting with the gang? Or was it her decision to make because she was the Aranrhod? One thing was certain. If she fought Balimm on his terms, she would fail. And yet he had to be defeated, Carys knew, even it meant the unthinkable, that she would lose her brother as well as her father. If ever Balimm got hold of the complete Aaron's Rod, even if his stone circle plan was foiled, he would find some other way to destroy the world. Out of spite, if for no other reason.

Merlin was to blame for this mess. Why did Merlin leave such a precious and powerful object lying around, and then make up silly rules to be obeyed and games to be played? The Finder and the Wielder? *By a silver circle in a silver circle?* Okay, it meant that Balimm couldn't find the rods himself, but there had been nothing to stop him taking the rods from Carys once *she'd* found them. And while Balimm couldn't withdraw the crucial third rod from the stone, there had been nothing to stop him murdering the rightful Cadwaladr and deceiving his naïve son into doing the final task for him. It was crazy.

Maybe it *was* all a game to Merlin. Maybe he couldn't care less what happened to Aaron's Rod. And yet it was the most powerful artefact outside the Ark and the Grail – didn't Dredge say that Aaron's Rod had been crafted from a branch of the Tree of Life, according to legend? What was Merlin doing, taking risks with such a legendary object?

Looking for the tiniest clue to help her decide what to do, Carys went over the events of the past two days, from bumping into Tom to crashing into Dyl; from meeting Beth and Zach to saying farewell to the Star Riders on their legendary horses. Carys had learned so much, heard so many wise words – from her mother, from her friends, from the Star Riders …

Carys took a deep breath. She knew what she had to do.

'All right, Dyl, I've made my decision. I'm not going to pretend that I believe any of the Professor's theories, but it's obvious that I can't beat him. My priority now must be to look after Mum and make sure I don't lose my brother.'

'You won't lose me, sis, I promise. Like I say, I'll look after both of you, you'll see. So what's the plan, then? When do we get the third rod?'

'I'll give it to the Professor at midnight tonight.'

'Why not now, when he picks me up?'

'It has to be by moonlight – he knows that. Midnight tonight, you and him, at the top of the hill. I will show him the third rod's location. I promise.'

'No tricks?'

'No tricks, Dyl. Like I say, we'd stand no chance against him. With the double rod, he's already like Superman. It wouldn't be fair to you or to my friends. Bye, Dyl.'

Carys kissed him on the cheek and ran to the house.

At the door, she turned and cried, 'I don't want to see the Professor now – you understand?'

'Fair enough,' replied Dylan. 'We'll see you on the hilltop at midnight. It's a full moon tonight – is that good?'

'I haven't the faintest idea. I don't make the rules.'

Carys disappeared indoors and went up to her room, where she could see the yard from her dormer window. After a couple of minutes, Balimm arrived, and exchanged a few words with Dylan. Balimm appeared uncertain and looked towards the farmhouse, weighing up Carys's proposition. Dylan spoke again, gesturing to the farmhouse and putting his hand on his heart. Balimm was convinced. He faced the house and used the rod to give a salute to his invisible foe. Then he gave the other end of the rod to Dylan to hold and they both disappeared, leaving a swirl of dust under the tree. The swing rocked to and fro as if the ghost of a child were playing on it.

Chapter 29 · Aranrhod's Legend

'The mullein train returns!' announced Tom, when they all trooped into Branwen's den.

Bethany presented a bagful of leaves to Carys. 'There's loads of the stuff. You can't miss it.'

'It's quite promising in terms of the riddle,' said Zach. 'Me and Beth went round the whole patch and it's roughly circular –'

'*Very* roughly,' added Tom, smiling. 'It's tricky to tell because it's a huge area.'

'How big would you say, Dad?'

'Maybe two football pitches? But I'm useless at that kind of thing.'

Zach took a handful of the leaves and began grinding them with the pestle and mortar. 'These leaves are greenish white. At a pinch you might describe them as silvery, but it would be stretching the definition, I think.'

Bethany laughed. 'Zach got so desperate, he was looking for a silver circle painted on the ground!'

'Dylan was here while you were gone,' said Carys abruptly. Everyone froze.

Zach gave the pestle and mortar to Branwen to finish. 'I bet he wanted to know where the third rod's hidden.'

Carys nodded.

'Well, we're not telling, are we Suzy?' declared Bethany.

Carys studied the backs of her hands. 'I'm … not so sure.'

Tom had been leafing through books. But now he put the books down and joined the others. 'You're seriously thinking we should give in?'

Carys shook her head vigorously. 'No, I didn't say we should give in, but nobody can say that our tactics so far have been brilliant. We've been on the defensive too much. Balimm always grabs the initiative and wins out in the end.'

'I think you've all been marvellous,' said Tom.

'Thanks, Tom. I know we've fought back when attacked and we've escaped when taken captive – with some help from our friends.'

'Maybe Merlin can help us,' suggested Bethany.

'That's what I mean,' said Carys. 'We've relied on outside help too often – including magic.'

Nobody knew what to say. There was an embarrassed silence.

'You've already decided what to do, haven't you?' asked Zach.

Everybody stared hard at Carys.

'I have, yes. I'm sorry. I felt it was my decision to make.'

Another silence ensued, with some shuffling of feet and clearing of throats.

Then Bethany spoke. 'Good! You're the Aranrhod. But I hope you'll still want me to help you, because you do have exciting adventures.'

Zach tossed his hair back. 'Beth's right on the nail, as usual. I've already told you, Cass, you're our leader.'

Tom agreed. 'I-I'm a hanger-on here. I'm still not sure if this isn't all a dream. I wouldn't feel qualified to decide on any future tactics. I'm with you, Carys.'

'So, what's the plan?' asked a voice of gravel. It was Branwen.

'In a word, to kill Balimm,' Carys replied.

'That's three words,' said Zach, 'but otherwise it's a great plan.'

The question on everyone's lips was 'How?', but no one dared to ask.

Carys understood. 'We won't be using jokes tonight. Our weapons will be faith and timing.'

'When and where?' asked Tom.

'The hilltop at midnight. Timing will be crucial, so Beth and I will need accurate watches. I don't have a watch – is yours any good, Beth?'

'The battery's flat – sorry.'

'Zach, how about yours?'

Zach removed his watch and handed it over. 'It's okay. It has a nice long second hand for countdowns, and it's luminous.'

Carys put it on. 'That's great. I'll have this, if that's okay? And yours, Tom?'

Tom showed Carys his watch. 'It'll do hundredths of a second if you want. And look, phases of the moon, a calendar, and Tetris for when sermons get boring – mine, I mean. And the battery's still working, for some reason.'

Carys handed it back. 'Sorry, Tom. It's a great watch but I can't risk the battery letting us down.'

'Drat,' said Tom, 'I'd always wanted to say "Synchronise watches!"'

Branwen called Carys over to her. After a few moments, Carys returned to the group.

'Mum has solved the timing problem. I suggest now that everybody gets some rest – sleep if possible. We'll meet outside at twenty to twelve.'

'Can I use your room, please Carys?' asked Bethany.

'Of course. It's –'

'It's all right, I remember which it is. See you later.'

'Zach, use Dylan's room.'

'Right you are. Come on Suzy.'

'Tom, do your best to rest down here.'

Tom replied, 'I'm concerned about Bethany. I know she won't want to duck out of this, but with her parents not being here, I feel –'

Carys interrupted, 'Beth won't be coming up the hill, don't worry. She has to stay here.'

'Is your mother lending her a watch, then?'

Carys smiled. 'In a way, yes. Beth will be using the grandfather clock in the hall. I'd forgotten, if it's fully wound, it keeps perfect time.'

Carys went over to her mother.

'Mum, I'm worried about the battery. The torch battery failed when I went down the well, and I hadn't even switched it on.'

Branwen spoke. Her voice was clearer. 'Don't worry. For a start, it's a bigger battery, and I won't let Bethany take it out of this room until thirty seconds before the time.'

'Thirty seconds? Isn't that cutting it fine?'

'It would be for me, but Bethany's a nimble little thing. I'll give her some practice runs – it'll give her something to do while you're climbing the hill. It'll work. It's a good plan, the bit you've told me – I'm proud of you, girl, and I know your father would be too. Now *you* go and rest.'

Tom stopped her on her way out. 'I'm puzzled. Why does the grandfather clock need a battery?'

'It's not for the clock,' replied Carys.

At twenty minutes before midnight, they all gathered in the farmyard. Bethany gave them all a hug, and said she was looking forward to the party when they all returned. When she hugged Carys, she whispered in her ear, 'Don't worry, I won't let you down. At the first chime of quarter past.'

As they were climbing the hill, the sound of the stones was strong, but Tom was coping well. He asked Carys how she'd persuaded Bethany to stay behind.

'Simple,' Carys answered. 'She's taken on her usual role as our secret weapon.'

When they came over the rise at the top, Carys could see what Zach and Tom had meant. The mullein was growing in a large, broadly circular area.

'It'll take all night to dig under all those Aaron's Rod plants to find Aaron's Rod,' said Zach.

'We won't need to,' replied Carys.

Balimm and Dylan appeared on the far side. They walked through the Aaron's Rod plants towards the centre, skirting outcrops of bluestone rocks, while Carys led her friends through the yellow-flowering rods towards her brother and the demon. When they were about three-quarters of the way to the centre, she signalled Tom and Zach to stop.

'I have to do this alone. Stay here and hold onto Suzy. I'll yell if I need your help, Zach.'

'Be sure you do.'

'Be careful,' said Tom.

'I will.'

Carys made her way to where Balimm and her brother were waiting.

'I am glad you have seen sense,' said Balimm. 'You have the rod?'

Carys pointed. 'It's here, in this circle of bluestones, in the moonlight, as Merlin prophesied.'

'But where *exactly?* I need that rod!'

'The double rod in your hand yearns for its completion as much as yourself. Let the rod in your hand guide you.'

Balimm held out the double rod and, sure enough, it turned him until he pointed to a particular spot, where an especially thick growth of mullein stood tall, like sentries keeping guard.

'Excellent. What next?'

Carys moved forward so that she was standing next to Dylan, no more than a metre away from where the rod was pointing.

'Strike the ground ... *there.*'

Balimm struck the ground.

For a moment, nothing happened. Then it began. The tiniest tremor at first. Then a rumbling sensation underfoot, but reminiscent of a deep sound rather than motion, as if the earth was breathing a sigh of relief. Then came the movement. Everyone lost their balance and had to adjust their footing as the ground shifted. Downwards.

Carys looked around. It wasn't an earthquake, for the earth wasn't shaking, not in that queasy way that makes victims feel they are on a ship instead of solid ground. They were sinking, not because the earth was acting like a liquid, but like a lift. They were descending on a gigantic lift.

The large, roughly circular area that contained every rod of mullein was sinking. The sides of what was now a basin were already half a metre high. The whole area of grass and stones and soil was pushing downwards, exerting pressure like a tectonic plate. The descent ceased when the sides of the basin were seven or eight metres high. Silence enveloped the scene like a ghostly mist.

Even Balimm was subdued. 'I have to say, I am impressed.'

Carys smiled. 'Yes, I'd say I chose the right spot.'

For there, equidistant between Carys, Dylan and Balimm, was an anvil-sized lump of bluestone granite, and sticking out of it, looking freshly minted, and glinting in the light of the full moon, was the third and final piece of Aaron's Rod.

'Yee … eeesss!' Balimm shouted to the stars in triumph.

Zach couldn't see what was happening, but he guessed. 'There was no burst of light,' he said in surprise to his father.

'Burst of light? That would have been OTT, don't you think?'

Carys glanced at her watch.

'Right, Balimm, there's your rod. But you have a problem. A serious problem. Poor Dredge thought Merlin's riddle was for him, when in fact it was for me. The first half of the riddle – *by a silver circle* – refers to my middle name, Aranrhod, which means *silver wheel*. That's how I was able to find all the rods. I was Merlin's Finder. Oh yes, I can see you'd like a word with Dredge now – what a pity you killed him. But I'm telling you, you have more reason to regret killing *someone else*.'

Balimm was trying to sneer at Carys's revelations, but his eyes betrayed a different reaction, one that the demon wasn't familiar with: fear. This girl had found all three parts of Aaron's Rod. While doing so, she had withstood Dredge's magic and reduced him to a gibbering rat. She had also escaped from a circle of demon guards, and it was rumoured that she had enlisted the help of Star Riders. Balimm listened ever more intently.

Carys continued, 'For you see, Balimm, Dredge didn't tell you a vital piece of the legend about the third rod and who is qualified to draw it out of the stone. He pointed you, correctly, to my father, who was the direct descendant of King Arthur Cadwaladr. But Dredge was either too stupid or too treacherous to tell you this – only when the direct descendant has a male heir does he qualify. So when you killed our father, you were wrong in thinking Dylan could do the job instead – at least straight away. Maybe if you call by in a few years, if and when my brother has a son and heir …?'

'Is this true, Professor?' asked Dylan, advancing on Balimm. 'You killed my father?'

The demon swept Dylan aside, knocking him to the ground. 'That has no importance now.'

'No *importance?*' Dylan struggled to his feet. He went to attack Balimm, but Carys put her arm out to stop him. For the moment Dylan was more confused than anything, so Carys could still control him.

'No importance *now*, Dylan, Balimm is right,' she insisted.

'Who's Balimm?'

'Balimm is Professor Nash's real identity, Dyl. He's a low-ranking demon –'

Balimm interrupted, as Carys knew he would. Pride was such a predictable sin.

'*Low* ranking? I command one thousand legions of demons …'

Carys glanced at her watch. *No time to lose.* 'Dylan, listen to me. I repeat: Balimm is right. More important than our father's murder right now is to prove to Balimm that I'm speaking the truth and that you can't withdraw this rod –'

'But I can … and I *will*. I must avenge our father's death …'

Carys held her breath as Dylan grasped the rod with both hands and began pulling at it with all his might. The sinews in his neck were bulging with the strain. Thankfully, Dylan believed her embroidered version of the legend, and so he couldn't budge the rod. *So far, so good.*

Balimm took a step forwards. 'How pathetic. It seems your sister speaks the truth, which is a nuisance, but nothing more. It means I need you in my employ for a while longer, Dylan, but at least now there's nothing to stop me disposing of *Carys!*'

Balimm spat out the word with venom born of frustration, resentment – spite. Then he took in a deep breath, opened his mouth wider than seemed possible, and began one of his deep, lethal roars. Carys felt the ground shifting beneath her feet. She was sinking. In seconds she was up to her ankles and unable to move. Dylan could do nothing either, rooted to the spot. With her thighs disappearing into the earth, Carys consulted her watch for one last time, and whispered, 'Three, two, one – Bethany … Now, Beth, *please!*'

A deafening clanging filled the air. Branwen's fire bell swirled and echoed around the basin. At the moment it rang out, everyone turned to see what it was – except Carys who was expecting it, and Dylan who'd grown up with it.

In that split second when Balimm was distracted, he ceased his deadly roaring. Carys leant over, drew the rod out of the stone, and tossed it to Dylan.

For a moment, Balimm was in shock as he realised what had happened, that *Carys* had withdrawn the rod from the stone, and now Dylan was holding it, with revenge in his eyes.

For that one moment, Balimm wasn't in control of the double rod in his hand, and that was the moment that Carys had banked on getting. It was all the time needed for the double rod in Balimm's hand to fly through the air to join the rod in Dylan's hand.

With Balimm unarmed and off guard, Dylan swung Aaron's Rod over his head and down, through the centre of Balimm's body. The rod met with no resistance, and all that remained of Balimm was a pile of clothing. Where the rod struck the ground, a black hole formed, a portal into a timeless abyss.

Dylan turned to face Carys. He raised his arms in triumph. But instead of returning his joy, Carys's face wore an expression of horror. Behind Dylan a huge serpent had appeared – Balimm's demon body. The serpent had broad mustard and orange stripes, and was writhing frantically, vainly struggling against being sucked into the black hole.

Dylan wheeled round but he wasn't quick enough. Lashing out wildly, the serpent knocked Dylan off his feet and sent Aaron's Rod flying. The serpent then wrapped itself around one of Dylan's legs, dragging him inexorably towards the hole. Dylan struggled and fought, but to no avail.

Carys had scratched away some of the soil, but it was packed tight and she knew she wouldn't get free in time to help her brother.

'*Zach!*' she cried, at the top of her lungs.

Zach dropped Suzy and raced through the forest of mullein rods, leaping over bluestone rocks in his path, until he beheld a scene from one of his fantasy computer games. Carys, half buried in the ground, and Dylan, only a short distance from being dragged down a yawning black chasm by a multi-coloured serpent.

'The rod!' yelled Carys. '*Use Aaron's Rod!*'

As Zach gripped the rod in both hands, there was an explosion of light and Zach was thrown onto his back so violently that he did well to keep hold of the … sword? Zach stared in disbelief. He sprang to his feet, holding a sword that glimmered like silver in the moonlight. The cross-guard was encrusted with jewels and the pommel was a huge, spherical ruby.

'Excalibur!' Zach breathed.

Despite Zach's slight build, the sword felt perfectly balanced in his hands. He ran to the edge of the hole. The serpent had seen the threat and was frantically uncurling from around Dylan's leg, the better to defend itself. Too late. Zach took aim and sliced off the serpent's head with one blow. Its body slipped into oblivion, leaving its severed head teetering on the brink. Then it opened its jaws further than seemed possible …

'Oh no you don't!' cried Dylan, giving the head a vicious kick with his foot. 'You've roared your last roar!' As the head rolled into the abyss, a stifled scream echoed around the basin.

By now, Suzy had dug Carys out of the ground with her powerful forelegs. The three children were about to celebrate when they heard something that chilled their souls.

It was like the sound of the stones, but many times more powerful. Carys, Zach and Dylan looked up and saw, silhouetted against the clear, moonlit sky, the outlines of dark, indefinable beings, thousands of them, moving and milling across the firmament of heaven. Carys and Zach knew what they were. The air above the entire basin was filled with Balimm's legions.

'Zach!' came a faint cry.

'Dad – I forgot about Dad!'

With Zach leading the way back along the path he'd cut through the mullein, the three of them and Suzy ran to find Tom. He was on his back.

'What's going on?' he asked. His voice was feeble.

'We killed Balimm,' replied Zach, 'with Excalibur!' he added, holding aloft the sword.

'But there's a slight matter of Balimm's legions …' said Carys.

They all looked up. The sound was changing. Less sonorous. There were shrill elements creeping in. Urgent. And the movement of the demon horde was becoming less chaotic. They were all beginning to move in the same direction. Downwards.

'What about using the ring again?' asked Tom.

'I didn't bring it.'

'You didn't *bring* it?' Zach shouted.

Carys shouted back, 'My plan didn't *need* outside help – and it worked, remember? Balimm's dead!'

Tom settled the argument. 'I'm sorry I mentioned the ring. Even the Star Riders couldn't have fought off this little lot. It isn't your fault, Carys.'

The mass of demons was lower in the sky. It wouldn't be long now.

'I'm glad we didn't bring Bethany,' whispered Zach.

Dylan hadn't paid attention to any of their talk, since he knew nothing about Carys's plan, nor about the Star Riders and the magic ring. So he'd been studying the movements of the creatures in the sky above them – and listening.

'They're not after us,' he declared.

Carys couldn't keep the scorn from her voice, even though she tried to allow for Dylan's lack of demonic experience. 'Of course they're after us, Dyl. We killed their commander. We've been attacked by demons before –'

But Dylan was unmoved. 'I don't think they've even *seen* us. I've not been attacked by demons, but I've played rugger, and I know what it's like to have a herd of monsters baying for your blood. You develop a sense for it. I tell you, those creatures are not after us. Listen, will you?'

They listened. What they heard was not war cries of anger, but the bickering panic of terror.

'You're right, Dyl,' said Carys. 'They're *not* after us. In fact, they're running scared. But what from?'

The problem for the demons was that the black hole was keeping them trapped inside the airspace above the basin, so the harder they tried to get out of it, the faster they ended up going round in a circle. Soon the mass of monsters was whizzing round like a tornado. All the Aaron's Rod plants were flattened. The group sat down before they got blown over. Tom was recovering his strength now the sound had changed, and he too was sitting up, watching.

'What's happening to them?' he asked, shouting to make himself heard above the wind.

Zach was holding on to his dad's cassock, using him as an anchor. 'I think I know.' With Excalibur, Zach pointed to the centre of the basin. 'When we killed Balimm, he was sucked into a black hole.'

The demon horde was looking more like a tornado every second. The mass had become a raging vortex, with a whirling funnel centred over the black hole. As soon as the tip of the funnel touched the rim of the hole, the process quickened. To the sound of screaming and wailing, Balimm's legions were sucked into the black back of beyond, out of this world, out of all worlds. As the last layer of demons slipped into the void, there was a distinct 'popping' noise, as the black hole closed.

A calm descended.

Chapter 30 Surprise Party

'Can you smell that?' asked Carys.

The air had a crispness, an electric tang.

'It's how the earth smells after a summer storm,' said Dylan. 'Fresh. Newborn.'

Tom got to his feet. 'I suppose the demons were lost once their leader had gone.'

Zach laughed. 'No, Dad, I don't think they were lost. They were damned by their allegiance. Where Balimm went, they had to follow.'

'Then I should have gone down that hole as well,' said Dylan.

Carys was having none of that. 'Rubbish, Dyl, you were tricked into following him. That's totally different.'

'Shush – listen everybody …' whispered Tom.

They listened.

'At last,' murmured Carys, 'that awful sound of the stones has stopped. I assume it stopped when –'

'No, no, listen again,' insisted Tom.

They listened again, more intently this time.

'I hear it,' said Zach. 'A kind of deep rumbling under the ground …'

'The demons can't be coming back, surely?' demanded Dylan.

'Maybe the lift is going back up,' suggested Carys.

Suzy had her own theory. She darted off, full pelt, in the direction of the hole.

'No, come back, Suzy!' yelled Zach, chasing after her, followed by the others.

The rumbling was getting stronger and the noise louder. Suzy had half her body in the hole, which was now an ordinary hole in the ground, if somewhat larger and deeper than most. Suzy's terrier instincts were informing her that a giant rabbit was about to emerge. She was right about the 'giant' bit, except it was a giant waterspout that shot from the hole, whooshing Suzy high into the air – surely her finest trick yet. She landed safely in Tom's arms.

'It's water!' screamed Dylan, in case anybody thought they'd struck oil.

Judging from everybody's reactions, it might as well have been oil, for they all began dancing and singing, shouting and barking. The water was refreshing, and it was cleansing. They could begin to wash away some of the ugly moments, and celebrate what they had gained. New friendships, new confidence, new faith.

Water began to force its way up from the earth in many other parts of the basin. Soon dancing became impossible, with water up to their knees. They all perched on a large bluestone outcrop and surveyed the shallow lake around them, getting deeper by the minute.

'I suppose I don't need to tell you,' shouted Zach, 'that this is how we'll get out. Take your shoes off and be ready to swim and tread water.' Tom took his cassock off as well, and the three children helped him to float on his back, since he wasn't too hot at the other stuff. The four of them took turns using Excalibur as a flotation device. Nobody stopped to question how a steel sword could do that – it was Excalibur, and that was good enough for them.

'Hellooo!'

It was Bethany's voice. She was peering over the edge to the swimmers far below. 'What happened here?'

'Carys decided that Merlin's Farm needs an Excalibur Lake for all the tourists that will be coming,' yelled Zach. He roared with laughter – until he swallowed a mouthful of water.

'Beth,' shouted Carys, 'tell Mum –'

'She knows. As soon as the sound of the stones stopped, we knew we'd won. How much longer will you be?'

Zach was counting on his fingers. He stopped. 'As long as it takes for this lake to reach the top!'

'Well, I'll go and tell Branwen you're all okay, and then I'll come back with a blanket so I can wait here for you. I can tell you jokes, if you want, to keep your spirits up.'

Voices rang out in unison: 'No, thanks!'

There was a thin sliver of light on the eastern horizon when four exhausted people and a dog clambered onto dry land. Tom fell asleep as soon as his head touched the grass, but the children were still too excited for sleep. Zach re-enacted for Bethany the events of the night, perhaps *slightly* embellishing his part.

Carys left them and went over to Dylan, who was standing by himself, holding Excalibur.

'Thanks, Dyl. I could never have done that. We only had that moment, and you didn't hesitate.'

'It's me thanking you, Cass, for having faith in me after I'd been so stupid. But I did believe he wanted to restore the earth, you know.'

'Don't be hard on yourself. He got you at a vulnerable time, remember.'

'Yes, but I did enjoy the money and the power. I'm going to have to live with that.'

'So what are you going to do?'

'I'm coming back home, if Ma will have me. For a while, at least. Then I'd like to get work, if I can, with an organisation that is *genuinely* trying to restore the earth's spiritual energy, rather than secretly plotting to rule the world.' Dylan laughed and his whole body shook.

Carys was pleased to see her brother laughing again.

'What do we do with Excalibur?' she asked.

Zach and Bethany came across. 'You hang it up inside the farm,' said Zach, 'so when the Arthurian tourists come –'

'Eh?' Dylan looked blank. 'What is it with Zach and tourists?'

Carys smiled. 'Take no notice, Dyl, it's Zach's crazy plan for how Mum should diversify. We all know that this legendary object is far too powerful to leave lying around.'

'And we all know where it belongs,' said Bethany, with a sigh.

'You're right, Beth, we do,' agreed Dylan. 'And it's up to me, since I'm my father's son …'

Nobody tried to stop Dylan as he ran to the edge of the lake and launched the sword into the air. It soared towards the middle of the lake. It landed flat but with hardly a splash – enough to produce a succession of ripples.

'Why isn't it sinking?' asked Bethany.

Zach chuckled. 'Funny you should ask that, Beth.'

Carys spoke more seriously. 'It hasn't finished, that's why. Look.'

The blade of the sword was shining with a silver light, brighter and brighter.

'Hey,' said Dylan, 'it's a light sabre!'

He couldn't understand why everyone laughed so hard at that.

The light from Excalibur spread outwards with the ripples on the water, until there was a glowing ring at the centre of the lake. A huge silver circle.

'That wizard!' said Carys.

'What a rogue!' said Zach.

The sword upended, so only the cross-guard and hilt were above the water. The diamonds on the cross-guard shone like rubies as they reflected the first rays of the rising sun. Then Excalibur was gone.

Bethany was looking puzzled. 'I wonder where Aaron's Rod went?'

Zach shrugged. 'Search me. I wonder if such legendary objects are ever *really* here at all.'

244

'I sort of know what you mean, Zach,' said Carys. 'The way the rod changed into a sword, it was as though a hand reached in from another dimension and swapped them over. Maybe these things only appear when they're needed, like when God gave the rod to Moses and Aaron in the first place.'

'You guys,' exclaimed Dylan, 'what are you on? Can we go and get some breakfast? I'm having more than three eggs this morning, no matter what Mum says!'

Everybody laughed. Zach woke his dad and they all set off for the farm.

They stopped at the crest to watch the sunrise.

'This is our second sunrise in a row,' said Tom. 'It's exactly twenty-four hours since the Star Riders rescued us – hello, I wonder whose dog that is?'

There was a dog ahead of the party, on the crest of the hill, silhouetted against the rising sun. Sitting there, waiting.

Carys's heart began beating in her throat. 'It looks like Vala,' she whispered.

'It'll be one of Dai's dogs, Cass,' said Dylan. 'Mrs Jones has probably come to see how Mum is.'

Carys began running on ahead. 'That's where Vala always waits for me when we have races down the hill!' she shouted.

'Carys!' Dylan yelled, but there was no stopping her.

Carys reached the dog and screamed, 'It *is*, it *is* Vala!' before disappearing over the hill with it.

'Poor kid,' Dylan muttered, 'she misses that dog so much.'

As Carys raced down the hillside with Vala, her thoughts were racing too.

Is this the vision I should have had when I held the final rod? Or am I so exhausted that I'm actually asleep by the lake, dreaming? Vala can't be alive. He's dead.

Tears were streaming down her face. She couldn't enjoy this, not like before, when she'd held the second rod down the well. This time all she felt was the pain and the sorrow of separation. Vala was surging ahead, as he always did. Carys rounded the last bend to see her father waiting at the bottom in his usual spot. Vala had reached him and was jumping up and down with boundless energy.

At least this will be the last time. No more rods to find. No more –

Bryn took her in his arms and swung her round and round. He kissed her and squeezed her until she thought she'd never breathe again. But it was only when she glimpsed Dylan haring down the hill, shouting 'Dad!' at the top of his voice, that Carys dared to accept the impossible.

'But *how?*' spluttered Carys.

'Your mother can explain – I think!' said Bryn, laughing exactly like Dylan. 'All I know is I got up an hour ago as usual, thinking it was the day after yesterday, the twelfth of January.'

'But Mum –?'

'It's all right. Branwen was forewarned by … a friend of yours, I believe?'

They came round the side of the house and there was Capella, seated at a large trestle table set up near the old tree. Her beautiful white horse, Procyon, was hovering nearby. Carys ran over to her, while Dylan went through the same experience of wonder, disbelief and joy that Carys had felt, as he embraced his father.

The four swimmers changed into dry clothes. The only thing in the farmhouse that would fit Tom was a voluminous flannel nightdress of Branwen's, which, he said, at least vaguely resembled a cassock. Carys was the last to come down. She had rifled through drawers that had remained unopened for months, and was wearing blue jeans and a bright yellow top. Everyone cheered and whistled. Branwen, with Capella's help, had prepared a party spread. Capella had brought the ice cream, so it was out of this world.

Branwen had an announcement. 'I've asked Capella to explain about Bryn and Vala, about … well, you know …' She sat down, too overcome to say any more.

The Star Rider stood up to speak.

BALIMM'S PRESENCE IN OUR UNIVERSE WAS ALWAYS A HUGE INTRUSION. WHEN YOU CHILDREN DESTROYED HIM, HE AND HIS DEMONS WERE EXTINGUISHED, NOT JUST HERE, BUT IN ALL TIME.

Branwen had recovered, and couldn't resist telling everyone the conclusion.

'It's as if Balimm never existed, so all the evil damage he did, never happened, including ... well, you know.' She slipped her arm round Bryn's waist. She looked twenty years younger.

Everybody applauded and cheered.

'And soon,' Branwen added, 'his memory will fade from our minds.'

More applause and cheering.

'Can I ask a question?' Bryn was puzzled. 'Branwen tells me you withdrew the rod from the stone, Cass. I can see that was vital to your plan, but how did you manage it? Legend says it has to be a male descendant of Arthur Cadwaladr.'

'It was something Capella and her friends said. *Legends are not laws to be obeyed, but stories to be told and re-told.* So I decided I would re-tell the Legend of Aranrhod, with that crucial detail changed. The Aranrhod would be both Finder *and* Wielder –'

'But what gave you the right to change it?' persisted Bryn.

'Something else the Star Riders said – *to make changes is the storyteller's privilege.*'

The party was over. Tom, Zach and Bethany were getting in touch with their families in Worcester and working out how they were going to get home.

It was time for Capella to go.

'Thanks for preparing Mum for the shock of Dad's return,' said Carys. 'Will I ever see you again?'

YOU CAN SEE ME ON ANY CLOUDLESS NIGHT. CAPELLA IS THE SIXTH BRIGHTEST STAR IN THE SKY, SO YOU SHOULD NEVER HAVE ANY DIFFICULTY FINDING ME. I AM THE STAR RIDING ON THE CHARIOTEER'S SHOULDER!

As Carys waved Capella goodbye, she saw her father by the old tree, leaning against the wall. She ran over to him. 'I've missed you so much, Dad, it's been awful.'

Bryn put his arms around her.

'The first thing I'm going to do, Cass, is make that swing I've been promising you for so long.'

'You don't have to, Dad,' said Carys. 'Now we've got water again, you'll be busy re-stocking the farm. You might even get Dyl to help you.'

'I don't think so, love. There's no future in sheep, not any more.'

'So what are you going to do? You won't sell up, will you?'

Bryn let go of Carys and leaned on the wall, looking out to the hill opposite.

'No, no, I'm thinking of diversifying.'

Carys leaned on the wall next to him.

'You haven't been speaking to Zach, by any chance?'

Bryn picked up a stone and lobbed it towards the well. It went in without touching the sides, and made a satisfying plopping sound when it hit the water. Bryn spoke with warm enthusiasm. 'Zach's got this great idea for a Merlin and King Arthur Theme Park. After a Wizard Tea, the tourists throw a replica sword into Excalibur Lake and ... why, what's the matter?'

Carys's laughter echoed down the valley.

THE END

Visit the Legend Of Aranrhod website

Ask questions and read the FAQs

Buy copies for your friends

Visit the author's blog

Solve the riddle

Win prizes

www.i4w2.co.uk/aranrhod

....

You can also order extra copies by post

Price: £5.99 - save £1.00 off the cover price!
Postage and packing (per copy):
UK: £1.00 (FREE if you buy 3 or more copies)
Europe (EU): £2.50, Rest of the world: £4.00

Send your name, address, number of
copies required, and your payment to:

ideas4writers
PO Box 49, Cullompton, Devon, EX15 1WX
(United Kingdom)

We accept cheques, postal orders and bank drafts
(British pounds only)

The Legend Of Aranrhod is Geoff Anderson's first novel.

Geoff has played: the guitar, squash, tennis, snooker, Subbuteo, and most card and board games ever invented.

As a living he has: built furniture, been a parish priest, and written.

To be outrageous, he has: lived in a commune, cycled over the Massif Central, and never done drugs.

For the love of it, he has: managed the St Petersburg Blagovest Ensemble since 2002. Olga Kozlova, their conductor, has invited Geoff to combine his book tours with their UK concert tours.

Geoff believes in: the power of the pen since he wrote a short story to convince his American girlfriend to come back to him, which she did. They now have four children and two grandchildren.

Geoff is an Associate Writer with the international publishers, Redemptorist Publications. He had an item included in the BBC Book of the Future, in which he foresaw cathedrals being converted into sporting venues – perhaps prompted by his own use of cathedrals as theatrical venues for his plays and musicals.

Geoff has written the book and lyrics for three musicals:

- Rock On Simon Peter
- The Damascus Roadshow
- That Saul, Folks!

These have been extensively performed and are available for hire.

Visit the author's blog at: http://aranrhod.wordpress.com